in a
FLASH

in a FLASH

DONNA JO NAPOLI

WENDY
LAMB
BOOKS

Text copyright © 2020 by Donna Jo Napoli
Jacket art copyright © 2020 by Qu Lan
Map art copyright © 2020 by Mike Reagan

All rights reserved. Published in the United States by Wendy Lamb Books, an imprint of Random House Children's Books, a division of Penguin Random House LLC, New York.

Wendy Lamb Books and the colophon are trademarks of Penguin Random House LLC.

Visit us on the Web! rhcbooks.com

Educators and librarians, for a variety of teaching tools, visit us at RHTeachersLibrarians.com

Library of Congress Cataloging-in-Publication Data
Names: Napoli, Donna Jo, author.
Title: In a flash / Donna Jo Napoli.
Description: First edition. | New York : Wendy Lamb Books, [2020] | Includes bibliographical references. | Audience: Ages 8–12. | Audience: Grades 4–6. | Summary: Caught in Japan and separated from their father when World War II begins, Italian sisters Simona, thirteen, and Carolina, ten, embark on a trying journey hoping to reach safety. Includes historical notes.
Identifiers: LCCN 2019039937 (print) | LCCN 2019039938 (ebook) | ISBN 978-1-101-93413-5 (hardcover) | ISBN 978-1-101-93414-2 (library binding) | ISBN 978-1-101-93416-6 (paperback) | ISBN 978-1-101-93415-9 (ebook)
Subjects: CYAC: Sisters—Fiction. | World War, 1939–1945—Japan—Fiction. | Survival—Fiction. | Italians—Japan. | Japan—History—1926–1945—Fiction.
Classification: LCC PZ7.N15 In 2020 (print) | LCC PZ7.N15 (ebook) | DDC [Fic]—dc23

The text of this book is set in 11.2-point Gamma ITC Std.
Interior design by Cathy Bobak

Printed in the United States of America
10 9 8 7 6 5 4 3 2 1
First Edition

To my grandchildren

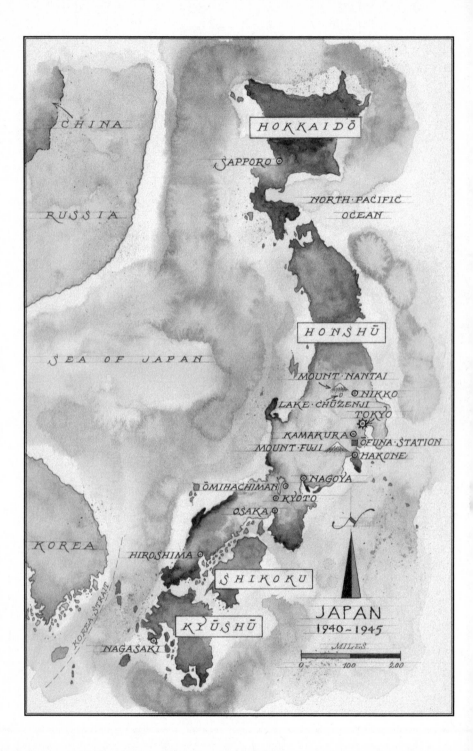

CHAPTER
ONE

24 July 1940, Lido di Ostia, Italy

I close my eyes and fall back into the sand with my hands clasped under my head. All I see through my eyelids is the red fire of the sun. All I smell is the sea. It makes me think of lemons. The waves pound close by as Carolina shovels sand into her tin pail. *Scrape, scrape.*

I wipe sweat from my eyebrows and around my lips. Everyone says the summer of 1934, when Mamma was pregnant with Carolina, was the hottest. I don't remember it because I was only two and a half. But they say this summer is nearly as hot.

I pinch my nose and prepare to be buried in sand by Carolina.

Nothing.

I sit up and blink. I see a dazzling spray of colors—blue

1

water, dark streaks in the sand, the white swan painted on Carolina's yellow pail. But no Carolina. My throat clutches. Where is she?

Salty water drips onto my head, stinging my eyes. I grin up at her as she sprinkles me with my watering can.

"Grow!" she screams.

I squat and gradually rise, like the enchanted bean plant in a fable. Soon I'm too tall for Carolina to water; I'm eight and she isn't even six yet. Carolina dances around me, laughing. "A giant Simona!" she shouts to Nonna.

Nonna sits on a turned-over wooden box, like all the other grandmothers on the beach. She shades herself with her pink umbrella and smiles.

"Lunchtime!" Nonna calls.

Carolina runs into the waves to rinse her pail and my old watering can, with the faded blue flowers. We didn't buy new ones this year. There weren't any in the shop because all the metal is needed for our wars. Papà said smart people are frugal these days anyway.

I brush the sand off the wooden box Nonna was sitting on and balance it on my head as we walk. Nonna holds her umbrella. Carolina holds everything else.

"Want to guess what I'm making for lunch?" Nonna asks, and smiles.

"Pasta." Carolina skips ahead.

"Of course. So guess what else."

"Zucchini flowers," I say.

"How did you know?"

"The vines are full of blossoms."

"Orange flowers, green salad, red sauce on the pasta," says Nonna. "The eye will be as happy as the stomach."

She loves cooking so much, it sometimes seems she must be Papà's mother rather than Mamma's. Papà is the best cook in Ostia; some say the best in all of Rome. Nonna says the best cook in all Italy.

Nonna goes in to start cooking while Carolina and I pick the zucchini blossoms. Then we walk inside to the welcome of the cool dark.

Papà is home! The way he is standing now, with his black curls tight to his head and his thin beaky nose, he makes me think of the black stork we saw in the marsh once. Carolina runs into his hug, crushing the flowers in her arms. Having Papà in the middle of the day is a treat.

I smile. Then hesitate. Lunch is the busiest meal at Papà's tavern. Why is he home?

Nonna sits at the kitchen table, hands limp in her lap. She should be at the stove.

A big suitcase stands on the floor beside Papà. I've never seen it before. "What's going on?"

"Your father has lost his mind," says Nonna.

Papà gives a quick laugh. "I'm going to be the cook in an embassy."

"That sounds . . . good," I say.

"I'll make more money," says Papà. "A man from the

Ministry of Foreign Affairs heard about my cooking and came to the tavern to taste it. I didn't know. Today he came back and offered me a job. Think of that. I'll be the cook at the Italian embassy."

I nod happily.

"In Japan," Nonna says. "Halfway around the world."

Carolina and I look at each other.

Carolina snatches her rag doll, Lella, from the shelf and goes to sit beside Nonna. Her fingers comb through Lella's yellow yarn hair, as though the conversation doesn't matter. But her shoulders bunch up.

"The new Italian ambassador to Japan has been in Tokyo barely a week, but he hates the food," says Papà. "He needs real Italian food. My food."

"Japan," says Nonna. "Luciano, Japan is at war with China."

Papà stands taller. "The man from Foreign Affairs predicts Japan's war with China will be over soon. Maybe even before I start the new job."

"Hasn't that war been going for years already? Maybe he'd say anything to get you to take the job."

"I doubt that. Besides, all the fighting is on Chinese soil. Japan is safe."

Nonna gapes at Papà. "Safe?"

"Safer than Italy. Europe is at war: Poland, Norway, Denmark, Belgium, the Netherlands." Papà counts off the countries on his fingers. "And now France."

"Germany invaded those countries." Nonna shakes her head. "Germany won't invade Italy. Mussolini and Hitler have a pact. The Pact of Steel. Italy and Germany are friends."

"But that pact is exactly the problem." Papà comes toward the table, palms together. He shakes his hands as he walks. "That's why Mussolini declared war on France and Great Britain."

Carolina looks at me, baffled, but I remember that announcement. On a Monday in mid-June—a month ago. Papà was home because the tavern is closed on Mondays. He was slicing tomatoes for dinner and listening to the radio news. He cried out in pain. I ran in because I thought he'd cut his finger. He sat me down and explained that because of the Pact of Steel, Germany's enemies were Italy's enemies; Germany was at war with France and Great Britain, so Italy was, too.

Now Papà puts both hands on the table and leans across toward Nonna. "Italian troops invaded France right alongside German troops. Mamma Raffaella, dear sweet one, you listen to the radio. You read the newspapers. You don't want to believe it, but you have to. There's going to be fighting in Italy," he says quietly. "Soon."

Fighting here? At school the boys dress in black shirts and gray-green trousers to look like soldiers' uniforms. It shows their loyalty to our leader, Mussolini, and the Fascist party. The boys have mock battles. Our teachers talk about real battles all the time, but those battles are far away—in Egypt,

Spain, Albania—and Italy always wins. No one says anything about battles here in Italy. My teeth clench so hard my jaw hurts.

Nonna has her hand over her mouth. Now she lets it fall into her lap again. "If you're so sure of that, how could you accept the job? Your poor girls. They've lost so much already. Their mother . . ." She stops. Then, "They'll miss you."

"Miss me? No, no. We're all going. All four of us. There's room for the whole family, right in the embassy."

Nonna is shaking her head again. She fingers her watch-band.

Papà looks at me, then at Carolina. "Do you want to go with me, girls?"

"Yes!" shouts Carolina.

A new country. A new school. But safe. With Papà and Nonna. I try to smile.

Leaving behind friends. And this house. Where Mamma lived, till she died in January.

Everything is different in a flash.

"I'm too old for this." Nonna puts on her headscarf and goes out the door. She shuts it so softly, it swings open again. She's going to church. That's what she does when she's upset.

Papà is looking at me. Waiting. "Don't worry about Nonna. I'll talk to her. We'll go for a year, two at most. Simona. Carolina. You'll get to see a bit of the world. An adventure. And . . ." His voice is nearly a whisper now. "A change would help us in lots of ways, Simona. We've all been . . . sad. . . . I don't know how to say it. But you're smart. You know what I mean."

Loss. Lost. Ever since Mamma died. Ever since she got so sick. That's what's in my head. And now, fear.

No! I mustn't be afraid. Papà wants a change. And it's only for a year. Two at most.

Papà looks at his watch and taps the face lightly, thoughtfully. "It's seven hours later in Tokyo than it is here. We'd be eating the evening meal if we were there now. So much would be different. But some things would be the same. Our family would be the same." He turns his face up to us and smiles. "Girls, will you help me pack? They're going to rush our documents through. I agreed to leave in four days. We'll take a ship—a long, long way. With good weather, we should arrive in time for you to go to school."

The smell of the zucchini flowers still perched in my arms is overpoweringly sweet. This room is overpoweringly dear.

I look at Papà. He is waiting. Hopeful.

I swallow. Then smile. I can bring Mamma's church scarf. It smells of her hair. I grab Carolina by the hand. "Let's go talk to Nonna. She might listen to us better." I nod to Papà, and we rush out the door.

We follow the path; it is so familiar, we could go there with our eyes closed. We sit on the wide stone steps of the entrance to the church, hot from the sun. Carolina herds ants with a leaf while I watch the door.

Nonna finally comes out. She gives us a small smile and plops down between us with an *Umpf,* taking off her scarf. Her gray curls spring up. "Is this an ambush?"

"It will be an adventure," Carolina says, patting Nonna's shoulder, as though she's the old lady and Nonna's the child. "You love adventure."

Nonna laughs. "Adventures at the beach or at a farm or wandering around the streets of town—that's very different from . . . what your father is talking about." She pulls Carolina onto her lap. "I'm old. And tired. Oh, my treasured girls, I can't face all that travel. A strange language. Different ways of behaving."

"We'll face it together," I say. "The whole family, like Papà said."

"I love you more than life itself, girls. But . . ."

"And we love you," I say. "We need you."

"No. I'd only hold you back. I've been thinking and praying. If you go, you have to go fresh and alert. I'm going to make a list for you. Things you should know. We'll talk about it a lot before you go."

"We're going in four days," says Carolina.

"Four days?" Nonna practically yelps, as though she's been pierced. Her dark eyes shine. "Then we'd better start talking now." She scoots Carolina off her lap and stands. "Stay alert. Always. Pay attention to everything and everyone. Pay attention to how things are done in your new country. Be kind. Be grateful. Smile a lot. Take care of each other." She's counting off on her fingers, like Papà does. Then she stops, takes us each by a hand, and lifts our hands high. "*Forza e coraggio—* that will be your motto."

Forza e coraggio. Strength and courage. I close my eyes and still my heart. We can do this.

CHAPTER
TWO

2 SEPTEMBER 1940, TOKYO, JAPAN

It's Monday, the second of September, my fourth day in Tokyo and my first day of school. Hatsu inspects me closely. She's on the kitchen staff here at the embassy. She and others make the Japanese food for the embassy employees, while Papà runs the kitchen and makes Italian food for the ambassador, his wife, and their guests. Hatsu has a daughter a little younger than Carolina, so when we arrived three days ago, it was decided that Hatsu will take care of Carolina while I'm in school, and her daughter will come to work with her, as Carolina's playmate. Right now, though, Hatsu smooths the cuffs of the little cap sleeves on my white shirt. She straightens the blue jumper-dress that goes over that shirt and nods, satisfied. She sewed this outfit for me fast. If Nonna had come with us, she would have sewn it just as fast. I blink now to keep from crying. Nonna promised to write often. Our uncle, Zio Piero, promised, too. Nonna lives with him now.

I could have made clothes for myself, because Nonna taught me. But I didn't know what school clothes looked like here. I couldn't even ask what I needed to make them; Hatsu doesn't speak Italian. So I just watched while Hatsu worked on my shirt and dress all day Saturday, and I smiled at her a lot and said "Thank you" in Japanese. But I'm glad. This is a pretty, deep-blue dress, and the shirt has a rounded collar. Hatsu undoes the top button and spreads the collar open like wings. That's good. That must be how they do it here. I touch the tip of the collar, nodding hard, and say, "I like it." She seems to understand.

Hatsu cut my hair on Saturday, too. I have bangs now. Her daughter, Botan, has bangs and two big white bows in her hair. I wish I had bows; they would hold my curls down.

Hatsu stands back, gives me one more sweeping look up and down, and smiles her approval. She hands me the book bag. I want to peek inside it, but she's rushing me. So I stick my arms through the straps while she says something in Japanese to Botan, who takes a seat on the floor. Carolina does the same. I'm not surprised. That's one of the things Nonna told us to do: "Pick out someone nice and copy them. That way you'll fit in." I need to find someone to copy.

Hatsu opens the door and looks at me.

I haven't been outside this giant embassy at all yet. I go to the door. Then hesitate. "Bye," I say to Carolina. "Have fun."

Carolina looks at Botan, who is busy twisting the bottom edge of her skirt, then looks back at me, frowning. She jumps up and hugs me. "You have fun, too."

"Thank you."

"Come back. Please. Right away."

"Of course I'll come back! As soon as school lets out." I squeeze her tight; this is her first day on her own, too. "You know I'll come back. Always."

"Nonna said we have to be best friends."

"Nonna's right. Go play now. Have fun."

I follow Hatsu out the side door to the gate. A man opens it for us. Hatsu bows her head to him, so I do, too. As we walk along the edge of the road, I'm glad to be walking steady; I don't feel like I'm still rocking on a ship, like I felt most of the weekend, after a month at sea.

Out on the ship's deck, I overheard Papà learning Japanese, and I heard lots of talk about war. News came through telegrams. Italy invaded Somaliland in Africa. One city, then another. Swift victories. Nothing about anyone invading Italy. And the news about Japan was good: Japan will conquer all of China soon, just like the man from Foreign Affairs told Papà.

I'm glad to finally be in Tokyo and see that Japan is safe. The people on the street are ordinary, not soldiers. I look closely at everyone we pass; no one carries guns.

I smile up at Hatsu, hoping for a smile back, but she looks straight ahead, over a big envelope she clasps to her chest, filled with everything she needs to enroll me. If the school officials ask me anything that isn't in those papers, I won't understand. The idea makes me a little sick. Maybe Hatsu's worried about that, too, and that's why her eyes are so intense.

A group of girls around my age walks ahead of us, dressed just like me. At the second corner, they turn right. We turn right. As we walk, I draw a mental map of the route in my head.

We're on a big street now, with sidewalks. Back home there are no sidewalks on my way to school. The girls ahead of us chatter and laugh. We walk past streets and little alleys. Cars and bicycles zoom by, horses pull carts that clatter, and my book bag thumps against my back. Then we turn right, onto a small street. Oh no, I lost count of the blocks! How will I ever know where to turn if I have to walk alone?

But that must be the school, at the end of the next block. Hatsu runs ahead, and I race after her. She stops one of the girls in the group and says a lot to her, then points at me. The girl glances at me and shakes her head. But another girl, shorter, nods to Hatsu and comes over to me. She says something; I smile and try to repeat it. She points at herself and says, "Aiko." Then she points at me and raises her eyebrows. So I say, "Simona." She gives me a quick head bow, and I bow, then look back at Hatsu.

Hatsu nods to me, and we follow Aiko through the main door. Hatsu flaps her hand at me: *Go with Aiko.* She smiles, waves, and goes into an office.

I watch Aiko walk up to a set of lockers, take off her street shoes, and put them inside. Then she takes out white cloth slippers and puts them on. She says something to me and points at the very last locker. I take off my shoes and put them in the locker. But there are no slippers in there. I stand in my socks, feeling exposed. Aiko looks doubtfully at me. She chatters and points at my book bag. I look inside. White slippers! Hatsu did good.

We go down a hall and into a big room where children are sitting on the floor. Aiko sits, so I sit beside her. A man stands on a low platform at one end of the room and talks at us. Everyone nods or laughs or speaks in unison. After the assembly I follow Aiko into a classroom. Aiko bows to the teacher and says something. The teacher nods. Aiko takes a seat at a wooden desk. There are two seats at every desk, and the desks are pushed together edge to edge, so that everyone sits in tight rows.

The teacher stares at me a moment. She looks at a piece of paper on her desk, then holds it up to look closer. Now I can see what's on it. She reads, "Simona?" I can't understand how that writing led her to know my name—it looks nothing like my name. I nod and smile. The teacher raps her knuckles on her desk, and everyone stops talking and looks at her. She says something to them. Then they all say something to me. I don't know what it means, but I repeat it. They laugh as though I'm stupid. I press my lips together hard and look down. The teacher points me to the closest empty seat.

That's how the morning goes. I learn all the words I can

without looking anyone in the eye. Some words are clear from how people behave—words for book and chair and desk. For girl (or maybe student?), and teacher. For blackboard and chalk. I repeat other words even though I can't figure out what they mean.

I love math class; it's just like the math I had last year. I'm good at it. And in another class I copy the symbols that the teacher writes on the blackboard. Some are hard to do; some are simple. It's fun, almost like doing art. In one class the girls sing, and I just listen. And in the fourth class I have no idea what's going on, so I watch and wait.

When the bell rings for the fifth time, a few girls leave the room, and the others open little boxes. There's food inside. *Bento*—that's what those straw boxes are called. Aiko catches my eye. She points at my book bag. But I know there's no *bento* box in there.

When I shake my head, Aiko comes over, peeks into my book bag, and takes out a cloth bundle. *"Furoshiki,"* she says. I can't tell if she's annoyed at me. *"Furoshiki."*

So that's what this cloth is called. I untie the *furoshiki,* and there's a rice ball, cucumber strips, and carrot chunks sitting in the middle. I know rice balls from home. I take a bite, but it's nothing like in Italy—no cheese inside, no tomato, no peas. I take a nibble. Sweet. I nibble till it's all gone. Then I eat the vegetables, which turn out to be pickled. They're good. Did Papà pack this for me? Or Hatsu?

The bell rings; we go to our lockers, put on our street shoes, and go outside. It's recess. I sit with my back against the sun-warmed wall and watch the girls skip rope. No one looks at me, not even Aiko.

We walk inside to marching music. Everyone takes ugly old cloths out of their book bags and gets to work rubbing off their desk. There's an old cloth in my book bag, too. I rub our desktop, while my deskmate rubs our chairs. Then we all push our desks and chairs to the edges of the room, and some students sweep with brooms while others wipe the blackboards and clean the chalk trays. I help carry the trash to a big basket.

When we finally put on our shoes again to go home, I'm too tired to be anxious. And I have a plan: If Hatsu isn't waiting to walk me home, I'll follow Aiko. She has to live somewhere past the embassy, because that's where she came from this morning. It won't be hard.

I go out the door. Hatsu isn't there. I look and look. I'm sure of it.

I turn in a circle. No Aiko anywhere. My stomach does flips.

A girl from my class walks by. She sticks out her tongue and puts her finger under her eye and pulls down, so her eye is distorted. She says something fast and pokes her fingers toward my face, and I know that whatever she's saying is nasty and is about the shape of my eyes.

Everyone pours outside and away from the school. Until I'm alone. Hatsu isn't coming. Aiko is gone. I quickly walk two blocks, and I'm at the big road with the sidewalks. I turn left and keep walking. I can do this. Except that nothing looks familiar. Maybe I can't do this. I taste salt, and I realize I'm crying.

A shout comes from behind me. I turn around. It's Aiko. I gasp with relief. She chatters at me and makes all kinds of crazy motions, and I know she's trying to explain something to me. Oh! She's mimicking sweeping and cleaning. She's telling me she had to stay late to do extra cleaning; she's apologizing. As I nod, it dawns on me that Hatsu must have asked Aiko to take care of me all day long, including walking me home. I slip off my book bag and take out the cloth—the *furoshiki*—and wipe my nose and try to smile.

We walk, and Aiko points at things and says the Japanese word for them. I repeat. It's not really that hard. I just have to memorize. There are so many words to learn, and I'm so glad to be learning them . . . and from Aiko.

When we get to the embassy, I turn to hug Aiko in gratitude. But she backs up fast, then runs off. I go in through the side door.

"You're alive!" It's the ambassador's wife. She's standing in the hall in a green dress, fingering the pearls around her neck. I can't believe how wonderful it is to hear Italian. "How did you ever manage?"

I don't know how to answer this woman, dressed fancy, talking so loud. I just smile. I've seen her only once before, on Friday night, the day we arrived. She came home from a dinner party with the ambassador, and her long hair was swept up with a tiara on top. Like a princess's.

"I told your father. When I learned that he'd sent you off to some horrible public school this morning, I told him. You should go to the Sacred Heart School, a good Catholic school. That's where foreign children go. The school is full of diplomats' children."

Papà appears in the hall. "Simona." He comes up and hugs me tight.

"Just look at her," says the ambassador's wife. "She must have had an awful day. You have to change her school immediately."

"I appreciate your interest in my daughters, Ambasciatrice," Papà says, using her title as ambassador's wife. "But the public school is free."

"She can't speak the language. She'll fail her grade. At the Sacred Heart School they teach the children Japanese."

"Indeed, that's quite right. But Sacred Heart is over in the Hiroo district. Mita Elementary, instead, is close. Simona can walk to it. And the school year starts here in April—not like in Italy. So she's entering in the middle of the third grade. She already finished third grade in Italy. That means she'll have time to learn the language before she has to move on to new schoolwork."

"What they teach in each grade here could be different from in Italy. Who knows? Besides, you can't learn a language that fast."

"Thank you for your concern, Ambasciatrice. But Simona's smart. She'll work hard and do fine." He looks at me. "Right?"

I do my best to nod.

"Now go find Carolina," says Papà. "Play. You can tell me all about your day tonight."

CHAPTER

THREE

8 December 1940, Tokyo, Japan

"You gobbled up the last piece of birthday treat after church, didn't you?" I say.

Carolina clutches her rag doll, Lella, to her chest and looks up at the sky, then along the wall around this yard, and finally at me. "I love lemons."

That wasn't exactly lemons, but it's as close to lemons as Tokyo has. It's my job to race through the markets to find substitute ingredients so Papà can make the ambassador Italian dishes. We've been here three months already, so I know the markets. "Pears would have been better, but there are none left."

"Lemon is perfect. I want crust with lemon every birthday from now on. So does Lella."

Papà made that treat last night for Carolina's sixth birthday. We ate it in the kitchen, after everyone else had gone home or to bed. It was a disappointment in comparison to birthday cakes back home, but it was still good. Papà mixed the fruit into a custard, and the smell as it baked was heavenly. Maybe I'll ask Papà to make that for my birthday, too.

"Konnichiwa!" Botan comes racing out the side door of the embassy, shouting the greeting that I know so well, and bows to Carolina and me. Carolina and I bow back

I'm surprised Botan is here. Today is Sunday, and Botan's mother, Hatsu, doesn't come on Sundays.

Botan chatters away, and Carolina nods happily. Carolina is learning Japanese as well as Japanese ways from Botan, so she'll be prepared for first grade.

Already Carolina knows a lot more Japanese than I do. Hardly anyone at school ever talks to me. I can speak some now, but slowly, and I have to search for words. Still, I'm starting to understand things, and I talk to Botan at home. I understand what Carolina and Botan are talking about now. Botan just learned a new game, *Daruma Otoshi*. She brought it in a bag, and she's explaining it to Carolina, who keeps asking more and more questions. I know that game from school recess. It's nearly impossible to explain it without showing it.

"Please," I say to Botan. "Please show."

Botan dumps the bag out onto the ground. There are four round stacking pieces, which she arranges into a tower. On top goes the fifth piece, a Buddha head. Botan picks up the only thing left, a little wooden hammer, and knocks out one of the round pieces. The whole stack falls. She makes a face and stacks them again and swings the hammer. All the pieces fall, and Botan makes an uglier face. The point is to knock out the bottom blocks, one at a time, without making the Buddha head fall.

Hitomi, Papà's best kitchen helper, comes out the side door. She makes a quick bow of the head. A boy stands half hidden behind her, staring.

"Party," Hitomi says to me loudly in Japanese. "Your sister. Carolina. Party. With friend." She clasps her hands below her stomach. "Naoki. See? He come. You have friend, too. Party."

Ah. Papà asked Hatsu and Hitomi to make this feel like a party for us.

Carolina and Botan stand up and hold hands. I stand beside them. In Japan, holding hands is considered babyish for eight-year-olds like me. I'm tense all the time, trying to figure out how things work here. The three of us just look at Hitomi. It's chilly outside, and our jackets are thin. The boy's jacket looks thin, too. Old and shabby.

"Play. All of you. Together." Hitomi bows again.

She's trying to be kind, talking to us slowly and using few words. That's how she talks to the ambassador's wife. The ambassador's wife hates Japan and refuses to speak a word of Japanese. We're not like her. I don't know how to tell Hitomi to talk normal without my seeming impolite, though—and in Japan nothing is worse than a child being impolite to an adult.

We all know what to do: bow. Hitomi goes back inside.

The boy is barely taller than Carolina, but he seems older. I smile at him. Naoki. I say a sentence I think I know how to say perfectly: "Do you go to school?"

"It's Sunday," says Naoki solemnly.

I almost laugh. He can't be that old, after all. "Want to play with us?" A second perfect sentence.

He looks at the scattered wooden pieces. "You can't play *Daruma Otoshi* on this ground. It's too—" He points to the pebbles, and I nod.

Botan picks up the pieces and puts them back into the bag.

"My mother is smart," says Naoki to me. "But she said something odd. So you must explain."

Hitomi is his mother? She's at the embassy every day all week. So who looks out for Naoki?

Naoki tilts his head. "Did your sister really have a birthday?"

"Yesterday," says Carolina. "Seven December."

"It's stupid to have a birthday in December. And it's stupid to have a party."

Carolina's eyes go big and liquid. I move to stand beside her.

"How old are you?" he asks.

"Six," says Carolina.

"That's not special," says Naoki. "When you turn seven,

23

it will be special. In the middle of November you'll visit the shrines and get to tie your kimono with a waist sash instead of a cord."

Really? I love kimonos—those beautiful robes. If Carolina gets one, I want one, too.

Carolina rubs her nose with the back of her hand, but her eyes stay on Naoki.

"You should know that," he says. "Any first grader knows that."

Carolina is not in first grade. She would have been among the youngest in her class here, and not knowing the language would have made her too vulnerable. So Papà is keeping her home till the start of the new school year, in April. I move closer still. My arm presses against hers.

"What games do you know?" says Naoki.

"My favorite is 'old home,'" says Carolina.

"How do you play?'"

"We sleep in that tree." Carolina points.

"You can't sleep in a tree."

"We lie back like this." Carolina throws her arms out to both sides. Lella dangles from her left hand. "We sleep high up, like in Italy. Not like here, on the floor."

"You'll fall. Foreigners are stupid."

"It's just pretend," says Botan.

Naoki looks at me. "Can you climb high?"

I shake my head. I'm not about to say anything more in

front of this boy unless I am absolutely sure I can say it perfectly.

Naoki twists his mouth. "Is that the only game you know?"

"What do you want to play?" asks Botan.

"I can fold paper in the air without using tools." Naoki glances at me. "Go get your best colored folding paper."

He's talking about origami. Everyone at school is an expert at folding paper.

"We don't have colored paper," says Carolina.

Naoki looks astonished. But his face lights up. "Then we'll play navy. Pretend you're on a ship. Japan has the best navy in the world. I'll serve on a ship someday."

"We came here on a ship," says Carolina. "But our grandmother stayed behind. She's old. Nonna writes to us. And we write back. Well, I draw pictures. But that's just as good. The letters take weeks and weeks to get back and forth, though. We got a letter just a few days ago. When we send ours tomorrow, we won't get an answer from her for over a month." Carolina pauses. "I miss her."

"Sometimes I miss my grandmother." Naoki looks away. "I missed her a lot last night."

"Where—" Carolina begins.

That's enough. *"Basta,"* I say to Carolina in Italian. "Don't ask anything else."

Naoki glances at me. His face is pinched. "So . . . what was the ship like?"

"Big," says Carolina. "Loud."

Remembering that ship makes me feel seasick.

Naoki smiles. "I know more about ships than you do. My uncle's in the navy. So I'm in charge in this game. I'm the navy! You're the enemy!"

"No," I yelp. "We're friends."

"Enemies are more fun."

I shake my head. "I don't want to be the enemy." At school the girls stand and watch the boys over the wall. The boys run at each other with sticks, shouting, "Kill the Chinese."

Carolina looks at Botan. A silent message must pass between them, because Botan says, "We'll play with you."

"But first I have to put Lella away. She doesn't like playing navy." Carolina runs inside.

When she's back, Naoki says, "Good. Go hide behind that bush."

The girls run off. I'm too cold to play anyway. I go inside and wander through the halls. The kitchen radio is on, blasting the news in Japanese. Above the radio noise, I hear Papà speaking Japanese in his halting way. I peek. Papà is short and thin, like me, but when he talks, he seems big and strong, and everyone listens. He's telling the kitchen servants to chop vegetables finer. None of his sentences are right, but they understand, because his hands fly through the air, showing exactly how to do everything. I'm guessing dinner will start with minestrone.

I retreat into the hall. On a mat in a side room lie two

stacks of colorful square cloths with fancy designs. I pick one up. A *furoshiki*, one of the first Japanese words I ever learned. Hatsu taught Carolina and me how to wind the sides of a *furoshiki* up the handle of a basket and make a fancy knot at the top. She taught me to fold a *furoshiki* into a perfect holder for chopsticks. The ambassador and his wife always use forks, like in Italy. But when Japanese guests come, chopsticks appear.

A couple of months ago, at the end of September, Italy and Japan and Germany signed a big agreement—the Tripartite Pact—and the next week the ambassador went to a huge party at some palace. Oh, the embassy is like a palace, too, but not huge. The ambassador came home smelling of tobacco. For weeks after, important men came to the embassy for dinner, and I folded their chopstick holders. Papà praised me, because the edges were perfectly matched: "You understand Japan. Already. My smart girl."

The *furoshiki* in my hands now is frayed and faded, like the others in this stack. But the ones in the second stack are lovely. Hitomi has sorted out this old stack to get rid of.

I smile. I know where Hitomi keeps the needles and thread.

I pick out four tattered *furoshiki* with patterns that fit well and arrange them in a big square on the table. I sew them together with my tiniest stitches. If I were working beside Nonna, we'd sing. So I sing now. But not an Italian song. That would make me miss her too much. And I won't sing an ugly marching song. We sing too many of those in school.

I choose a sweet song: "Momotaro-san." My classmates sing it at recess, and I listen closely and sing in my head. It's about a woman who is washing clothes in the river when a peach—a *momo*—floats past. She and her husband take a bite, and—*plop*—out falls a boy. They're so happy to have a child. They name him Momotaro. When Momotaro grows up, he goes to an island to kill ogres, and he makes friends with a dog and a monkey and a pheasant. And somehow they help him, so that he winds up rich forever after.

Nonna might like this song. I'll tell her about it in the letter I'm writing now. I add to that letter each night.

I'm just finishing up when Naoki and Carolina and Botan come in.

"What are you making?" asks Carolina.

"A present."

"For who?"

Naoki elbows Carolina in the ribs. "You, of course." His voice is sharp. "You don't even need it. You're spoiled, living here. But your sister will make something for you anyway."

"That's not so!" We're not spoiled. I suddenly realize who I'm making this present for. "It's for you, Naoki."

Naoki's face freezes. Then he shakes his head. "That's not boy cloth. Everyone would laugh at me."

"You could use it like a blanket," says Botan.

"No."

"There must be something," says Carolina. "Simona sews good."

"I guess you could make me a *horo*," says Naoki.

"What's that?"

"The old samurai wore them. They're cloaks like big bags. When the samurai galloped on horses, the bags blew up. That way no one could shoot them with arrows."

"That sounds funny," says Carolina.

"Samurai are fierce!" Then Naoki smiles. "Maybe it was sort of funny, too."

"Wait." I run to our room and rush back with paper and pencil. "Draw it."

Naoki sits down and draws. "I've always wanted a *horo*."

After dinner, I go to the bathing room and roll back a tiny section of the slatted boards that cover the deep tub. I splash myself. Then I stand in the middle of the room and scrub myself with soap so hard, my belly gets red. I dip a wooden bowl into the water and rinse off, watching the dirt and suds swirl down the drain in the floor. Now I roll back more of the slatted boards, enough so that I can climb in. Japanese baths are one of the best things in the world. The coal fire under the tub keeps the water so hot that it hurts, but not bad hurts, and everyone uses the same water over and over. So long as you go in clean, the water stays clean. I ease in and slide down till the water reaches my chin.

This has been the best day in Japan so far. I haven't made friends at school yet. It's hard, because the other girls have been together since first grade. And I can't say half the things I want to say. Aiko still whispers to me now and then, usually to let me know I'm doing something wrong. But she never smiles if anyone else is watching. And she stays away from me at recess. It doesn't matter, though, because maybe I'm making a friend here at the embassy. When Hitomi told Naoki it was time to go home, he said, "Can I come back next Sunday?"

Usually I spend most of every night practicing writing. I do at least a page of characters. I have to memorize how to draw them and what they mean. And I write lots of words in *kana*—symbols that stand for sounds. But this next week I won't do that. I'll finish sewing Naoki's *horo*.

There's a knock on the door. It opens without anyone waiting for an answer. Carolina and Botan stand there, shy.

"Can we come into the bath?" Carolina uses such charming little-girl Japanese that I want to hug her. But why is Botan still here?

Carolina laughs at my puzzled face. "Botan's mother is letting her sleep with us tonight. Because of my birthday. So . . . can we come in?"

I take baths with Carolina all the time, but we've never invited anyone else in. It's a wonderful idea, though. There's a public bath nearby; people who don't have a bath at home go daily to soak with others—women in one area, men in another. Carolina and I went once with Hatsu and Botan, just for fun.

But both these girls are small enough that the tub water would go over their nose. That's why Carolina has a special low tub stool. I point at it now and look at Botan apologetically. "We have only one stool."

"Botan can have it," says Carolina.

"Thank you, Karo-chan," said Botan.

I press my lips together in envy. *Chan* is what you add to the end of a girl's name when you like her a lot. Carolina has a real friend, one who calls her *Karo-chan*. Botan is sweet to Carolina.

But Carolina is sweet to Botan, too. Carolina deserves a friend. "How generous of you," I whisper in Italian.

"I'll sit on your lap," Carolina whispers back in Italian.

I laugh. So she wasn't sacrificing after all.

We stay in the water till our skins are as wrinkled as the dried salted apricots that Hitomi chops and stuffs into rice balls to eat when you have a cold. Hitomi believes in the values of the Shinto religion, and she makes different kinds of rice balls, each special somehow in helping one be pure and in harmony with nature. The apricot rice balls smell like they taste, stinging and wonderful. I feel almost calm, almost harmonious.

CHAPTER
FOUR

16 December 1940, Tokyo, Japan

My school lunch is wrapped in a *furoshiki* that sits on the little table near the servants' door. I could buy a used *bento* box at the market, but I like the *furoshiki* because that's become my favorite Japanese word. Papà packs me whatever the servants are going to eat each day, and it's always yummy. He still cooks Italian food for the ambassador and his wife, but he makes Japanese food for the rest of us. Papà learned to cook Japanese style so that he could make everyone happy.

"Your fingers must be sore." Carolina comes up beside me. "From sewing on Naoki's *horo* every night."

I smile. I gave the finished *horo* to Naoki yesterday, and he pretended to gallop around the side yard while Carolina shot imaginary arrows at him, all of which sailed right through the billowing cloth, missing Naoki. Each time he triumphantly laughed. I pretended to be the servant who kept repairing his *horo* when an arrow pierced it.

Carolina puts a rice candy on my palm. "For being so good to Naoki."

The candy is misshapen, and bits of rush grass are embedded in the outer layer of rice paper, the part that dissolves in your mouth immediately. But these candies are delicious. I haven't seen any in the market for weeks. Many things are rationed now. "It's dirty," I say, wrinkling my nose.

"I hid it under my futon. It got pressed into the tatami mat. If you don't want it, give it back."

I close my fist around the treasure. "Where did you get it?"

"Pessa."

We call the ambassador's wife Pessa now—short for *principessa*—princess. She hardly ever leaves the top floor of the embassy except for the evening meal. And then she talks only to the ambassador, though it's clear she loves Papà's cooking. She uses bread to wipe every last drop of sauce off her plate.

Why would Pessa give Carolina candy? "You don't bother her, do you?"

Botan and Hatsu come through the door with a burst of cold air. They bow a greeting and plant their shoes on the shelf by the table.

Carolina sets a small *furoshiki* beside my bigger lunch one. "From Papà," she says, shifting to Japanese. She and Botan walk off holding hands.

I wonder how Carolina's doll Lella feels about Botan. The rag doll has been sitting in our room alone lately. But I guess that's good. Carolina is growing up.

I tie on my school shoes, then pick up both *furoshiki* and step outside. It's earlier than I normally walk to school. I check my jacket buttons because of the cutting cold. This is as warm as I'm going to get.

The gray wall of the embassy yard has an iron fence on top. Sharp points at the top stab the dull air. It might rain today. I wish it would snow. Then the bitter cold would be worth it. Papà says snow in Tokyo is as rare as snow back home.

I walk around to the front and out the gate, and smile big at the guard without showing my teeth. Aiko taught me that girls my age don't show their teeth when they smile. The guard never smiles back.

After a couple of blocks, I open the smaller *furoshiki*. It holds leftovers from the ambassador and his wife's breakfast: the crusty end of a loaf of bread, buttered. I can't remember when I last had butter. I nibble slowly.

"Breakfast?"

I turn my head.

"Don't look back. Walk as though I'm not here."

It's Aiko. How lucky. I've never come across Aiko walking alone. Maybe I should always walk to school earlier.

"I can smell it from here. Something odd."

"Butter." I take another bite.

"Last week you came to school smelling of plum."

"Plum jam." It was delicious. I nod.

"Don't nod," she snaps.

My heart beats hard. Why are we walking like this, her behind me?

"And before that it was something else. You shouldn't eat fancy food."

I swallow the last bite of bread and butter.

"People say the Italian embassy is full of gluttons. With expensive food. Eggs all the time. Meat. Foreign food. They have a nickname for you: *ishuu.*"

I know that word. It means different religion, and it sounds like the word that means stink. Someone's being mean and clever. I feel sick.

"I'm going to pass you now. Don't look at me." Aiko walks around me swiftly. Why is she taking this risk for me?

I stop in the middle of the sidewalk. My eyes burn. I miss Nonna more than ever.

Aiko meets up with a group of girls on the corner. They walk together toward Mita Elementary School. All the other kids walk in groups. Except me.

Last week Naoki said we're spoiled because we live at the embassy.

We're servants. We don't live like the ambassador and Pessa, but people here don't know that.

What matters now is that Aiko has done me a favor. She's trying to help me.

I walk back half a block to the closest pine tree. I rip off a handful of needles, stiff with winter. I stuff them into my mouth and chew. They poke the insides of my cheeks. I chew harder and swipe at my eyes. Pine scent finally. I gnash my teeth, grinding out every last bit of pine juice.

I march to school, eyes on the sidewalk. If anyone gets close enough, I'll breathe on them. They'll think they're in a forest.

I don't meet anyone's eyes all morning.

When it's time to clean the classroom, the teacher tells us to put on our shoes instead. We're going on a bus ride with women from the Adult Assistance Group. Everyone else seems to know about it. Our teacher must have announced it last week. Or maybe she wrote it on the board and I couldn't read it.

On the bus, I sit by a window. People file in to sit in twos. I look out the window. Finally someone plops down beside me. I dare to peek. It's Aiko. She stares straight ahead.

A girl named Mutsuko gets on. There are no more free seats.

"Sit with those two." A woman points at Aiko and me. It makes sense; we're the smallest, so there's room.

Mutsuko perches on the edge of the seat and talks softly with Aiko.

We drive through so many streets. I see women of all ages, but the men are old. The young ones are off at war. I lean my forehead against the cold glass as we bump along.

We get off at a huge park, and I look around in awe.

"The Komazawa green," whispers Aiko. "People play golf here."

No one is playing golf now; instead, soldiers train everywhere I look. They are boys, with skinny necks. They wear floppy pants and bands around their heads, and their shirts are dark with sweat, despite the cold.

Three women lead us out onto the field. "Clean it up!"

Girls form pairs. I expect to work alone, but Aiko stays with me. She glances around, and when she sees that no one is looking, she gives me a small smile. We pick up cigarette butts and scraps of paper and throw the rubbish into a trash cart.

The women herd us through the streets now, and we collect metals. The military needs iron and copper and brass for war tools. We take the metal strips off the bottoms of doors and from the edges of roofs. We gather old metal teapots and broken hibachis. We go into a Buddhist temple with a huge tree out front. The leaves shine green, even though it's December. An old woman stands at the base and hugs the main trunk. I wish someone would hug me.

"I'll be back," whispers Aiko. "Act normal."

I go inside with the other girls. We take the altar lamps, the brass bells, the incense burners. Even the beggar bowls. I feel strange, like this is a sin. But Aiko told me to act normal, so I hold one of the big bags while other girls stuff things into it. The women who lead us around keep telling us what a good job we're doing.

When we go back outside, Aiko appears again. "Did anyone notice I was gone?"

"I did."

Aiko covers her mouth and laughs.

I put something into her hand. I've been clutching it all day, ever since she warned me about my plum-jam breath, hoping I'd find the right moment to give it to her.

Aiko holds her hand close to her belly and looks down into it. She gives a little gasp. Then she pops the rice candy into her mouth. She didn't even pick out the bits of grass.

I imagine that soft cube oozing sweetness across her tongue. I wonder what flavor it is.

The woman in charge calls, "When you turn twelve, if this war is still going on, you can take jobs in the munitions factories." She beams.

"I don't want to quit school at twelve," I whisper to Aiko.

"Me neither."

Our group walks to a station and gets on a streetcar. When the car passes the imperial palace, the woman tells us to lower our heads and pray for the peace and prosperity of Emperor Hirohito and the imperial family, because Emperor Hirohito is a direct descendant of Amaterasu—the sun goddess who made the world. I bow my head like everyone else.

When we get off the streetcar, we're sent home.

"Walk ahead of me," says Aiko.

We get to the corner where she joined me this morning, and I stop. As Aiko passes me, she hands me something wrapped in folded paper. "This is better to chew than pine needles." And she's gone.

I unfold the paper. In the middle is a pile of green shiny leaves. From that huge tree! I bury my nose in them. Camphor. A girl in my class back home took camphor for her asthma. A bit of this in my mouth will cover any smell.

I tuck the leaves in their paper into my pocket. Tonight, in my ongoing letter to Nonna, I'll tell her about the woman hugging that ancient tree. And about Aiko helping me. And admitting to me that she doesn't want to quit school at twelve.

Tomorrow I'll leave for school early again, and hope to see Aiko.

CHAPTER
FIVE

24 JULY 1941, NIKKO, JAPAN

The train bumps along hour after hour. It's summer vacation, at last. We're on our way to the summer villa that belongs to the embassy, and Naoki is with us. Even more amazing, Aiko is here, too. I've never been happier. One year ago today, Papà told us about his job offer at the embassy. Forever ago.

Nonna's last letter asked when Papà was going to bring us back home. It's my privilege to read her letters aloud, while Carolina sits on Papà's lap and listens quietly, practically memorizing every word. But when I read that question, Carolina yelped, "We're not going back to Italy yet, are we? Not yet. Please."

I looked at Papà.

Carolina started first grade in April, and Botan is in her class. Carolina loves school, and no one is mean to her. Or if they are, she's handling it, because she never talks about that. But school is still hard for me. My spoken Japanese is getting good, but I'm way behind in writing. The *kana* aren't so bad, because there aren't that many of them, under a hundred. But the characters are a challenge because there's a different one for each word—everyone else has been memorizing them for years. You have to memorize hundreds and hundreds, maybe thousands, just to read a newspaper. It's hard to catch up. And I'm left at the edge whenever groups form at lunch or recess. But Naoki and I play all day on Sundays. Most important, Aiko and I are friends, secret but true. Sometimes we meet at the major public library and whisper as we look at the atlases. And even at school we find ways to be together when no one will notice. Aiko is fascinated by the world outside Japan. She asks me about food in Italy, and she brings me Japanese lunch treats. She asks me about being Catholic, and she tells me about being Buddhist. She asks me what people in Italy say about war, and she tells me what people say in Japan. She told me there are only two people in the world she can be completely honest with, and I'm one. I don't know who the other one is. But I'm so glad to be one. I'm not ready to leave Japan yet, either.

When Papà finally answered, "No, we're not going home yet," I let out my breath in relief.

We miss Nonna, though. Her letters remind us of everything back home—the manger scenes at Christmas, the carnival masks at the end of winter, the dove-shaped cakes at

Easter, and the great big church in the center of town. The church of peace. She wants to make sure we don't forget Italian traditions. But she always includes advice on how to get along here, and even though she's never been here, her advice helps us. Carolina and I memorize it and remind each other often. Nonna ends every letter with the words *forza e coraggio*—strength and courage.

And Zio Piero has written twice. He sent a card for Carolina's birthday last December and another for my birthday in February. When we write to Nonna, we always address the letter to him, too.

The train wheels screech, and Hitomi stands up. We're here. Finally. We've arrived at Nikko, a town way north of Tokyo. Papà and Hitomi have big sacks roped to their backs and bundles in both arms. Carolina, Naoki, Aiko, and I only carry sacks filled with our clothes. Still, we're tired after two crowded trains.

Tokyo was sweltering when we left, but Nikko is fresh; the cool hits us now like wind off water. It feels like we've moved backward and we're at the start of spring. We stand outside the train station, where bushes are in bloom, and I look down the road to the mountains I've read about.

"There's no snow," I whisper to Aiko.

"It's July. What did you expect?"

But I know she was hoping for snowcapped mountaintops, too. We stared together at the photo book in the Imperial Library at Ueno Park.

"I'll find out about the local bus," Hitomi says as she puts down her bundles.

"I'll go with you." Naoki crosses the street, walking just a few steps in front of Hitomi, chest high, as though he'll protect her.

"Look!" Carolina runs over to a man with a donkey attached to a cart.

I step closer to Aiko. For an instant, it almost feels as though we two are here alone. The ambassador and his wife will come in a few days, after we have the villa cleaned and the kitchen in running order. The ambassador told Papà he needs a perfect vacation; he has too many headaches in Tokyo. The Japanese foreign minister has been complaining because Italy keeps losing battles in Ethiopia and Albania.

Hitomi and Naoki come back. Hitomi says, "The next bus isn't for four hours."

"We can go in the donkey cart," Carolina says, popping up beside us again. "It's cheaper than the bus—one fare for all of us. And faster, because the donkey can go on a direct path."

The donkey owner nods at us.

"I wonder if that's what people around here call a taxi," I whisper to Aiko.

"The ambassador and his wife will be surprised," she whispers back, and we giggle. It feels good not to worry about being seen together by the girls at school. It feels great!

The donkey owner leads the way, and Papà and Hitomi walk behind the cart. Our bundles line the cart, and we children perch on top. We move slowly, and I'm feeling like I could fall asleep to the creak of the wheels, when I hear rushing water. The donkey hoofs clop and the wooden wheels clatter as we cross an old red-lacquered bridge.

"The Daiya River," calls the donkey owner.

I look over the side of the bridge. It's a long way down, and the river is fast and noisy. Carolina grabs me with one hand and Aiko with the other. Naoki does the same; we are all connected in a circle. And I'm grinning, even though I can't bear to look down again.

I'm so glad Aiko's mother let her come. Her father is in the army in Indochina. But her big brother, Gen, is home, so at least her mother isn't alone. Aiko's mother told Papà that Aiko has never been out of the city, so the villa is a wonderful opportunity. She thanked him over and over. We have the whole of summer vacation together, an entire month. Aiko made me promise I won't tell anyone that she came with me, and I know we have to go back to hiding our friendship in September. But for now we are free.

There's the villa. Huge! We dump everything in the small corner room reserved for the servants, and dance across a sitting room, a dining room, and a study. One side of the villa faces a lake, with windows and windows and windows. The other side looks out on forest. It feels like we're animals in the wild. I wish we could go outside, but it's raining now.

Hitomi goes upstairs to clean the ambassador's private quarters. Papà is already clanging things around in the kitchen.

"Come see!" Naoki lies on the dining room table. It's a Western-style table, like in the embassy, with chairs all around. "Come look with me."

We four lie like paintbrushes in a box and stare up at the ceiling, where airy bamboo poles cross every which way. It seems as though the whole villa could just float away on a breeze if someone opened a door wide.

"A cat." Naoki points.

"A frog," says Aiko. "Two!"

"A bunny!" Carolina laughs.

I see them now! The pole crossings make funny shapes. "Like origami animals."

"Exactly," says Naoki. "Now you will learn." He goes to the servants' room and comes back with squares of colored paper. "Every Japanese person needs to know how to fold paper."

Carolina and I are not Japanese. I hold my breath and wait. But Naoki doesn't say anything else. I smile. Naoki has just said Carolina and I are honorary Japanese.

Naoki is a good teacher. Patient, especially with Carolina. Aiko is already excellent at origami. It's like folding *furoshiki* into chopstick holders—but more complicated. We fold paper for a long time.

"Look." Carolina holds up her creation. "What is it, Simona?"

Oh, please let me guess right.

"A fish," said Aiko. "With a fine tail." I wonder if she was listening as Naoki instructed Carolina.

Carolina smiles. "I made something good. Can we go play now?"

So we count the stones in the fireplace. A gecko runs across the top. Naoki grabs at it, but the gecko gets away. Naoki's left with a tail in his hand.

"Bad you!" says Carolina.

"The tail will grow back," says Naoki. "That's how geckos work."

"I love geckos," I say. "They're cute and quiet and quick, and they eat mosquitoes. Let's be nice to them."

We go stand on the porch and watch the rain bounce on the surface of pure, deep-blue Lake Chūzenji.

"The volcano is the lake's emperor," says Naoki. "Mount Nantai."

We look to the right. Beyond the point of land that sticks out into the lake, far, far beyond, Mount Nantai shimmers. Papà told us it's Japan's Mount Vesuvius, and it's important to listen to it. If it rumbles, you run.

"Kegon Falls is out there, too." Naoki points across the lake to somewhere we can't see. "With giant waterfalls."

"Let's go out onto that platform," Carolina says. "See it?"

The platform is a big wooden square with a handrail around it. We pick our way carefully down the steps and across the pebble beach. Soon we're drenched, but the rain is stopping. And it's warm and lovely as a bath.

Carolina squeezes my arm. "Simona!"

A big monkey comes out from the woods, followed by more,

until there are six, with two babies, one on a mother's back and the other hanging below her. They're gray with pink faces, and they walk on all fours. One turns, and I see a pink bottom.

They head toward us, cautiously.

"Monkeys are dangerous," says Naoki.

They're between us and the house now.

"Here." Aiko beckons toward a hole in the side of the support under the platform. "Get in, fast."

We crowd into the dark hole and squat. Carolina squats right behind me. She grabs the back of my shirt.

The big monkey walks up to the opening, and sits on his haunches. The other monkeys settle behind him.

I smell the leader's wet fur, like rotting tree bark. His golden eyes are beady, sunken into his face. His fur hangs long around his mouth, like an old man's whiskers. Hair runs all the way down his long fingers to his light gray fingernails. "The leader is looking at me," I whisper.

"Don't look back," whispers Aiko.

"Looking back is a challenge," whispers Naoki.

I drop my eyes and pick up one of the broken planks that has fallen inward. I hold it with both hands, ready.

An adult makes a *coo.* I peek. One monkey picks something off another one and eats it. Now all of them are doing that.

Finally they walk away, their short, stumpy tails wagging, and disappear into the woods.

"The daddy looked mean," says Carolina. "I'm glad Lella is safe in our room. Will they come back?"

I wait for Aiko or Naoki to answer. They know about monkeys. Finally I say, "Why should they?"

"Tell me they won't come back, Simona."

"They won't come back, Carolina."

Carolina relaxes against me, even though she told me what to say.

"There's a box under this platform," says Aiko.

I turn around, staying in a squat, because the platform isn't high enough to stand under. "Where?"

"Behind me."

We're all feeling the sides of the box now.

"A pirate chest," says Naoki.

"Push it out into the open," says Carolina.

We push. It doesn't budge, but the top lifts easily. I force away images of spiders, and Aiko and I feel around in the hazy dark. "Wooden shoes," she says. "But not the ordinary kind."

We skitter out the opening one by one. I straighten my legs and arms stiffly.

Aiko holds up a fancy pair of wooden shoes. They are flat wood on very tall bottom supports underneath the heel and toe.

Carolina grabs them. "Whose are they?"

"The pirate wife's," says Naoki. "She's going to come back and snatch you away for stealing them."

Carolina stares at him. He grins, and she laughs.

We go up onto the platform and take turns wearing the fancy shoes. Even Naoki.

"*Kata-kata, kata-kata,*" we sing, mimicking the *clickity-clack.*
It's hard to balance in them, so we fall, and laugh.

"Let's go swimming," says Carolina.

Naoki bumps into me. "I can't swim," he whispers to me.

I nod, and say to the others, "When Naoki goes to help his mother, we can have a girl swim without him." How will Naoki ever manage in the navy if he can't swim? Maybe I can teach him.

But I'm so glad he's here. I look behind us at the sides of the villa, where the dark and light pattern of the wood is like a checkerboard. It's just right, among these trees. We four fit together just right. I wish we could stay here forever.

CHAPTER
SIX

7 December 1941, Tokyo, Japan

Carolina's stomach growls. She giggles, even though we're in church. We haven't had breakfast yet, because the adults and I are going to take Communion, and our insides must be clean and empty, ready for the wafer. Carolina should have nibbled on something before church, but she likes to fast because I do it.

Papà doesn't scold her for giggling, and neither does the ambassador, sitting beside Papà, nor Pessa. In Italy children giggling in church isn't bad behavior. But Japan is different.

I look around. Denenchōfu Church is packed with a mix of foreigners and Japanese. It's tiny in comparison to our huge church in Italy. And it's made of wood, not bricks. The brass altar bells that were here when we first came are gone. So is the altar candelabra. But the incense smells the same, and the

Latin words are the same. I love this church. Everyone does. People stand in the side aisles and at the back. The church couldn't hold one more body.

It's the seventh of December, and Carolina turns seven today; we're having a party. We're not calling it a party, though, since no one in Japan has birthday parties.

After Mass everyone spills out the front doors. We wait our turn to bow to Friar Inayou. He's the only Japanese priest at this church; the others are from Europe. He likes Carolina and me. Last autumn Carolina gave him an origami boat. Since then, after Mass he gives each of us an origami animal. This is a Franciscan church, and Saint Francis loved animals. Today the priest's animals are birds in flight. A yellow one for Carolina and a blue one for me. We bow again.

We pile into the official embassy car to ride home. Papà sits up front beside the driver. The ambassador and his wife sit in the back, with Carolina and me between them. I take Mamma's church scarf off and tie it onto Carolina. I get to wear it during Mass, and she gets to wear it on the way home. Most girls her age don't cover their heads in church. We fly our origami birds in wonderful swoops.

I think of Nonna. We've been waiting and waiting for a letter from her. It has to come soon; she'd never fail to wish Carolina a happy birthday. Zio Piero's card isn't here yet, either. Papà promises they will appear any day; the Italian mail can be late, but it always shows up in the end.

The ambassador leans forward and taps Papà on the

shoulder. "Foreign Minister Matsuoka will be coming on Wednesday. We need to serve him a Japanese banquet."

"Of course," says Papà.

"A celebration." The ambassador sounds annoyed. "He hinted something about the Soviet Union."

"I can buy herring roe, and with the perfect light soy sauce, I can—"

"Do whatever you think is best." The ambassador reaches past Carolina and me and pats his wife's knee. "Just make sure that for the rest of the week you make my wife's favorite dishes. Your cooking is such a relief."

Pessa sighs. "Oh, Mario." She looks out the window, her hands twisting and twisting.

It feels strange to hear the ambassador's first name. Carolina laughs.

Pessa turns and gives Carolina a small smile. Pessa takes Mamma's church scarf off Carolina and drops it onto my lap. Then she smooths her lace mantilla and puts it on Carolina's head. "It's your birthday, I heard. From now on, you can look like the big girls in church."

Carolina's mouth falls open, and her eyes say it all: she wants to be wearing Mamma's church scarf.

"Thank you, Ambasciatrice," I say. "But your gift is far too fine and expensive."

Pessa smiles. "I need a new one anyway."

Carolina sits like a stone.

I pinch her thigh lightly.

"Thank you, Pessa," she manages.

"Pessa?"

"Carolina thinks of you as a *principessa*," I say. "Because you're as beautiful as a princess." I look at the ambassador, with his slicked-back hair, parted in the middle. He isn't a prince; he's more of a frog. The princess and the frog.

Pessa touches Carolina's cheek. She says to the ambassador, "The bay, please."

The ambassador says to Papà, "Tell the driver to take the route along the bay."

Papà is writing something in the little notebook he always carries. He doesn't seem to hear.

"Please take the route along the bay," I say to the driver in Japanese. "The ambassador's wife wants that."

The ambassador looks at me as though he's just realized I was there. "Such good Japanese," he says.

"I know it, too," says Carolina.

The ambassador nods at me. "I watched you with the Japanese children last summer at the villa. How old are you?"

"Almost ten."

"Only ten." He taps his fingertips together.

Today is bright and clear. No clouds. But there's a cold wind. We can see the bay now. I wish the windows were down, so I could smell it. The Tokyo Bay is enormous, with lots of ports and many rivers that empty into it. The five major ones are the Tama, the Sumida, the Edo, the Obitsu, and the Yōrō. At school I stand in front of the big map and try to memorize every detail of this area. The others in my class learned all this in first grade; I'm always working to catch up.

The water in the bay is choppy, and there's a gigantic battleship out there. The waves slosh over the decks, but the ship barely sways. Naoki says the Japanese navy is invincible. He must be right.

When we get back to the embassy, Papà prepares breakfast for the ambassador and Pessa.

"Don't forget the canary," says the ambassador, in Italian, and he and Pessa disappear up the stairs.

Papà turns to Hitomi. "The ambassador's wife wants a canary bird. Can you find one? Today?"

Hitomi's eyes widen. "She already has so much to eat."

Papà laughs. "She wants it as a pet. A live canary."

Papà grinds coffee beans with his mortar and pestle. The smell coats the air. He sets out fresh bread and bowls of jams. But my mouth doesn't water at the sight like it used to. Now I love Japanese breakfast. I love all Japanese food.

Carolina and I run into the room off the kitchen, where Naoki waits for us every Sunday. I think he's extra glad on Sunday, because it's his one day with his mother. She works such long hours at the embassy. I don't know if he has a father. He talks about his uncle, but never a father.

We sit on mats and eat rice balls rolled in dried fish flakes and sesame seeds. And we nibble pickles. A wonderful breakfast.

Hatsu arrives with Botan, but Hatsu doesn't stay. It's not her job to look after Carolina ever since Carolina started school in April. I don't know what job she has now. I watch Hatsu leave; she's thinner than before. Maybe Botan is thinner, too.

The girls immediately sit beside each other and share food. They're together in class all week, but you'd think they never get to see each other, the way they talk now.

Finally Aiko arrives, and we five play games all morning.

Papà comes into the room. "Do you want to help me prepare your lunch?"

"What will we make?" asks Carolina.

"There's leftover pasta. And spicy leaves. And eggs. Not the powdered kind that we buy in the ration lines. Fresh eggs, that beat into the right froth. So I thought we'd make—"

"Frittata!" shouts Carolina. "We'll help."

"Western food?" Naoki wrinkles his nose.

"It's omelette, one of Papà's specialties," I say. "You can crack the eggs."

Naoki smiles.

We make the best frittata ever. All the servants share. Then Papà serves Carolina's birthday cake, a giant crust with lemon-like custard. Enough for everyone.

We play outside all afternoon.

Evening falls early these days. Aiko leaves by herself; I know that she lives close enough to walk alone, though I've never been to her house. Hitomi and Naoki also live close enough to walk; Carolina and I went to his house once. He leaves with Hitomi, and Hatsu arrives to take Botan home.

I bow and hand Hatsu a *furoshiki*. "Old foods. Half-rotten. I'm so sorry to bother you with them. If you cannot use them, dispose of them, please."

Hatsu bows deep.

We avoid each other's eyes.

"Maybe Botan can come every Sunday," I say. "Otherwise Carolina is lonely while I play with Naoki. It would be a service to us if you brought her here."

Hatsu bows again. She and Botan leave.

Carolina hugs me around the waist. "I won't tell Papà."

She's right, it's a secret, because in a sense I stole the food I gave Hatsu. The food is supposed to be for the employees of the embassy, including the day servants and the live-in guards, and Signor Rosati, the consular officer. And I may have made a problem for Papà; it's his job to feed us all within the budget. But Hatsu and Botan look hungry—hungrier than any of those others. So I'm a thief, but maybe not the worst kind.

The next morning, ready for the start of the school week, we go to the kitchen, where the servants are sitting on their heels in a circle around the radio.

Hitomi jumps up and gives us each a breakfast tray with rice and salted plum.

I whisper to Hitomi, "What's going on?"

"The Americans think they can tell Japan what to do in Indochina. The white pigs. But we won't let them. So before dawn this morning, our air force bombed them in Hawaii. Pearl Harbor. Now they know how strong we are. They will remember the eighth of December forever." She rushes back to her spot on the floor.

The eighth of December. But Tokyo time is seven hours ahead of Italy time—so it happened on the seventh of December in Italy. In America, too. I don't correct Hitomi, though. Whatever the date, everyone will remember today. Japan bombed America!

The radio announcer describes how boats were sunk in the harbor of an American island. Many people died. A surprise attack.

Papà rushes down the stairs into the kitchen. The ambassador and Pessa must have had breakfast in their rooms. He chews on his bottom lip as he throws our lunches into *bento* boxes. When Carolina started school, Botan told her that everyone uses *bento* boxes, so now we use them, too. Papà walks with us to the side door.

I touch his hand and whisper, "Hitomi says this is good news. Your face says it isn't."

Papà puts one hand on my head and one hand on Carolina's head. "America has stayed out of the war that Italy and Germany are waging in Europe and North Africa. It has stayed out of the war that Japan is waging in China and Indochina.

But now that Japan attacked, America can't stay out of these wars. And America is unbeatable."

"America will declare war on Japan?" I clutch his arm.

"And on Italy."

"Italy!" I cry. "But Italy didn't drop bombs on the American harbor."

Carolina watches us.

"When America declares war on Japan, Italy will declare war on America," Papà says. "Remember the Tripartite Pact, Simona? Germany, Italy, and Japan fight together. The enemy of one is the enemy of all three." Papà's hands smooth our hair tenderly. "Go to school."

Carolina and I go out to the street. The group of girls we usually walk with is halfway down the block. We run to catch up. They're talking about the attack.

"Our air force killed hundreds."

"Thousands! Many thousands."

"After we defeat America, everyone will have plenty to eat."

"Japan will rule the world."

As we walk, more girls join us and talk. Maybe everyone in every home in Japan is talking about the surprise attack.

Aiko whispers to me, "America is huge. It has more soldiers than Japan, and more planes, more ships."

And Papà said America is unbeatable. How do Aiko and Papà know these things?

I walk closer to Aiko and pull Carolina with me. Aiko took a chance to whisper those words to me; it would have been awful if anyone else had heard. This is another secret between me and Aiko—the way we can talk about things the radio doesn't say, the way we can share our own opinions. And she knows things I don't know.

I look around at the group of girls. Does anyone else have opinions they can't speak out loud? What do they know?

It's Monday, and we start the school week with morning assembly. The principal says that today is a stupendous day for Japan. We stand and shout the traditional cheer, *"Banzai!"* Marching tunes play nearly all day long, so it's hard to even think. We stay late for extra songs and marching around the school grounds. On the way home, soldiers stand in the streets and hand out the evening editions of newspapers, with giant headlines: JAPAN DECLARES WAR ON U.S., BRITAIN AT DAWN and DEADLY AIR STRIKE ON HAWAII. Loudspeakers on public buildings blast out marching tunes. Men walk past us talking about how much money they are making today, how Japan's stock market is soaring. Everything feels like a giant celebration.

When we get home, Papà doesn't say anything about Pearl Harbor. But the radio in the kitchen is constantly on. Papà was right: the next day America declares war on Japan. Days later, Italy and Germany declare war on America. And America declares war on them. But no one in Tokyo talks of fear. Not out loud, at least. The radio spews praise for the imperial Japanese forces, for our victories, for our glorious future.

CHAPTER

SEVEN

4 April 1942, Tokyo, Japan

The interpreter stands outside the ambassador's office door with a pile of newspapers in his arms. I peek. The headlines are about *Daitōa Kyōeiken*—the Co-Prosperity Sphere—how this war will liberate Asia from control by Great Britain and France, and Asia will prosper.

The interpreter gives me a small head bow. I bow back, much deeper, and hurry to the servants' door.

The school year ended in late March, so Carolina and I are home on school break, and today we're going shopping with Papà.

Papà pulls his apron off over his head. It's all one piece, black, crisscrossing in the back, with big pockets on the sides—so different from the white jacket he used to wear in Italy. The three of us walk out the gate and along the street.

"What are we going to buy?"

"Dried salted roe," says Papà.

"Pessa wants it," says Carolina. "One. Two. Ha! Look, three, four." She's counting the rising-sun flags that hang from windows. The fourth of every month is flag day. People display flags to celebrate how well Japan is doing in this war.

I remember dried salted roe. Back home, Papà grated it over ripe tomatoes or asparagus or plain flat bread. It smells and tastes wonderful. "Do they even sell it here?"

"They do."

"Thirteen," says Carolina loudly. "Pessa wants it grated over pasta." She goes back to counting on her fingers. Lately, when she's anxious, she counts.

"Pasta?" I turn to Papà. "I thought the flour was gone." The wheat harvest failed.

"I bought more."

I almost ask how. But I stop. Tokyo is full of illegal black markets these days. Those are places where people sell food beyond what the government rations out. My teachers warn against them.

"Eighteen," says Carolina.

A man in uniform passes with a stack of folded red papers in one arm—the call-up notices for military service. The notice is always hand-delivered. My heart flutters. I'm glad Naoki is only ten. The war will be over long before he's sixteen.

We go to Papà's favorite fish vendor. He isn't there. We go to another. Closed.

"Pessa will be sad if we don't get it," says Carolina.

The way she says it makes me jealous. They have a bond. I remember the rice candy that Pessa gave Carolina, and the beautiful mantilla that Pessa wanted Carolina to wear to Mass.

Then I think of Denenchōfu Church. After the bombing of Pearl Harbor, the military police took all the foreign priests who weren't German off to prison. Friar Inayou is still there. He's Japanese. But Papà says there are no Masses anymore.

I miss that priest and that sweet little church.

Still, Sundays are special. Botan comes to play with Carolina, and Naoki comes to play with me. I can't wait for tomorrow.

The third fish vendor is closed. Even the fishermen have gone to war. We get on a streetcar and go to the market at Tsukiji, the one Papà doesn't like because it's big and confusing. He speaks Japanese decently now, but not quick enough for that market. So we help him, and hurrah! We find dried salted roe. Carolina dances in a circle.

"Dancing?" says the fish vendor. "Are you on your way to the cherry blossom festival on the Meguro River? Will you gobble up candy?"

Carolina stops; her face begs Papà to take us there.

I want to go, too. But ten-year-olds don't beg. Most girls in my class planned on going to the festival the day after the school year ended. Our teachers say the cherry blossom is important. Soldiers are like those blossoms, fated to have short lives. It is something to be proud of, to die for one's country. The cherry blossom symbolizes the proud and loyal Japanese spirit.

We went last year with the ambassador and Pessa. I remember the pink and white overhead, so dense that it screened out the sunshine. I remember the constant buzz of bees, and the bitter and sweet smell of the blossoms everywhere, coating my teeth.

Now we're on another streetcar. This isn't the one to take us back to the embassy—but the one to see the trees!

Soon we walk the path beside the Meguro River and look down at the high walls along both sides. Fewer people stroll here than at last year's festival, though it's just as beautiful. Most of the cherry trees are in bloom. A wind comes in off the water, and petals drop; it rains velvety pink. The river surface is instantly awash in pink. Carolina skips ahead, her hands out to each side, palms upward. Papà and I stand on a bridge, and the pink accumulates in our hair.

Carolina runs back to us. "The shop up there sells seafoam candy."

Seafoam candy is like the lovely mix of beaten egg whites and sugar that birthday cakes are made of in Italy. It comes in different colors and shapes. Papà nods, so I go up to the shop. There's a man on a chair behind the candy counter, dozing.

I give a formal greeting in my gentlest voice.

The man stands up and turns. His face opens in surprise. He's so thin, his cheekbones look like they might pierce his skin. "From your voice, I thought you were a Japanese girl. You sound like you come from Tokyo."

I beam at him.

Carolina chooses white candies shaped like mice. I choose pink ones shaped like cherry blossoms. Papà surprises me. He picks a candy—just one, but even one sweet is unusual for him—green and shaped like a giant teardrop.

"Come back at night," says the candy vendor. "See the lanterns lit up. It's even more beautiful then."

On the way home, I eat my candies slowly, so they'll last the whole way. I ask Papà, "Do you think they have any idea how much trouble they make for you?"

Papà smiles. He doesn't ask who, and I'm glad. I don't want to say bad things about Pessa in front of Carolina, though I'm pretty sure she isn't listening. The seafoam candies take all her attention. She's licking them, the best way to make them last. "It's my job, Simona. I love my job. I make people happy with food. But . . ." Papà's voice lowers on that last word. "I'll save some dried salted roe for us." His tone is conspiratorial. "We can put it between thin slices of raw white radish—and garlic bulb stems. That's how the Japanese eat it."

As we get closer to the embassy, we see a boy swing a bamboo pole with a string on it toward a tree. The tip of the string hits a bird. The bird falls, struggling against the string. Something sticky must hold the bird fast.

The boy rips the string away and stuffs the squawking bird into a bulging cloth bag. He has other birds in there.

Carolina runs up to him. "Set them free!"

The boy looks at her as though she's crazy. "Everybody needs soup."

Carolina's mouth drops open.

My face burns. He's as thin as the man who sold us the seafoam candy.

I have two seafoam candies left. I hand them to the boy.

He stares, as though he doesn't know what they are. What good is candy? I might as well have put two stones on his palm. But I have nothing else to give.

Carolina looks at me. She has one candy left; she's been so good about making them last. She adds her candy to the boy's palm. "Lick them," she says. "Slowly."

We walk on.

Papà pats Carolina on the head. "I'll tell Nonna about you two in the next letter. She'll be proud."

We step inside the embassy to find an envelope from Nonna, almost as though Papà's words made it appear. It's my turn to open it. The tissue paper inside is rolled. We go to the table and unroll carefully. Seeds appear. Zucchini, melon, spinach, parsley, beets, carrots. Seeds and seeds.

Carolina and I immediately set about preparing a kitchen garden. Over in one corner of the embassy grounds there are two piles, one of dirt, one of rocks. The ambassador bought them to build a rock garden for his wife. But Pessa doesn't want one. Carolina and I lug the rocks to the side yard and arrange them in a square. This garden will be even larger than Nonna's.

In the gardener's storage space we find buckets and hedge clippers. No shovel. But, oh! There's the perfect tool. "A *zappa*," I say happily, calling the hoe by its Italian name. Nonna always says that's all a gardener really needs.

"A *kuwa*," says Carolina, the Japanese name.

I didn't know that word. Sometimes I wonder if Carolina speaks Japanese better than Italian these days. In Nonna's last letter she begged us to speak Italian to each other, to remember who we are, and to come back soon. It's been nearly two years here, and she guesses how much we've changed.

We fill the center of our square from the pile of dirt. It mounds up beautifully, just like a garden in Italy. Hitomi comes out into the yard and nods approval. She makes me think of my teachers; they say vegetable gardens are the best way to be patriotic.

In this moment, we are the best kind of Japanese girls.

CHAPTER
EIGHT

21 April 1942, Tokyo, Japan

I stand in the side yard and watch the canary cage in the upstairs window. A shadow passes. Once. Twice. Now the person
comes to the cage and stays. Pessa. She feeds the bird from
her palm.

"Come on." Carolina kicks the side of my shoe. "I don't
want to go to school any more than you do. But we have to."

Since when did she become so grown-up?

She goes out the gate of the embassy ahead of me. We walk
slowly. Other children on the street go slowly, too. It's Tuesday,
the twenty-first of April. Three days ago, American planes
bombed Tokyo. Their machine guns strafed in wide swaths.
They destroyed factories and warehouses.

But that wasn't the worst.

They came right before noon. Most children had gone home, since Saturday school is a half day. But some stayed to help clean classrooms. A child at Mizumoto Primary School was killed. A child at Waseda Middle School was killed. Those schools used to seem far away from the Minato ward, where our embassy is. Now they seem close.

Adults died, too. But it's those children that everyone talks about. Children, killed in their schools.

Yesterday our teachers told us not to be afraid. Japan is strong. America is weak. Otherwise America would not have targeted schools. We must come to school without fail, to keep Japan strong. Everyone counts on us. They said it over and over. They made us repeat it after them.

We stomped around the room singing military marches. We sang about the goodness of the emperor and the divine origins of Japan, about admirable Japanese mothers sending their sons off to war so bravely, about Mount Fuji and New Year's Day customs and village festivals, everything we love, right down to pounding rice cakes. We sang about how Japan outshines all other countries.

I try to sing these songs to myself now. I want to stop being afraid. But I keep looking up at the sky as we walk to school.

Over the past three days the interpreter has brought the ambassador piles and piles of newspapers. After he leaves, I read the front page of all of them. It's hard, because I don't know all the characters yet. But more than half is written in *kana,* and I know *kana.* Japan swears to get even with America. It will kill thousands of Chinese people, men and women and children, to show America that Japan is strong.

How does killing Japanese children prove that America is weak, but killing Chinese children will prove that Japan is strong?

Could I be right and the newspapers be wrong? My stomach's jittery; I should be ashamed of such thoughts.

And I can't stop scanning the skies for planes.

Keiko and Aiko join us at the corner, and we greet each other, as usual. But Keiko's face is stern, and Aiko doesn't look at me.

"What's wrong?" I ask.

"Nothing is wrong." Keiko stands tall. "Everything is right. Tell her, Aiko."

Aiko glances at me quickly, then away. Her face is tear-streaked. "You tell her."

"Our brothers received the wonderful welcome yesterday—the call-up notice for the imperial army." Keiko's voice is brittle. "It's on red paper."

A chill goes up my spine. "I've seen it." I hadn't realized Aiko's brother, Gen, was sixteen already.

"Do not look like that, Simona!" Keiko says. "Do not make that sad face."

I look down.

"They have been honored. They go for the military physical next week. They will pass with top scores and go to Toyama for combat training."

Everyone gets top scores on their physicals these days. The military turns away no one. Everyone who is called up must serve.

"It's the emperor's orders," says Keiko. "Our brothers will lift their hands in salute and say, 'Long live the emperor.' I am so proud." She smooths the front of her skirt. "They are delivering military call-ups all over Tokyo today."

Of course! Because of the bombs on Saturday. Big brothers are being taken away because of the American bombs.

Shizue and Yoshie and Noriko join us at the next corner. Keiko shares the news, and the girls congratulate her and Aiko. Everyone smiles.

Aiko falls back. Carolina and I fall back with her.

"Gen must be proud," I say softly. "You must be proud."

"Would you be?" The corners of Aiko's mouth quiver.

I touch the back of her hand. Just one quick touch, so no one sees. "Don't be afraid. Japan is winning the war."

She looks straight ahead, but her eyes blink fast.

"It's in the newspapers," I say.

"Don't act like an idiot, Simona. All the men are gone. Now all the boys are going. If we're winning, how come no one ever comes home?"

My stomach clenches. Aiko hasn't heard from her father

in so long. It will be just Aiko and her mother now. "It's . . . it's going to be all right."

"You sound like our teachers. First they say we will win. Then they say it's an honor to die. They don't even see the contradiction. They're crazy. Crazy liars."

Her words echo my own thoughts from the past days. I'm ice inside. "You can't say such things," I whisper.

"I didn't. And if you ever say I did, I'll deny it." Aiko looks at Carolina. "Don't you ever say I did, either. Or I'll do something mean. I'll . . . cut off a lock of Lella's hair."

Carolina looks stricken, though she hardly ever plays with Lella anymore. "I wouldn't say anything even if you stayed nice."

We pass a tobacco shop. A line stretches from the front door, around to the corner, and down the side street. People in line bicker. There's never been a line at the tobacco shop before.

The train station has a long line, too.

"Look around," whispers Aiko. "Look at our wonderful, organized country. Nothing works anymore."

"We still have school," I say.

"Till we're twelve. If we don't starve before that."

"We're all planting kitchen gardens," says Carolina.

"How many will they feed? Japan is full of mountains and forests and riverbeds, so we have no big farms. And two years of drought ruined the rice crops. The wheat. And those typhoons." She wipes away a tear. "Things are falling apart."

"No," I say.

"What do you mean, no?"

"No." I walk more quickly. "Your brother will not die."

"No one can promise that," says Aiko.

Aiko and I look at each other.

"I promise anyway." But inside, we know we are crying.

CHAPTER
NINE

20 June 1942, Tokyo, Japan

Naoki stands in the kitchen doorway, and I stand beside him, trying to calm my jumping stomach. He says, "I'm going home."

Hitomi stops stirring. "You just arrived. You wanted all Saturday afternoon together with Simona in the garden. This June weather is perfect for weeding and thinning the root vegetables."

"I changed my mind."

"Working in the kitchen garden is a contribution to the country. Tell me what happened."

Naoki glances at me, face pinched. It will hurt him to tell on me.

"I said something that Naoki didn't like," I say.

"About?"

"The war."

"The Shinto gods hold this war holy." Hitomi's voice is as stiff as her words.

I know how she feels about her gods. I give the smallest nod.

"What did you say?"

"Maybe . . . maybe we shouldn't be fighting."

Hitomi puts down her stirring spoon. "Those words are an offense to the gods. We'll go home together, Naoki." Her voice gives no hint of emotion. "Simona can explain to her father why we cannot be in her presence today."

I wish she would shout at me.

I wish I didn't have these doubts.

As Hitomi is about to leave the room, Naoki in tow, she stops. "Naoki, wait for me outside the door." Naoki goes without a word or glance. Hitomi moves close and says very quietly, "You read the ambassador's newspapers. I see you. Maybe you hear the ambassador say things in his own language. Different things from what the radio says. You think you are smarter than you are. That is a white-pig flaw. All Westerners have it. You may have it worse than most because you speak Japanese so well, so you think you understand. Do not be fooled. Japan is triumphant throughout the Pacific. The Americans lost many men at the Battle of Midway. Your words and thoughts are an offense to the gods. Learn. Cleanse yourself."

And she's gone.

My breath hardly comes. My eyes well with tears.

Papà comes into the kitchen, takes one look at me, and rushes over. He hugs me tight.

"Hitomi and Naoki left because they're mad at me. Maybe Hitomi hates me."

"Oh, Simonuccia," croons Papà into my hair. He hasn't called me Simonuccia since I was little. It feels good. "We can talk about this after Carolina goes to bed tonight. Without an audience."

I look around the kitchen. We are speaking Italian, and no one understands anything we say. No one has even paused in their tasks. I doubt they heard what Hitomi and I said to each other. But I'm sure they saw my tears. This is not how a Japanese child my age should behave. I step back and nod.

But I'm already realizing what I can and cannot tell Papà. I can tell what I said to Naoki—that if we're doing so well in this war, how come people are so hungry? How come the emperor keeps taking more men and boys from their homes? I want to know what Papà thinks. But I cannot tell Papà what Hitomi said about Westerners. She was angry; she couldn't mean it.

"The midday meal is already prepared," Papà says to the servant Masaaki. "You know how to serve it. My daughters and I must do errands." He turns to me. "Go get Carolina."

Carolina is still outside in the kitchen garden, weeding around the sunflower stalks. The government handed out seeds, and when the flowers are ready, government personnel will take them to press for oil to be used by the military. We've been talking about how wonderful it will be to see cheerful sunflowers. Carolina is waiting for Naoki and me to come back and help weed. Will Naoki ever come back? He must. We're friends.

I call Carolina inside, and we meet Papà in our room.

"Put on kerchiefs and tuck your hair up under them." Papà wears brown pants, a brown shirt, and a field cap. A citizen's uniform, what men who aren't in the military wear to show their loyalty. People wear them more often since those bombs dropped on Tokyo. "We'll do the errands Hitomi was supposed to do this afternoon. Inconspicuously. You walk behind me and look down like obedient daughters. I'll keep my face down, too."

Does he really think people will take us for Japanese? Carolina and I walk like Japanese girls, but Papà doesn't walk like a Japanese man at all. Every step gives him away. People are going to know we are Westerners. Maybe they'll think we're horrible white pigs.

We go straight to the laundry. I've been here many times, because Hitomi takes Carolina and me on errands if she needs extra hands to carry things. When we part the curtain to enter the doorway, bells chime. The washerwoman calls a greeting. Papà and I place the dirty laundry on the counter, and we all straighten up, because the washerwoman is blind. It doesn't matter whether our faces show. I do all the talking, so even if it she hates Westerners, like Hitomi, she'll never know that's who we are.

She sets our laundry to the side and takes two pieces of

paper from a box. She folds one piece of paper into a mushroom. Then she folds the other into the exact same shape. She puts one origami mushroom on the stack of our dirty clothes, and she hands the other one to me.

Every time we come to her shop, she makes us a different shape. She's smart. Writing numbers on a slip of paper as a receipt won't work for a blind person. But when we come back and hand her the paper mushroom, she'll go straight to our stack of clean laundry, and her fingers will check the little paper mushroom sitting on top and know that it's ours.

I'm good at origami now. I can make a mushroom like the washerwoman's, but not as fast. And not with my eyes closed. It's a marvel that those rough red hands can move so precisely. The first time I saw her hands, I asked Hitomi about them. She said it was because the washerwoman has to pluck laundry out of boiling soapy water and scrub it, then drop it back in, and then scrub again. How can she get out the dirty spots when she can't see them? Do her hands constantly hurt?

We leave, and my arms feel light without that bundle of sheets. For no reason at all, I'm happy. "Can we go to the department store?"

Papà turns his head to me sideways, keeping his face down, but I see the surprise there. His mouth opens, and I watch his lips go to form *no*. I can rattle off all the reasons myself. I never should have asked. But instead he says, "Why not?"

Carolina squeals and makes a little skip. "We can buy treats," she says in Italian.

Papà presses his finger to his lips, and I'm afraid Carolina has just ruined it. But then he says, "Speak only Japanese." He switches to Japanese on the last word. "If we buy anything, let Simona handle it."

"I speak Japanese, too," says Carolina. "As good as anyone. Simona still says things wrong now and then."

"Yes," says Papà. "But Simona knows how to handle situations."

I look away, trying to hide my smile from Carolina.

We ride the subway to the Shinjuku Station. Carolina whispers that the yellow cars are like sunshine streaking below ground, making it warm. Her words feel like poetry, like the haiku we study in school.

We walk through the station to the huge department store, behind a woman with two daughters. The older daughter must be seven or eight. The younger is a baby wrapped onto her big sister's back inside a wide sash at the waist just for that purpose. The baby sleeps, and her head hangs backward.

That baby has to feel very loved, to be carried like that. And that big sister must feel very loved, to be trusted like that. I imagine a baby on my own back.

Carolina has the same reaction. She drags us around the store looking for a child-size sash, so that she can carry Lella in it.

We go to the roof first, to the children's play area. But no other children are around, so Carolina quickly jumps off the swing. The pet supply section is gone; the garden supply section is nearly empty. The last time we were here, the store bustled, but that was more than a year ago.

We go down floor by floor, searching for a child's sash. The shelves are half-empty. No pottery. No lacquerware. Our footsteps echo in the aisles.

All the pretty children's kimono sashes are gone. No bright colors. Nothing to make Carolina smile.

In the basement grocery and food court, people crowd in a corner. Oh! Someone is making tempura. Papà is the world's best cook, of course. But he never makes tempura. I've eaten it only three times in my whole life. It's crisp and delicious.

The fish sizzles in the bubbling oil. Everyone murmurs about how long it's been since food counters have served anything but miso soup. We are lucky to go by this counter at this very moment on this very day. The cook quickly drops the fried fish into bags and seals them up. We buy a bag and hurry outside to find a place to eat. Tempura is best hot.

Beside the department store stands an old building, like an ordinary house. This part of the city has big new buildings beside little old ones, all helter-skelter. Along one side of that old building is an alley with a plum tree in a tiny plot of dirt. A trash cart is parked under the tree, the two-wheel type. A man sleeps in it.

We sit on the stone bench near the cart, and Papà rips open the bag. A stench comes out—the fish is bad. Carolina drops her hands onto her lap and moans.

A mangy dog hobbles along the alley. Big splotches of his fur are missing, and his ribs show. I take the bag and walk after the dog. He growls; he'll bite if I get close. I set the bag on the ground and go back to the bench. The dog finishes off that rotten fish in three gulps, and licks his chops. Then he turns down the alley. I pick up the ripped bag.

We hear a door slide open. A tiny woman comes out of the low building, and we stand. When the woman's eyes meet ours, she hesitates. She didn't see our faces till now. She carries a wooden box.

She comes closer, and we all bow. "Sit, please."

We don't sit, of course. That is her bench, under her plum tree. "We were just resting a moment," I say. "We didn't mean to disturb you."

The woman tilts her head. "I saw. You must have bought that unlovely fish at the department store. Many people have had that misfortune today. The dog you gave it to is an Akita. That's a special breed. Did you know that the police have been ordered to kill dogs they see wandering alone? No one is allowed to feed them."

I tense up. "We didn't know."

"That dog will live a little longer because of you. Animals are innocents." She takes the lid off the box and sets it on the bench. Then she holds the box toward us with both hands. She's so skinny, her hands are birdlike. "This is not fancy tempura, but the fish is not rotten."

There are three perfect sticks of fish glazed with teriyaki sauce. Studded with sesame seeds. They smell so good.

She bows. "Please enjoy them."

Papà bows back. "Thank you," he says in Japanese. "You are kind and generous." He turns to me. "Simona, explain that we were disappointed at the rotten fish, but we are not hungry," he says in Italian. "We cannot accept fish, not when she's hungry herself."

"She gave it as a gift, Papà. We have to accept her gift."

"Make her understand, Simona."

I look at the woman. "My father is proud," I say very softly, as though Papà won't be able to hear. "He wants me to tell you we are not hungry. We have eaten far too much today to accept your delightful fish."

The woman looks pleased. "I make so many mistakes. These sticks of fish are not for you or your father. They are for the little one."

"Thank you," says Carolina. She bows. "I love fish on a stick." She takes one before Papà can stop her.

"You have two hands," says the woman.

Carolina gives a second bow and takes a second stick. "Thank you."

"Would you mind disposing of this last one for me?" The woman holds the box toward me.

I bow and take the stick of fish. "Thank you. You humble me."

The woman bows. "You do me an honor." She goes back inside.

We walk out to the main street. Papà takes the extra fish stick from Carolina, and we huddle together as we nibble. Papà smiles at us.

All it takes is one good thing to change everything.

CHAPTER
TEN

1 AUGUST 1942, NIKKO, JAPAN

"All right," I say, looking at Carolina and Aiko, "we have a choice. We can go north along the lakeshore, then east up the hill, or we can bushwhack through the forest."

"The forest is shorter," says Aiko. "Two kilometers instead of three."

She knows because we went to the falls three times last summer. But Carolina never came; Papà said she was too little to go without an adult.

"The forest has monkeys," says Carolina. "And we don't have Naoki to protect us."

We've been at the ambassador's summer villa for a week, and we haven't seen monkeys yet. Anyway, Naoki didn't protect us last summer when the monkeys came. But I don't point those things out. The memory of the monkeys makes my insides quiver.

"We could ask Naoki's mother to go with us," says Aiko. "She looks fierce enough to scare any monkey."

"She's doing laundry today." Here at Lake Chūzenji we don't have a local woman to go to for laundry. That responsibility falls on the servants: Hitomi and Papà.

But Aiko is right. Hitomi is fierce. Whenever she passes, she glares at me. When Hitomi told Papà Naoki couldn't come this summer, I chewed on the inside of my cheek to keep from crying. Naoki loved it last summer, even more than the rest of us. He did martial arts exercises on the pebble beach every morning. He shot imaginary enemy ships on the lake. I miss him. I missed him every Sunday in July, and I miss him now. Who is he staying with while Hitomi is here? I hope it's the uncle he loves.

"The only time we saw the monkeys last summer was on the shore," says Aiko.

"But they came out of the forest," says Carolina.

"How about we go through the forest one way and along the shore the other way?" I say. I don't know if monkeys can swim, but we can. If we're on the shore, we can always jump into the water.

"Then let's take the shore route going there," says Carolina. "That way I can see the famous Kegon Falls before I die."

"Die?" says Aiko.

"Before the monkeys kill me on the way back."

"The monkeys are not going to kill you," says Aiko.

"Promise?" asks Carolina, but she's looking at me, not Aiko.

I don't like this game of hers. But I say, "Promise."

"Just don't look them in the face," says Aiko.

The walk along the shore is easy, but as we go uphill, the lowest cedar branches scratch at us, and the last stretch is steep. Who minds? The scent of the trees is like a mix of lemon and pineapple; it makes my skin tingle.

The hills that surround the lake teem with birds, and their songs are a pleasure. Cuckoos and nightingales. In Tokyo it's rare to hear birdsong these days. Even pigeon coos have disappeared. Everybody needs soup.

We come out on top into the open air. The highest waterfall always takes my breath away, literally. The water drops so far and so fast that the air forms a chilly mist that hits us in the face and steals our breath. Behind that fall and on both sides are maybe a dozen other smaller falls.

"The baby waterfalls are like leaks," says Carolina over the roar of that falling torrent.

I look out from this wonderful viewpoint, over the forest and over the huge marshy expanse that stretches to the foot of Mount Nantai. Dead trees poke up through the marsh, gray and spiky and lonely.

A young man squats at the edge of the trees. He wears a loincloth like the poorest field-workers. I haven't seen a man his age in the fields for a long time. Only old people and children work the fields. Men his age are soldiers.

His back is to me, and he's busy at something. A sheen of sweat coats his shoulders.

I walk over and stand behind him, close enough to see what's in his hands. Two rocks. He grinds them together. His back muscles move around his rib bones with each breath. He's as skinny as anyone I've ever seen.

Carolina and Aiko join me.

"What do you want?" He doesn't look at us when he talks. But he must sense we're children, because he speaks in the Japanese adults use with children.

"Nothing."

He keeps grinding the rocks together. "Did you come for *shinrin-yoku?*"

I have no idea what that is. I raise my brows at Aiko.

"Bathing in the forest scents is beneficial," says Aiko in her most formal language, "but we did not come for that. We came to see the falls."

"How old are you?"

"Eight," says Carolina, counting years the Japanese way. She won't really be that for four more months.

"Ten," says Aiko, though both of us are close to eleven.

"You're still in elementary school. I went to elementary school. But my grandmother wouldn't let me go to agricultural school because it was in the city. No one who left our village to go to school ever came back. She didn't want to lose me."

"Our grandmother lost us," says Carolina. "But we'll go back one day."

"Is Nikko your village?" I ask.

"I'm from Toga. It's a speck in the western mountains of Toyama prefecture. No one knows where it is unless they live within a hand's throw of it." The man grinds the rocks harder and faster. "But I've traveled. I went to Manchuria. I bet you don't even know where that is."

Of course we know where Manchuria is. It's that part of China that stretches to the north of Korea. In Tokyo all schoolchildren know that. But we don't want to be rude, so we don't answer.

"I went with the imperial army to Manchuria. In 1935. To secure the long western border with the Soviet Union. We pushed our way through bushes, up and down mountains. Just like hiking here today. The next year, they called me to service again. In central China." He stops grinding the rocks and clacks them together for a while. Then he grinds them again.

"My brother is serving in the imperial army," says Aiko. "But I don't know where."

"Poor him."

Aiko stiffens. I have to hold my hands together to keep from putting my arms around her.

"I hope your brother never comes to Kegon Falls."

"Why?"

The man stands up and looks at us. If he's surprised to see Carolina's and my Western faces, he doesn't show it. He drops the rocks and walks into the forest. "Are you coming?" he calls without looking back. "I can teach you something. Besides, I have a gift for you. Something that matters to your brother."

Aiko hurries after him. Carolina looks at me. The man doesn't seem threatening. He's skeletal; the three of us could overpower him if we had to. Besides, now we are one more if monkeys should come. Carolina and I join hands and follow.

The man walks without saying a word until we are at the foot of the mountain. He finally squats by a large old tree and puts his arms around the base of the biggest, ugliest mushroom I've ever seen. It's black and curly. He tugs and tugs at it, and I can see that he's strong after all. Beetles tumble off the mushroom and fly away. Finally the base of the mushroom rips free, sending the man backward onto his bottom.

"If you clean this mushroom properly—get all the slugs and larvae out of it—it can be delicious. Eat it with . . . ah, it used to be perfect with noodles . . . but now eat it with whatever you have." He shoves the mushroom in front of us.

"Thank you for the gift," says Aiko.

We all bow.

How will we ever get this mushroom home? It must weigh half as much as Carolina.

"This is not the gift," says the man. "This was my lesson: the forest can feed you." He walks to a pile of neatly folded clothes not far from where he ripped up the mushroom. He pulls on tattered pants and a shirt. Under them is a magazine. "This is *Chikakiyori*." He bows to the magazine. I've never seen anyone do such a thing. "This is the gift. Read it. But keep it hidden, because adults will not want you to read it. They can't risk you knowing the truth. When you see your brother again, he will be grateful that you know." He gives a final bow to us and to the magazine. Then he walks across a small field and disappears into the forest beyond.

"He talked like he wasn't real," says Carolina. "I didn't understand him."

"He's real. I think maybe he ran away from the army—a deserter." Aiko sits on the ground, already reading. "This magazine is not like the newspapers we read at home."

I read over her shoulder. An article about the Japanese victory at Kokoda in New Guinea. We know. News about the victory is on the radio, and it fills the headlines in the ambassador's papers. But this article also talks about the Japanese forces lost in the battle. It predicts that Japan will not be able to hold on to Kokoda.

My eye moves to the next article. It's about Poland. In Europe. It says Jews are kept in a walled-off area. They were gathered up and forced to live there. Now they are being taken away to Germany to be killed. I gasp; my stomach goes cold as ice. I re-read, to make sure I haven't mistaken it. Killed. It definitely says killed. What did the Jews do? I think of the old synagogue in Ostia. Nonna and I used to turn on the lights for them on Saturday, their holy day, when they aren't allowed to do the "work" of flipping switches.

"I don't understand," I say.

"This is an underground publication," says Aiko. "Gen told

89

me about them. They tell us what the government doesn't want us to know."

Carolina screws up her face. "I can't read most of those words. What does it say?"

"Nothing." Aiko stands up. "We never saw it. It's dangerous. Do you understand, Carolina?"

"Saw what?" She smiles. "We have a perfect hiding place for nothing under the platform by the pebble beach."

"Good thinking," I say, though my heart is beating so hard, it may pop out of my chest. Reading such a magazine is disloyal. Our teachers would be appalled.

And angry, like Hitomi.

Aiko closes the magazine and shoves it under her shirt. She looks fat. "How are we going to get this mushroom back to the villa?"

"We could drag it on a broken cedar branch," I say.

It turns out to be not so easy to break cedar branches; they cling to the tree. But we manage to get one, and we drag that mushroom home. Hitomi and Papà are delighted.

They have no idea about the issue of *Chikakiyori* under the platform by the pebble beach. If Hitomi knew, she would destroy it. Papà . . . would want to read it, too. But he's an adult. If he got caught with it, who knows what would happen? That magazine is a danger to him.

We're just children; we can't get into real trouble.

For now, it's best we stay children with a secret.

CHAPTER

ELEVEN

3 FEBRUARY 1943, TOKYO, JAPAN

The ambassador sent for me, and I have no idea why. I stand in the open door to his office, not daring to step in. I hope he won't make me late for school.

Important business happens in this office. Carolina and I have never been inside it. Paintings in fancy frames hang on the walls. They're odd. Not mountains with isolated houses that have curved roofs, or women in kimonos half-hidden behind fans, or dragon boats in the middle of wild seas, like the scenes on the folded screens in the rest of the embassy. These are different—a seated man, three nearly naked women with yellow hair, a landscape with a gnarled tree. It makes me think of the olive trees all around Lido di Ostia. Oh! These are Italian paintings.

The ambassador works, bent over his desk. Maybe he doesn't demand Italian food just because of the taste. Maybe he's homesick. Like Signor Rosati, the consular officer. He left last month without even waiting for a replacement, he was so homesick.

The ambassador finally looks up. "Come in, Simona," he says in Italian.

I walk to the edge of his desk.

"You talk with the servants. You play with their children. Are you surprised that I know this? I watch everything, you see. Your father tells me you get good grades in school. You help him bargain in the market."

What do all those things have to do with each other? I look at him.

"So I'm guessing you speak Japanese well."

I recall the words of the seafoam candy vendor under the cherry blossoms last spring, and I've learned so much more since then. "I speak like anyone born in Tokyo."

"If that's true, you're the only Italian in this embassy who knows Japanese well enough to pick up on the little meanings. Is it true? This is important. Think before you answer."

"It's true."

"I'm going to give you a chance to prove that. Every day, as soon as you get home from school, you're going to put yourself in that corner, right there"—he jerks his head toward a corner—"and listen to the conversations I have with my visitors."

I gulp in surprise. "Why?"

"Once they've left, you'll tell me what they said in Japanese to each other."

This feels important. And somehow wrong. "Your interpreter does that."

"My interpreter is Japanese." He looks at me hard. "Do you understand what I'm saying? You're a big girl. Turning eleven this month, your father tells me. He trusts you with your little sister. Last summer he even allowed you to take her up onto the mountain where the waterfalls are. So you're responsible." He comes around the desk to stand beside me. "A big, responsible Italian girl who knows Japanese as well as anyone." He leans over a little. "My interpreter might not tell me things he doesn't want me to know. I get the feeling sometimes, when he's translating newspapers, that he skips things. You've seen him come in with stacks of newspapers, right?"

Has someone complained about my reading the newspapers before they are thrown out each day? Maybe Hitomi? But the ambassador wouldn't understand if he overheard the servants saying anything like that, anyway. I nod.

"He might even lie to me."

The interpreter is polite to me, and sometimes he smiles. I pull on my fingers. "He seems nice."

"Anyone can lie, Simona. I was the ambassador to Serbia before this, and they lied there, too. Even ambassadors lie. The past ambassador to Japan lied to me about what it was like to live here. He said it was fascinating. He claimed to like their revolting food. Anyone can lie. You know that, right?"

I nod and practically wrench my fingers from my left hand.

"Even if my interpreter is honest, he might not explain to me the importance of how things were said . . . or not said."

I nod again and fold my hands to hold them still.

"Off to school now."

Carolina and I race to catch up with the others. The cold, wet February air numbs my windpipe. We all greet and talk, but my head spins. I tug on Aiko's sleeve, our signal to fall behind.

"What's the matter?" Aiko whispers.

"I'm going to be a spy."

She giggles. "You're bad at this game. Spies don't tell."

She's right; I shouldn't tell anyone. But I'm about to burst. "The ambassador wants me to check whether the interpreter is telling him all the news and all the truth."

"That's dangerous." Aiko's cheeks go ruddy.

My stomach clenches. "Don't hate me."

"I can't stand it when you act like an idiot. I will never hate you."

"Good. Because I want to know what people tell the ambassador."

"Yes."

"And if the interpreter lies to him, I want to tell him the truth."

"Yes."

I let my elbow touch hers. "I might even be able to bring

him other information." As I say it, my throat burns. "From *Chikakiyori.*"

"Don't say that word!"

"How can I get copies of that magazine? Regularly?"

"Don't ask me."

"You knew of it before that man at Kegon Falls gave it to us. You must . . . know someone."

She looks at me, silent.

"You don't have to be in the middle," I say. "Tell me who, and I'll find them."

She looks away.

"A name. That's all I need."

"No."

"But—"

"No. I will be in the middle," says Aiko. "I will help."

"Really?"

"All these lies to win the war, when there's no point in winning a war if it means we're all ruined. Thank you, Simona. Thank you for this chance."

After school, I rush home. Carolina trails behind me. "Hurry up!" I call.

"Why are you walking so fast?"

"I have something to do as soon as we get home."

"What?"

"Something stupid you won't care about."

"You have a secret with Aiko. I could tell when you two were whispering on the way to school. What is it?"

"Nothing."

Carolina catches up. "You've trusted me with other secrets. The secret under the platform by the pebble beach."

"That's because you were there at the waterfall. You had to know. I'm sorry, Carolina, but this one, you don't have to know." I shake my head. "Sometimes . . . there are things you're better off not knowing."

Fear flashes across Carolina's face. "Don't get in trouble, Simona."

"I won't. I promise."

"Tell Papà about it."

"Good idea."

We go inside the embassy, and I put my things away, then hurry to the ambassador's office. The door is open.

"You're just in time, Simona. A visitor is coming in a moment. Stay in that corner and listen."

"But everyone will see me."

"He'll barely notice you. Japanese officials often seem to have servant girls your age waiting off to the side. You won't matter to him."

I go to the corner and sit on my heels on the floor.

"What are you doing?" The ambassador smacks his hand on the desktop. "Stand up! Act proper."

I stay where I am, with my legs folded under me, and bow forward, letting my forehead touch the floor, though we normally don't bow to the ambassador. Then I sit up tall and work to slow my heart. "This is how a Japanese girl sits." I speak as steadily as I can manage. "It will make your visitors more comfortable if I behave as they think is proper."

The ambassador blinks. "You're cleverer than I thought."

I'm glad. The ambassador has given me a job, and I will do it right.

Soon a man enters with the interpreter. I lower my eyes and stay where I am. It's cold in the corner. A draft comes in through a side window. I shiver, but I don't hug myself or rub my arms. I won't do anything to bring attention to myself. Spies have to blend in.

Everyone talks freely, as though I can't hear. They have no idea I will report on them. I listen to every word.

After they leave, the ambassador says, "Did the interpreter do a good job? Did he tell me properly what the Japanese man said?"

"Yes."

"Did you notice anything odd at all? Anything suspect?"

"No."

"You can go now. I'll see you tomorrow. Right after school. Be prompt."

I turn to leave.

"And, Simona . . ."

I stop.

"That skill of observation . . . of noticing and then behaving as you think is best . . . behaving strategically . . . it's a good skill. It will serve you well. Work hard at it."

My ears ring with the praise. But it was easy. The

interpreter is honest. Maybe spying won't make me have to do awful things after all.

Later, I tell Papà what happened.

"Did it frighten you?"

His question almost surprises me. I'd somehow pushed all thoughts of danger out of my head as I boasted to Papà. I can't answer.

"What, Simona?"

My pride of a moment ago vanishes. Everything crumbles inside me. I want to run, flee. "The ambassador seems homesick. And so was the consular officer. Sometimes I am, Papà. We've been here more than two years. Lots more. You said . . ."

"I know." Papà shakes his head. "Last April, when the bombs fell and killed those school children, Signor Rosati and I tried to find a safe way to get back to Italy. But all ships leaving Japan are targets. Rosati gave up finally and just took his chances. I have no idea how he left or where he is now. But I have you and Carolina; I have to find us a safe way."

So much goes on that I don't know about. I truly thought Signor Rosati had left only because of homesickness. I feel small and ignorant.

"In the meantime, Simona, do you want to do this for the ambassador or not? If you don't, I'll tell him no."

And I remember how Aiko reacted. This is important. "I want to do it."

Papà puts his hands on my shoulders. "All right, then. You

will help the ambassador. But this task is a burden. Every time, come tell me what happened. You'll share the burden with me, so it's not so heavy in your heart. Understand?" Papà cups my cheeks and kisses me on the forehead in the most solemn way. His hands smell of olive oil. Somehow Papà managed to buy a small bottle last week. I remember Carolina's baptism years ago, how she smelled, anointed in olive oil with balsam. Papà's kiss anoints me now. I can do the job the ambassador wants me to do—I can do it well. Especially with Papà beside me. And maybe I can help Papà find a way to get us home.

CHAPTER

TWELVE

22 MAY 1943, TOKYO, JAPAN

A letter came from Nonna yesterday, but Papà was busy late last night because the ambassador had important people to dinner. He said we'll read it tonight. I hold up the tan square envelope. There are five stamps on it. Normally Nonna's letters have only four. I shake it. It seems heavier than usual. There are postmarks all over it, some Italian, some Japanese—front and back. One stamp says this envelope has been deemed safe by an examiner. Safe for what? I can't wait until tonight. "I'm going to open it."

Carolina crawls from her futon, across the tatami mat, and snuggles up beside me. "I'm ready."

I tear the thin paper carefully, so as not to rip what's inside. A photograph slides out. It's Nonna, standing under the old spreading fig tree by Zio Piero's house. Off to one side in the background is an almond tree in bloom, heralding spring. Nonna's holding a round low cake and smiling big. There are candles on it. Of course! Her sixtieth birthday. This is the first photograph she's sent. I stare at every detail. My eyes well. I can predict what's in the letter with this photograph; she will tell us to speak Italian so we don't forget who we are. She tells us that often. But now, with this photograph, she's telling us that simply with the hopeful look on her face.

"I recognize her," says Carolina at last.

Her words startle me. Of course she should recognize Nonna. But, oh, Carolina hasn't seen Nonna for nearly three years, and she was only five and a half then. I put my arm around her and pull her close. It's time to go back to Italy.

Carolina places her fingertip on a bird sitting on a branch of the almond tree. "A magpie."

I look closer. Unmistakable black-and-white markings.

"Nonna will have good luck," Carolina says.

"But . . ." In Japan, magpies mean good luck. But in Italy they mean bad luck.

"But what?"

"But Nonna better chase him away from the almond tree. Magpies are fruit and nut thieves."

"She will. She's smart. Right, Simona?"

The rasp of footsteps on gravel comes from outside the window. It isn't the clacking *kata-kata* of servants coming to work in their wooden clogs. This sounds like Western shoes.

I roll off my futon and walk to the window. A man in high

black boots ducks as he gets into a red car with shiny chrome trim. The embassy guard has already pulled wide the gate, and the car zooms outside the wall.

A car like that stands out on the streets of Tokyo. The ambassador got one last month. Papà said it was a mistake to show off. No one should put chrome on their cars anymore—this war takes all the metal.

The sight of that rich car puts a lump in my throat. I want nothing to do with show-offs. I remember how the girls at school used to treat me when they thought I was rich just because I lived at the embassy.

"Who was that?" Carolina stands beside me.

"Some visitor. It doesn't matter. We can read Nonna's letter later, when we get home from school."

"No we can't. You'll disappear, like you always do."

Carolina knows I go into the ambassador's office. But I never mention what happens inside there. "Then we'll read it tonight with Papà, like usual." I put the photograph and the unread letter into the red lacquer box beside my futon, with all the past letters from Nonna. "You know what? I'm going to teach you how to read Italian tonight, so you can read Nonna's letters to me and Papà from now on."

"You can't teach someone how to read a language in one night. It takes years."

"Learning to read Japanese takes years. But reading Italian is different. You'll see."

We dress and have breakfast, and I take one of yesterday's newspapers off the stack that is to be thrown away. I put it into my book bag. Hitomi once asked me what I planned on doing with a newspaper at school. I said it was like padding against my back; it helped when my back hurt. That seemed to satisfy her. She didn't ask why my back hurt, and she never looked at me funny when I took a newspaper again.

When we meet up with the others, Aiko smiles and says, "There was a white-cheeked starling outside my window this morning. He sang, 'Kyur-kyur.'"

I come to attention; mentioning a bird is our signal that Aiko got a new issue of the magazine *Chikakiyori* to pass to me.

"Our grandmother sent us a photo of her with a magpie in an almond tree," says Carolina.

"Your grandmother climbs trees?" says Yukiko.

The other girls laugh.

I do, too, looking at Carolina.

Carolina is only a half second behind in joining in. She understands; pretending not to notice an offense deflects it. That's what all the big girls do. Carolina's smarter every day.

"But, Aiko," says Yukiko, "what's all this talk about birds? This must be the fourth or fifth time that you tell us about some bird outside your window, but they're not even special ones. So who cares?"

My fingers tighten around the straps of my book bag so hard that it hurts. I don't look at Aiko.

"I smile at the flag outside my window. It greets me every morning," says Aiko. "So I say hello to the birds at the same time. And when the birds seem particularly cheerful, then I tell all of you."

Aiko's answer is perfect! I glance at her in awe. Aiko looks like any other girl—bangs, long hair, open expression with clear eyes. But she's a genius.

"Just as you should," says Keiko. "I look at our flag each day as evening comes."

"Pretty soon we'll see fireflies in the evening," says Misato.

And everyone sings *"Hotaru Koi,"* the firefly song. It shows our loyalty to the beautiful traditions of Japan. We sing it over and over all the way to school, behaving just as we should, every last one of us.

It's Saturday, so school lets out before lunch. By the school's front door, I meet up with everyone, including Carolina and Botan. All spring, Hatsu has been allowing Botan to come home with Carolina on Saturday afternoons. "Please walk at your own pace," I say to my friends. "I may lag behind. Take Carolina and Botan with you."

"Your back hurts again?" asks Yukiko. "I thought you were better."

"It's good that you don't complain," says Keiko.

"Maybe you shouldn't play so hard at recess," says Aiko.

I understand her message: Act like I feel bad on the days when Aiko sees a bird outside her window. At recess, sit in one place and watch the others play.

"I can wait and walk with you if you want," Chizue says, and gives a small smile.

"That's kind of you." I smile back. Chizue has never tried to make friends with me before. "But it's good to be alone sometimes. I enjoy stopping to think before I walk."

They finally leave, and I lean against the sun-warmed wall until they turn the corner onto the big road. Then I hurry to the postbox on the next street over. It's the best one for Aiko and me because it stands on four short legs, rather than being perched on a pole, so there is a small, protected space underneath it, just right for hiding an issue of *Chikakiyori*.

The street is empty. I go straight to the postbox, put my book bag on the ground, unbuckle it, take out yesterday's newspaper. Fighting the urge to glance around for prying eyes, I reach under the postbox, grab *Chikakiyori*. The latest issue—good. I fold it inside my newspaper, put it all into my book bag, slip my arms through the straps, stand, open and close the little door on the postbox slot, keep my eyes on that door. I act like everything is normal; I'm a schoolgirl who just mailed a letter.

My ears buzz. If anyone catches me with this magazine, something bad will happen. That's why Aiko never passes it directly to me. If one of us is caught, at least the other is safe.

I walk back to school, forcing myself not to run. Once I'm on the right street, out of sight of anyone who might have been watching the postbox, I race back to the embassy, and get there just as Carolina and Botan are going through the gate.

I enter the ambassador's office without a word and sit on my heels in my corner. The ambassador is listening to the interpreter and doesn't seem to notice me. A telegram has come—in German. Everyone says this interpreter is as good in German as he is in Italian. The ambassador makes the interpreter translate that telegram over and over, so many times, I practically memorize it. It says Italy is falling apart. Cities are in ruins. But Germany won't put up with an Italian rebellion; Italy is on Germany's side, and it has to stay there. If Italy makes trouble, Germany will reduce Italy to mud and ashes.

Mud and ashes.

The ambassador repeats those words as he paces.

I'm dizzy. A rebellion in Italy? The ambassador points at me, and my heart jumps. But he says, "Bring me coffee." That makes sense; I don't know German, so I'm useless here.

I run to the kitchen and gobble down rice balls with salted plum inside while Papà makes the coffee. I whisper, "Germany is afraid that Italy might rebel. What would that mean, Papà?"

"It's what Signor Rosati feared. But it won't happen, Simona. It can't. We have a pact."

I hurry back to the ambassador. Now the interpreter discusses the Japanese newspapers. He talks about Admiral Isoroku Yamamoto, the commander-in-chief of the Japanese navy. The imperial headquarters announced his death on Friday, but he died back in April. A hero's death on the front line. He was a military genius; he planned the attack on Pearl Harbor in America in 1941. The navy will do even better now, with its morale heightened by the loyal example of this super-lative admiral.

When the interpreter stops talking, the ambassador says, "Thank you. You can go now."

I flush. This is rude. The ambassador doesn't even bow. But the interpreter takes it in stride. He and I exchange slight head bows, and he leaves.

"So, did he do well on translating the Japanese news?"

"Yes. But a new issue of *Chikakiyori* came out." I pull it out of my book bag and lay it out on the ambassador's desk. "The cover—it's all about this admiral, too."

The ambassador goes around to his side of the desk and looks at the magazine thoughtfully, like always, though I suspect he can't read a word. "But a different viewpoint, right? Maybe different information?"

I open the magazine. "It says he was shot down on 18 April. Nearly a month ago. Over Bougainville."

"That's all?"

"I'm reading as fast as I can," I say, keeping a steady voice. "Bougainville is one of the Solomon Islands. The Americans shot him down."

"Of course they did. He was a strategic idiot, to attack Pearl Harbor. That's what made the Americans enter the war. That's what's going to make Japan lose."

He doesn't mention Italy. And he's not in a hurry. For once, he's not in a hurry. This is my chance.

"Please, sir, I have a question."

He looks at me.

"What did the Polish Jews do?"

"What do you mean?"

"I read that the Germans are killing them. What did they do?"

His mouth hangs open for a moment. "What does the magazine say?"

"I didn't read it in this issue. I read it last summer. Back at the country villa. What did they do, those Polish Jews?"

"Maybe nothing."

"You can't kill people for doing nothing."

The ambassador's face is blank. He drops into his desk chair. "I don't know the answer. No one tells me anything. Forget the old magazine, Simona. Tell me what this one says."

I turn my eyes back to the magazine. "Oh," I gasp. "It says here that the Americans broke the Japanese code—they deciphered it. They knew Admiral Yamamoto's locations and times on his final journey."

"Good heavens." The ambassador taps the ends of his fingers together faster and faster. "God only knows what else they've figured out."

"It says that the Japanese navy has no chance of being effective now."

"Just the opposite of what the newspapers say."

"It has news about Germany, too."

"Battles?"

"Last month German aircraft were shot down over Tunisia. A big defeat."

"North Africa is lost. I don't know why anyone insists on keeping up the fighting there."

"There's news about Jews again."

"Stop, Simona." The ambassador sighs loudly. "You must understand. I have to keep my eye on the Pacific. And even then, I can't do anything to affect what happens. I can only react. I don't want to know about Europe unless Italy is directly involved."

"But this is good news. Sort of. In April, Jews in the Warsaw ghetto gathered explosives. They killed over one hundred Germans."

"How many Jews died?"

I swallow. "More than a thousand." I keep reading. "Maybe . . ." My voice cracks. "Maybe thirteen hundred."

"That's good news?"

"They fought back."

My words sound foolish.

The ambassador is silent. Then he nods. "The Jews fought back, yes. That has to be good. Resistance matters."

I shiver. To talk like this is treason. Death. I must forget this conversation. But the ambassador's words play in my head: *Resistance matters.*

"All right, Simona. You did well. Someone from the Vatican embassy is coming after dinner. Eat fast and get back here."

Anyone from the Vatican embassy will be Italian. The conversation will be in Italian. So why does the ambassador want me there? But the look on his face keeps me from asking.

I go to the kitchen and pick at my dinner.

Papà glances at Carolina. Then he says softly to me, "Did you learn something . . . dreadful?"

Carolina jerks to attention. "Dreadful?"

"I'm not hungry." I look at Papà.

I hurry back to my corner in the ambassador's office. Soon I hear an engine outside. Noisy. It must be that showy red car.

When the man comes into the room, the ambassador lights a candle and the two of them stand in the glow and talk. I watch, invisible. The Vatican man says that Italians are tired of starving for a war they don't understand. It's as bad as Japan, he says. Soldiers desert. Italians threaten revolution. It's time to tell the Allies how to reach victory over Japan.

I have to keep myself from jumping to my feet. How could he say that!

The ambassador asks, "What do you mean—precisely?"

"I recommend you and your wife leave Japan."

"Safely? How?"

I strain to hear. But the man only shrugs, shakes the ambassador's hand, and leaves.

The ambassador slaps his hands on his desktop and leans there, looking into the dark. "Why doesn't Rome tell me what's happening? I can't get through to anyone."

He stands there so long, I finally cough.

He says, "In Italy most people distrust the rebels—the underground. Did you know that? The underground bombs bridges so military equipment can't be transported to the battle front. They blow up arms factories. They say this war is not about regaining Italy's past glory, but about killing off whoever Hitler hates so he can rule the world. People don't know who's telling the truth."

I swallow.

"But here, the underground feels like it's our best friend. Without that magazine you bring me, I might think that the Vatican was exaggerating, as they usually do. I believe that magazine."

I want to run away.

"Go to bed, girl."

I walk to our room, stand beside Papà's futon, and listen, hoping he's awake. No sound but breathing. I creep past Carolina onto my futon, and stare into the black night. I want to talk to Papà.

But, really, everything I could say, Papà knows already. Signor Rosati was right to leave when he could, even if passage wasn't safe.

Because we aren't safe here.

CHAPTER

THIRTEEN

10 July 1943, Tokyo, Japan

I dress in my white shirt and dark-blue checked pants. School clothes. Girls used to wear jumper-dresses, but in April, at the start of this school year, everyone changed to pants; they cost less.

An engine roars outside our window. I watch that red car from the Vatican embassy disappear out through the gate. The fact that it was here can't mean anything good.

I hurry to the staff room, where Papà sits on the floor with the rest of the servants. They have box trays in front of them, each holding a steamed sweet potato in a bowl. It's been months since we ate rice at breakfast. Papà is at the edge of the group, and no one is looking at him, so I lean over from behind and kiss his cheek, as though we're in private. Or in Italy.

"Go into the kitchen," Papà says in Italian. He rests his elbows on his knees and doesn't look at me. "I'll meet you there."

I whisper, "Why did the Vatican embassy send a man in that stupid car again?"

Papà turns to me. "Didn't you hear me? Go." His eyelashes are wet. He's been crying! He hasn't cried since Mamma's funeral.

In the kitchen, Carolina is holding both our lunches. "You got up early," I say.

"I'm surprised you didn't. The ambassador woke Papà."

"Why?"

Carolina shrugs. "Eat fast."

Papà comes in, and I clutch his hand. "What's going on?"

His eyes dart to Carolina.

Carolina tugs Papà's sleeve. "I'm going to learn about it anyway."

"The man brought a message from the Vatican, so we'd know before the radio announced it." Papà leans down and pulls us close to his face. "The Americans invaded." He puts one hand on my shoulder and the other on Carolina's. "They're in Sicily."

I step backward in horror. Sicily is the big island in the south of Italy. "Let us stay home," I say. "Please. It's Saturday. We can all be together for two whole days. Please."

Papà shakes his head. "We can't bring trouble upon ourselves." He looks at Carolina. "Both of you are clever; you understand. If trouble comes on its own, we'll deal as best we can. But, for now, we act the same as always." Papà kisses one of my cheeks as he pats the other. He does the same to Carolina. "Not one word about this to anyone," he whispers. "It's still the middle of the night in Italy. The invasion started only hours ago. No one outside the embassy knows yet. It's impossible to predict what will happen next. Sicily is lost, but who knows what will happen to the rest of Italy. To Japan. To the world."

Hitomi comes into the kitchen.

Papà steps away from us. "Go to school," he says loudly in Japanese.

"We're going," says Carolina in Japanese. "But eat your breakfast first," she adds to me. "Quick."

I take a bite of sweet potato. Sicily has been invaded.

Another bite. Papà is afraid.

I finish my sweet potato, though it makes me feel sick.

We walk out the embassy gates, and my head buzzes. How far is Sicily from Rome? How far are the Americans from Nonna and Zio Piero? The map of Italy in my head has blurred.

The ambassador and Papà think that the Americans can beat anyone.

Japan and Germany and Italy—all of them are doomed. And Italy might be first.

When we aren't even a block from the embassy, a girl comes running from the side street with a boy chasing behind; his outstretched hands are red and wet. The girl clutches a dog to her chest. It's Mutsuko, from my class. Tears drip down her face. Carolina and I run and get to the corner just as she does.

The boy catches up to Mutsuko and yanks at her arms. His hands are bloody!

She shouts, "No! Go away!"

"Stop!" I yell. I step closer. "Leave her alone."

"Go home, *ishuu*," says the boy.

That old nickname. I want to put my hands over Carolina's ears. We're the only foreigners.

The boy pushes Mutsuko hard and grabs the dog as she falls. He stomps away with the howling dog. Mutsuko sobs. I take her arm.

"Let go!" She twists free. "It's your fault."

"Me?"

"Your dumb people are such bad fighters, we have to fight that much harder."

"Sicily's not my fault."

"What's Sicily?"

Oh no. I press my lips shut.

"And now they're killing our dogs."

"Who's killing dogs?"

"Everyone. In Minami-Azumi in Shinshu they killed every dog and gave the hides to the army. For making clothes. Now people want to do it here, too. I hate you." Mutsuko runs ahead.

I turn to Carolina, who looks shocked. "Don't listen to her," I say. "She didn't mean that."

"Maybe she did," says Carolina. "Some people hate Westerners."

"Americans and British and French. That's who they hate. We're Italian. We aren't like the other Westerners."

"Maybe they don't know that." Carolina walks ahead a few steps. "Come on, Simona. We have to go to school. That's just how it is."

She sounds like she did last year, when the Americans bombed Tokyo. All grown-up.

We see Mutsuko join the group of girls ahead of us. They close around her like a protective blanket. No one waits for us. When we move a little faster to catch up, they go even faster.

Only Aiko glances back. Once.

It's as though everyone agrees with Mutsuko. They're protecting her from us.

"They'll get over it," I say to Carolina.

I expect her to make me promise.

But she doesn't.

CHAPTER

FOURTEEN

15 JULY 1943, TOKYO, JAPAN

Five days later, I hold out my math exam as the teacher collects them. I clean my ink brush and put it away with care. It has to last. We used to get new brushes when the old ones lost their softness, but no more. The factories in Japan make nothing but weapons now.

It's the middle of July and the end of this school term. School terms always end in hideous exams. For three days all the girls say *ganbatte*—persevere—to each other. It's as close to wishing luck as we get.

Today the school day is short because we have an air-raid defense practice. The morning radio gave sermons about the value of military drills and teamwork. So we broke into teams; some cleaned our classroom, some cleaned the halls, some cleaned the playground. Then we took exams. Now the Adult Assistance Group is bringing a treat. We wait with folded hands.

Women march into our classroom holding placards that say TOKYO-TO. We jump to attention. Two weeks ago, the government declared that the name of the capital city would change to cover the whole prefecture area, so it's Tokyo-to now. A bigger, more important name. We bow low from the waist and cry, "Tokyo-to."

The lead woman blows a whistle. Even though it isn't an official air-raid drill, we drop to the floor, facedown. Something pokes my back. I squirm away. It pokes harder.

"Get up."

I stand.

The woman turns to my teacher. "Who is this child in the pants?" Somehow all the other girls are in kimonos today.

"Her father works in the Italian embassy."

The woman's face grows stony. "Italy?" She leans toward me. "That Mussolini of yours has made a fine mess. If he had any honor, he'd commit suicide."

I don't even blink. Mussolini is prime minister of Italy, but I don't care about him. I don't remember what he looks like. He has nothing to do with the Italy in my head—Nonna's Italy.

I'm not shocked, either. People mumble about the honor in suicide.

What bothers me is the look on her face. Does this woman hate me just because of Mussolini? What he does isn't my fault. She's an adult; she knows that. I lift my chin and will it not to tremble.

Thump! Thump, thump, thump! Two women dump folded cloth onto the floor at the front of the room—stars and stripes—American flags. They tell us to spread them out and jump on them. "Remember the Battle of Attu. Let it never happen again! Don't let the Solomon Islands be a repeat!"

I steal a glance at Keiko. Her brother was killed at Attu. But Keiko's face shows nothing. She gets in line like everyone else.

We jump on the flags. I trample with all my strength. America is my enemy, too, doubly so. My classmates may be thinking only, "Remember Attu," but I'm adding, "Remember Sicily."

The women produce big puppets of the British prime minister, Winston Churchill, and the American president, Franklin Roosevelt. They give us bamboo spears and tell us, "Stab them!"

We shout "Die! Die!" as we stab. I hate Prime Minister Churchill. I hate President Roosevelt. We don't stop till the puppets are shredded and our spears lie in splinters.

At lunch I sit in the circle of girls, beside Aiko.

"I'm sorry they talked about Attu," says Aiko softly. "I'm sorry about your brother, Keiko."

"Don't be." Keiko is on Aiko's other side, but she speaks loudly so we all hear. "I'm not envious that your brother is still alive," she says. "Every night my family expresses our gratitude to Riku's spirit for having brought us honor."

"A hero's death," says Misato.

"Right. My mother says, '*Okuni no tame ni.*'"

Okuni no tame ni. For the sake of the country.

"*Okuni no tame ni,*" come quiet repetitions around the circle.

Aiko's lips move, too, but I can't hear any noise from her mouth.

I bow my head, so no one can see my face. If a brother of mine died in battle, I wouldn't be grateful to him. I'd want him to come home again and be my big brother. I'm sad for Keiko. And angry. Today, I'm furious.

We walk home in our usual group, with Aiko and Carolina and me at the rear. An old man in a kimono and fat pants that end in a puff at his knees waddles down the street. I point. "Those pants! Doesn't he make you laugh?"

Aiko puts both hands over her mouth. Then she whispers out of the side of her mouth, "That clothing shows patriotism. You have to wear it for all air-raid drills now, and whenever else you're told."

"Were people told today?"

"Yes."

So that's why everyone else wore a kimono. "How were they told?"

"The radio this morning."

Papà plays the radio in the kitchen while he chops food on the big board. This morning, though, he didn't turn it on.

I had gotten up early to study extra for the exams. He didn't want the radio to distract me.

Everyone else heard, though. Everyone else wore kimonos. What must they think of me and Carolina?

We're scrutinized all the time. I can hardly bear it.

Just two more days till the term ends, and we go to the country villa. Aiko isn't coming this year. She said she can't tell me why, only that it has nothing to do with our friendship. We are best friends. Forever.

It will be all right. Being just Carolina and me until September will be all right.

An escape.

FIFTEEN

25 July 1943, Nikko and Tokyo, Japan

We arrive at the villa after the long, crowded train rides—Hitomi and us in coach class, and the ambassador and Pessa in first-class. The train was crowded today. I can't wait to swim in the lake and wander under the cool halo of the forest trees.

The ambassador puts his hands on his hips, and his chest swells as he takes a deep breath. "It's good to be out of the city. Let's drop our things and walk along the lakeshore for a while."

"I'll go prepare supper," says Papà.

"No. Let the Japanese woman make something simple. I want a walk. It'll do us good." A look passes between him and Pessa. "The five Italians."

This feels odd. I don't like leaving Hitomi out, no matter what she thinks of me.

Oh, what if the ambassador has something private to tell us about Italy?

But as we walk along the shore, the ambassador stays silent. He was right: the wind off the water soothes our spirits. I sense a calm spread over us.

"Back now," says the ambassador, turning and lifting both arms as though he's a bird about to take flight. "Let's put on bathing suits and swim."

Pessa lets out a small laugh, and Carolina and I run ahead.

A man is waiting on the pebble beach, a servant from the embassy. He bows to the ambassador. "Your excellency, Mussolini is no longer in power. Badoglio is the new prime minister."

"Badoglio, the army general?" the ambassador says slowly in Japanese, but turning to me.

The man nods. "The king declared martial law in Italy."

The ambassador repeats the Japanese words, stunned, "Martial law?"

"In Italy, the army has taken over. Soldiers patrol the streets. No calls are going through. No telegrams. You're needed in Tokyo immediately."

The ambassador looks at me, and I translate.

"Tell him we're coming, Simona."

We pile back onto the next train.

"Let's pretend this train is taking us to Italy," says Carolina in Italian.

I don't like it when she speaks Italian in front of Hitomi. Hitomi might suspect we're saying disloyal things about Japan.

But I know Carolina's disappointed that our vacation has been stolen. I am, too. So I answer in Italian, "You know a train can't get us there. Tokyo is on an island."

"Honshu Island."

"Yes."

"Can't you pretend just for a while? You're not that big, you know. Let's pretend it's months ago. It's spring and we're on the train so that we'll get to Italy in time for Nonna's sixtieth birthday."

"Look at the cherry blossoms," I say.

Carolina dutifully looks out the window. There are only massive cedar trees. But she nods. "They're beautiful. The best pink in the world. Like kitten tongues."

"Kitten tongues?"

"Botan's cat had kittens. She said their tongues are the color of cherry blossom petals."

I'm surprised Hatsu still has a cat. No one has extra food for pets these days. I pat Carolina's leg. "Listen to the wheels. They're turning fast. We'll be in time for Nonna's birthday."

Carolina snuggles against me despite the heat in the train car. "Tell me about Italy. I can't remember. Tell me everything."

"Everything?" I smile.

"People eat chocolate on bread," says Carolina. "Tell me about that."

"You already know about that. See? You remembered it."

"Tell me. Tell me something new about Italy."

"In the summer, you put lemons in ice." I remember those

hot heavy days. "Then you cut them in half and sprinkle them with sugar and suck on them." I remember each little sack of juice before it burst in my mouth. The scent. The perfect sweet and sour. The crystal cold in the stifling heat.

"Oh, that sounds lovely." And in moments Carolina's asleep.

I'm grateful. I can barely think well enough to talk. Martial law in Italy. What does that mean for Nonna? Is she afraid of men walking around with guns? Can Zio Piero take care of her? Will he be called to service in the army?

When we get back to the embassy, I go straight to my corner in the ambassador's office, and we're bombarded with details from the interpreter and the newspapers. Mussolini was voted out of power and thrown in prison.

Over the next few days, the ambassador keeps me at his heels. He growls constantly. He even yells at Pessa.

Papà gets up earlier than ever and turns on the radio first thing. The Japanese servants are jittery and never smile. Papà says none of them trust each other, and we mustn't trust them, either. At the end of the day, they disappear without a word. Some servants don't even come to work.

Hatsu doesn't bring Botan to play with Carolina, even though the girls miss each other.

And I never get to see Aiko. Which means I don't get the new issue of *Chikakiyori*. I'd have to find out where Aiko lives, meet up with her, and go through passing the magazine along under the postbox. And Aiko might have to do something unusual to get the issue. With school out, our regular patterns are broken. And doing something unusual can be dangerous.

I could tell the ambassador all this, but I'm afraid he might guess I'm talking about Aiko. She's gone to the country villa twice, and he knows her.

So the only news we have is what the interpreter brings.

CHAPTER

SIXTEEN

13 AUGUST 1943, TOKYO, JAPAN

The interpreter stands in front of the ambassador's desk with his stack of newspapers. He's about to go through them, when the ambassador says, "Tell me about revolution."

I'm shocked—so abrupt. The poor interpreter must find the ambassador rude beyond comprehension.

But the interpreter doesn't hesitate. "I beg your pardon, Ambassador. Has someone been reading *Chikakiyori* to you?" He doesn't look at me, but I feel like he knows. I clasp my hands. "I bring you the right magazines and newspapers. I don't bring you that particular magazine because it is a dirty rag. Japan will never have revolution."

The ambassador looks surprised, and I know why: the interpreter misunderstood. The ambassador was asking about revolution in Italy, not in Japan.

So both countries are on the verge of revolution. Sitting in my corner, I press my arms hard against my sides and tuck my hands in the crease of my knees to hold myself steady.

The ambassador comes around from behind his desk. He folds his hands together, trying to act composed. "But this . . . dirty rag . . . says the Japanese people will revolt?"

"Lawyers and professors say that. They're talking about the Katakura silk workers in Tokyo and the . . . No! I should not give dignity to their rubbish by repeating it. Premier Tōjō scorns them. The scholars say the Americans have a million bombs! They say the American military budget is more than double Japan's entire national budget." The interpreter laughs. "Impossible. The scholars know nothing."

"What if they are right?"

"Their claims are worthless. But, even if they were true, think of Kurifugi," says the interpreter. "You know who she is?"

His question is almost an insult. Kurifugi is the most famous name in Tokyo, after the emperor. She's the mare that wins every race.

The ambassador knits his brows and hesitates.

I hold my breath. Has he really never heard of Kurifugi?

"The racehorse?" he asks.

I breathe deep, in relief.

"Japan is like Kurifugi. Defeat is inconceivable."

The ambassador sighs. "Read me the newspapers you brought."

And so the interpreter spreads out a paper.

The ambassador looks at me. "Look over his shoulder, girl," he says gruffly in Italian. "How many times do I have to tell you to improve your Japanese?"

Does the interpreter realize I'm spying? But I walk to stand behind his chair as he reads that America will surrender soon.

The ambassador says, "Who knows if that's true?"

The ambassador's words are like a punch. Yet the interpreter just reads on: crime is on the increase.

The ambassador says, "Crime in Japan must be out of control for the newspapers to mention it."

The interpreter doesn't seem offended. He reads, "Burma has been granted independence from Japan in exchange for declaring war on England and America. Hotels in Osaka have no sugar or salt or butter to serve their guests."

"Ha!" says the ambassador. "Something true."

The interpreter reads, "The German and Japanese armies are undefeated. It is only the lack of steel that prolongs the war. Postwar meetings have begun."

Now the ambassador's eyes question mine. The interpreter read correctly. I give a quick nod.

"Postwar?" says the ambassador. "How could there be postwar meetings if Japan just got Burma to enter the war on our side?"

"You understand the complexities better than I do," says the interpreter.

The ambassador sets his hand down in the middle of the

newspaper and puts his face close to the interpreter's. "Are you afraid?"

They are silent.

That night I tell Papà what I heard, but I still don't tell him about *Chikakiyori*. So I can't talk to him about the things that worry me most.

"You're doing a good job, Simona. I'm sorry you have to do it, but I admire you for doing it so well."

My papà admires me.

"Obedience," says Papà. "You are practicing obedience. That's the only choice. For the moment."

"For the moment?" I ask. "What do you mean?" Has he found us a way to get home?

"Everything changes. Stay ready." He kisses both my cheeks.

I crawl to my futon and lie awake with words repeating in my head. The ambassador's question to the interpreter: "Are you afraid?" Papà: "Stay ready."

After a long while, I crawl over to Carolina's futon and snuggle in against her. She snuffles but doesn't roll away. Lella is tucked inside her arm. When did she start sleeping with Lella again?

Shouts—outside in the street. Papà is up in an instant, and out the door. I run to the window. Carolina wakes and comes to my side.

I touch her shoulder. "I'll go find out."

"I'm coming with you."

"No."

But Carolina follows me to the front door, where Papà stands with the Japanese night guard and the ambassador, facing the police.

"No light can show from any house," the lead policeman says harshly. "Not even cigarettes. Nothing should be visible from the air, in case of a raid."

"It's a blackout drill," Papà explains to the ambassador in Italian.

"I understand that. But why are they bothering us? We have no lights on. We've even taped paper over keyholes, so that if someone has a candle burning, light can't leak out. The Light Police never roused us before." The ambassador turns to the policeman and tries to explain this in his halting and stupid Japanese.

The lead policeman barks, "No. You failed to cover your windows with black curtains."

The ambassador grabs me by the shoulder. "Tell them we don't use lights at night, so we don't need curtains."

I bow and explain.

The lead policeman shakes his head. "Moonlight reflects off glass, so you need curtains no matter what."

I translate. The ambassador shakes his head right back. "Tell him we have no curtains."

I tell the policeman.

The policeman says, "You have shutters. Close them!"

"We will take care of it," the ambassador says in Japanese.

131

The policeman looks at the shoes inside the entrance hall. "Leather is needed to make boots for soldiers. I will notify someone to pick up your shoes. Everyone must do their part."

The ambassador hesitates, then nods. He turns to Papà and practically snarls in Italian, "Get these buffoons out of here."

Papà clears his throat and bows to the policeman. "It is my fault the shutters were not closed. I will do it immediately." He turns to the ambassador, bows, and says in Japanese, "I am sorry for this error." He turns to the policeman and says the same, three times, bowing each time.

The policeman stands a bit taller. He looks from Papà to the ambassador, and seems satisfied.

The ambassador once said that I behaved strategically; I must have learned it from Papà.

I pull Carolina by the hand back to our room. We stand at the window and listen to Papà and the Japanese night guard closing shutters as the police leave. A policeman in the street shouts and waves his arms. A car screeches to a halt in front of him and turns off its lights. The idiot. You can't drive with lights anymore.

When Papà finally comes into our room, he presses his lips against our cheeks.

We lie in the sweltering heat, all closed up, like clams steaming in sake.

CHAPTER
SEVENTEEN

26 AUGUST 1943, TOKYO, JAPAN

I've spent August in my corner in the ambassador's office, listening carefully to the men who visit. I am nearly crazy with alternating fear and boredom. We never see Naoki or Aiko or Botan. I don't know how Carolina spends her time. She hardly speaks, and I can't remember when she last smiled.

But this morning we are outside, and it feels like the best treat ever. We stand in line with Papà at the food depot, waiting for rations. Most of the people in this line are women with their woven baskets and sacks; all are in Western clothes. "No one here has Japanese clothes on," I say under my breath.

"That's because of so many thieves these days," whispers Papà. "You can't run fast in a kimono."

We pick up our rice. It's even less than what Papà brought home last time, but at least it's white. None of us liked the gummy brown rice the government tried to promote. The woman who loads our basket breaks a tomato with her thumb just by picking it up, the thing is so old. The wrinkled eggplants have brown spots. The chunks of pumpkin curl, dry at the edges. Cabbages and radishes make the pile seem substantial, but this is for the whole embassy; it's pathetic. Papà carefully wraps our ration of matches in a small *furoshiki*—six per person per week.

We could be eating decently from our own vegetable garden, except this year the vegetables disappear as soon as they're close to ripe. It's impossible to climb over the embassy walls. So the servants are stealing. No one dares steal the sunflowers, though. The military police would get angry if they went missing.

I think of Naoki. Sometimes I see him with the boys' martial arts groups. He's thinner than ever. I hope Hitomi is giving him good things from our garden.

The only things we harvest these days are basil, oregano, parsley, fennel, garlic, and rosemary—flavors not used here. Japanese food is full of ginger and horseradish.

As we walk home, Carolina counts the lines of laundry we pass. It's been a while since she counted things like that.

"The basket is light." Papà swings it in complaint. "We'll go down to two meals a day."

Self-pity is as bad as being a coward, my teachers say. "We won't starve, Papà. It's fine to be poor."

Papà stops and looks at me. "It's not poverty I object to,

134

Simona. It's unfairness. You're working for the ambassador now. You should understand these things."

"I understand plenty."

"Maybe not enough. Let's get home, and then I'll show you."

We put the food in the kitchen, and Papà picks up another list and checks his money supply. "Carolina, I want you to stay here. You can play by yourself for a while."

"I play with Lella. All the time. Every day." She nods, almost as though numb, and walks toward the door to the side yard.

"Please let her come, Papà," I say. "She's alone too much."

So we all go, back to the shopping area, down long, narrow alleyways, past the bread store, the tofu store, the soy sauce store. Half the shops are boarded up, because the workers have gone to war or been conscripted to work on the home front. All the barbershops are closed, all the little places to eat.

We turn a corner, and everything changes. It's a marketplace, but the small tables are bare. All the goods are underneath the tables, in boxes. People talk quietly with merchants. Money and goods exchange hands, often under the cover of a *furoshiki*.

Of course—a black market. Now I see why Papà didn't want Carolina to come. I want to hook my arm through hers to keep her safe. But that isn't done here. So I move to the outside, squishing Carolina between me and Papà.

"Japan has become a country of two kinds of people,"

Papà says in whispered Italian. "The military and big shots on one side. The others stand in lines, then receive too little. It's wrong."

"This market is illegal," I whisper back. "We can get in trouble."

"The military police could show up at any moment. But they won't. They'll pass on by at the end of the road. They take bribes. If your pockets are lined, your eyes can go blind." Papà rubs his fingers together in the "money" gesture.

"Let's get out of here," I say.

"The ambassador likes oranges," says Papà.

"Oranges? What are you talking about?"

"Carolina, you just lost another tooth, right? It takes food to make your next, the permanent teeth. You're both still growing." Papà shakes his head. "We all need oranges. *Pancia e coscienza.*"

Pancia e coscienza—belly and conscience. Nonna used to say that all the time. It means that we should try to do the right thing, but we need to eat, too. Nonna said, "We have to hold body and soul together."

Like Aiko said: What's the point of winning the war if everyone will be ruined? Energy surges through me.

We go from table to table, and buy. It feels reckless. We're about to leave when Carolina pokes me in the ribs. A woman is selling persimmons, Carolina's favorite fruit.

"Persimmons, Papà," I say.

The merchant looks at me. She holds two fruits low, by her waist so we can see but no one else can.

"We need them ripe," says Papà. "We'll buy next week."

Next week we'll be back in school and Papà will forget. "Hitomi showed me a way of ripening them," I say.

Papà's smiles. He loves to learn new food tricks. We buy a persimmon.

We wander down an alleyway of regular shops again, and enter the few that are open. Bells tinkle as we part the curtains. The shopkeepers look up, smiling, but distrust follows the instant they make out our faces. We pack into our basket dried cuttlefish, pink bean cakes, pickled vegetables. The ambassador and Pessa won't eat these things, so Papà is getting them for the servants—for us. A feast. It's reckless to spend money, but I'm giddy.

We turn down the cloth merchants' alley. Several shops are open, but only one type of cloth is for sale: silk. The whole world, it seems, boycotts Japanese silk because of the war. So here in Tokyo silk is cheaper than anything else.

I remember the interpreter's words to the ambassador: the silk workers want a revolution. Those words seemed odd then. Why would silk workers care one way or the other? Now I know why.

I stop in front of a shop. "Carolina, you've outgrown just about everything."

Her eyes jump to attention. "You have, too."

Papà nods.

I know I'm taking advantage of his strange mood that's making him buy so much. He'll regret it later. But we really do need new clothes. Carolina chooses a floral bolt for her dress, and I choose a pattern of flying cranes for mine.

I rest my hand on a bright yellow bolt. "Sashes?" I say to Carolina.

"I love sashes."

The shopkeeper moves closer and bows. "That yellow would make perfect sashes to go with kimonos in both those patterns," she says in Japanese. "Are they for you?"

"It's for dresses, not kimonos."

"I will measure you."

"We only want the material," I say. "I'll sew them."

"Dresses are hard to make," says the shopkeeper.

"We want simple ones," I say.

"No dress is simple to make. And you are a child."

"Simona makes all our clothes," says Carolina. "And they're pretty."

The woman flinches. She's insulted.

I bow. "What my sister means is, I always choose the material and do a little part of the sewing." I bow again. "You are kind. But we have someone to help, to do most of it."

"I will give you a better price than this other person. And I am an expert. I am famous for my kimonos. I will do a better job at a better price."

"Everyone needs to eat," Papà says in Italian.

I remember the boy with the birds; everyone needs soup.

"Fix it, Simona," Papà says. "Make her understand. As kindly as you can. You know how."

I bow to the shopkeeper. "I'm sorry. We do not have someone to help us. We sew ourselves. We're not as good as you, I'm sure. But this is part of our job."

The woman looks incredulous. "You're servants? Who would hire Western servants?"

"Western people. We work at the Italian embassy."

"Italy is part of Japan's ruination." Her voice turns harsh. "You pay double."

Papà's face flashes anger. "Measure the material you need, Simona."

"I'll measure," I say to the shopkeeper.

The woman steps aside.

I measure out enough for the dresses. Then I measure out enough for the sashes. I step away and fold my hands in front of my waist in a gesture of finality.

The shopkeeper cuts the material and wraps it in rough hemp cloth that smells strongly of camphor. She announces her price.

Papà hands the package of material to me. He puts half the amount she asked for on the table and picks up his basket. "We will be back if we need more."

"No!" The woman reaches for the package in my arms.

I twist away.

"Tell her the material is already cut, Simona. Tell her that cheating us will not bring back her dead. Nothing will bring back her dead, just as nothing will bring back ours."

I translate.

The shopkeeper looks at Papà, and for a moment I think she might slap him. Then she turns and goes to sit on a stool in the corner.

Papà marches ahead of Carolina and me, stops outside a low building, and hands Carolina the grocery basket. "Wait here."

"Let us come with you."

He just looks at me.

We lean against the wall and wait. A boy on a bike skids to a stop and watches us. I stand in front of Carolina and glare at the boy.

Papà comes out, and the boy rides off.

Carolina runs and hugs Papà.

Papà kisses the top of Carolina's head. He pulls a *furoshiki* out of his pocket. "Simona, you can use this to cover . . . my treat!" With a flourish, Papà uncorks a long-necked bottle under my nose.

I jerk back. "It stinks! What is that?"

"Pig wine," he says. "Bootleg liquor. From sweet potatoes. Dresses for you; drink for me. These might be our last treats." He smiles, but his eyes are as sad as his words. "Remember, it's me who did this—not you. But it's your job to keep quiet. You're my silent partners. The best kind of partners."

Even if what we're doing is wrong, it feels good to conspire with Papà. Almost like being a hero in one of the Japanese songs at school.

I wrap the bottle in the *furoshiki* and carry it in both hands while Papà takes the basket. With Carolina between us, we make our way out to one of the busiest roads and weave through pedestrians and bikes and cars and little two-wheeled carts that hold a person and are pulled by a running man. Soldiers in reddish-brown uniforms rumble past in trucks that spew black clouds of exhaust. They wear caps with five-pointed stars at the front, and neck flaps at the back. Most are Papà's age. How many of them are fathers?

When we get home, I put the persimmon into the bottom of a crock and pour rice over it. That's the secret. Leave it under rice for a few days, and it will turn sweet. And the fruit doesn't hurt the rice at all. Papà watches and smiles. He puts his hand on my back, and I lean against him.

Three days later my family shares the sweet persimmon.

CHAPTER
EIGHTEEN

8 September 1943, Tokyo, Japan

It's September and we're back in school, but this term consists of only two things. The first is studying popular culture, or, as Papà whispered to me, propaganda. Papà's attitude toward me has changed since he told me he's looking for a way to get us home, and even more since our rebellion at the black market. He shares little whispered criticisms like that because he trusts me completely. Just as he helps me when I overhear things in the ambassador's office, I now share his burden.

Popular culture studies include the teachers telling us that the Chinese are dying of starvation because of the failed Asian wheat crop. But Japan is better than China because Japan will not starve. Japan can get through anything. We must listen for dissenters, but not listen to them. We must report them to our teacher so that the Special Police who monitor how we think can arrest them. Even teachers should be reported on, to the principal. The good schoolgirls in Surugadai reported on teachers for spreading nasty rumors, so their school closed and they go to different schools now, with good teachers. They're a model for us.

Third graders and up—so Carolina is included—are automatically in the regiments of the Great Japan Youth Association, which tells us it is honorable to sacrifice for the nation. Good families give up their annual vacation in favor of working. If our family has not yet made that decision, we should help them make it. When we go to the movies, we must remind our brothers and grandfathers to remove their caps whenever the emperor appears in a newsreel, or they'll get arrested.

Women from the Great Japan Women's Association write slogans on the blackboard. We copy and memorize them. "Be frugal and save." "Luxury is the enemy." One by one, we stand and take our turn holding documents at arm's length and reading them aloud—all declarations about Japan's history and glory.

When we read these things, I glance at Aiko. She always looks earnest, just like everyone else. She doesn't glance at me. *Resistance matters*—those were the ambassador's words—even if it's only in our heads. Still, our resistance must stay a secret.

The second thing that fills our school day is war work. We make robes out of blue silk for wounded soldiers in hospitals, and underwear out of white silk for volunteer nurses. Unmarried women have an obligation to the nation. If you don't want to do factory work, you must "volunteer" to help on the battle front.

Some of the girls use the treadle sewing machine that's been installed at the rear of the classroom. I hand stitch. Right now I smooth the silk on my desk, pin the pieces of material together, and sew. Our teacher walks around, looking over shoulders. As she gets to me, I bend low, concentrating on my work.

"You are quick and your stitches are even," she says.

My cheeks burn in unexpected pleasure. Just yesterday she announced that Christians are a scourge. I'm the only Christian. Today she's praising me.

At a special morning recess we walk to the boys' school and watch them practice fencing with wooden swords. I think I see Naoki, but I can't be sure at this distance.

Music comes on, and the boys march inside single file. How I wish I could find Naoki and talk to him.

We girls troop back to our classroom and sew till lunchtime. Then some of us go off, like always. I know now that they're the poorest ones, who go into a special room for food the government provides. The rest of us get our *bento* boxes from the shelves and eat in the classroom. Noriko produces a white sash covered with red stitches, the threaded needle still attached. She adds another knot stitch. "Who's next?"

Keiko takes it. "Congratulations on your brother going to war."

My stomach lurches. I didn't know. How many have brothers at war? Or dead brothers?

"Thank you," says Noriko. "He's happy to serve the nation."

Keiko stitches, then passes the sash. Each girl adds a stitch and congratulates Noriko. When the sash reaches Yoshie, she makes a stitch and leans past Shizue to hand it to Yukiko.

"I want to make a stitch," says Shizue.

"You're still eating," says Yoshie.

Shizue blinks and bows her head. What's going on? Shizue is usually included in everything. I bite my lip. I remember when I used to be left out.

The sash passes on till it gets to me. I make a stitch in an instant.

"You're quick," says Mutsuko, with an edge to her voice. "You should make a second."

I make a second stitch. "Noriko?" I say. She looks at me. "Your brother is brave."

"Thank you."

I want to say she is brave, too. But she probably doesn't want to hear that. "Can you tell me, please, what the sash is for?"

"It's a *sennin bari*. Once it has a thousand stitches, my brother will wrap it around his body for safety, right under the flag. Every knot will be like a drumbeat, helping him be a good warrior."

I know those words. *Sennin bari.* Everyone helps. Everyone.

I stand up. I feel dizzy, but I carry the sash to Shizue. "I see you've finished eating," I murmur. I hand her the sash with the needle. Shizue quickly makes a knot stitch. Then I go back to my place and pass on the sash.

When I finally dare to look around, Aiko's eyes meet mine. Her eyes smile. The sash goes around the whole circle a few more times.

At the end of the lunch period, Yukiko whispers to me, "Sew slower, thief."

Thief? What's she talking about?

We go to second recess right after lunch, so I sit outside and try not to meet eyes with anyone.

Aiko sits beside me. "You did a good job of *inaoru.*"

Inaoru. Sit tall for what you believe. I did good at *inaoru.* It feels good to be told that. I run my finger around the edge of my shoe. "Yukiko called me a thief for sewing fast."

"Her mother sews robes and underwear and sells them to the government. Most mothers do. If schoolgirls sew too fast, mothers can't earn. They'll have to make more comfort bags."

"What are those?"

"Bags with gifts for soldiers. Our mothers assemble them and get a small price. But sewing pays more. Everyone needs the work."

"I'll slow down."

"You know what you said about Noriko's brother being brave? No one is brave anymore. But Oto, Noriko's brother, can't stand being a burden to the family. Their father was wounded and can't work. The neighbors scorn them. They say it's better to die fighting than to hang back so that you survive." She digs her finger into the dirt. "The family can't afford milk. Only families with small children get milk rations now, but Oto's family needs it, because his mother is pregnant again." She digs her finger deeper. "So Oto enlisted."

"But he could work in a factory."

"Those jobs pay less all the time."

"A mine, then."

"Koreans work the mines. For free." Aiko looks at her dirty finger, then brushes it off. "They're forced to. And it's horrible work."

"But war . . ." I hesitate and look around.

"Right," whispers Aiko. "War is horrible work, too."

"You and I," I say as quietly as I can, "we don't believe half the things they tell us. Yet you always look like you do."

"I know how to compose my face. You should learn. You must learn." Aiko takes a deep breath. "Oto is going to war because his father says it is honorable, the best way to help his family." Aiko makes fists of both hands. "Oto-kun is scared out of his mind."

It's funny to hear her put –kun after his name. It's like putting –chan after a girl's name. It feels very dear. "How do you know?"

"He's my sweetheart."

I drop my head forward in disbelief. "You're eleven."

"What does that matter? I spent the summer vacation talking with him. That's why I didn't go to the villa with you."

I look around at the girls skipping rope. It's still a favorite recess game. They sing and laugh like little kids. Do any of the others have a sweetheart?

My eyes settle on Shizue, sitting alone. "Why is everyone mean to Shizue today?"

"Her mother was caught stealing food. The police brought her home and fined her. Shizue's father is dead. Her oldest brother is in the army. She has three little sisters and a baby brother at home, plus her grandmother. There's no one to help them."

I grab a skipping rope off the pile beside me. "Shall we get Shizue?"

"Yes."

NINETEEN

8 SEPTEMBER 1943, TOKYO, JAPAN

Going home today, I'm happy, because Aiko and Shizue and I played all recess. Carolina skips ahead, excited by the promise of a fancy meal for supper. Two nights ago, a naval captain from Italy showed up at the embassy. He's in charge of the Italian fleet in the Far East. The ambassador and the captain sat up drinking and talking. Today he's coming back, so Papà is preparing a feast.

What's that up ahead? Military police cars in the street outside the embassy. "Carolina! Wait!" I catch up to her, and we run. The gate stands open.

A policeman blocks our way. We bow. I force myself to speak slowly, though I can hardly think. "Please. We live here. Our father is the cook."

The gate guard comes over. "They're the ones I told you about." He doesn't look at us.

The policeman moves aside.

We run through the side door, rip off our shoes, and race inside. There are policemen everywhere. Carrying guns. The ambassador sits at the dining table, his head in his hands. I grab Carolina's hand, and we race to the kitchen. No Papà there; not in the staff room, nor the little workroom off the kitchen. We run to our room. Papà opens his arms, and we rush to him.

"What's going on?"

"Rome signed an armistice with the Allies. With our enemies—the Americans, the British, the Soviets," says Papà, "last week, on 3 September. But it only got announced today."

"What's that mean?"

"Italy surrendered."

"But what does that mean?" I shout now. "What's happening?"

"Let's all sit," says Papà in a strained voice. "We're together. That's what matters."

We huddle on the mat. "Tell us. Please, Papà."

"I don't know much. The ambassador only found out when the police showed up. The naval captain has been in the Pacific for a year, and he didn't know, either. That's what the ambassador told the police. And the naval captain told them the same thing."

"How do you know what the captain said? Is he here?"

"He's wounded—in a clinic."

My heart stops. "They shot him?"

"No. What he told the police is that he got a telegram on his ship yesterday—saying that the fleet should make for the open sea fast, and if they didn't think they could get there before the Japanese found out about the armistice, then the captain should sink his ships so that the Japanese couldn't get them. The men threw equipment overboard, and opened the valves to flood the ships. And they made it to shore in smaller boats. That's when they were captured. The captain fell and got hurt."

"Do you really think he just fell?"

"I don't know, Simona. The police showed up this afternoon. They've been questioning the ambassador ever since."

"The captain must have told the police he'd been here at the embassy. He shouldn't have! The police could think we knew about the plans to sink the ships. Those terrible plans! The captain got us all in trouble!"

"They knew the captain had been here, Simona. They knew already, when they arrested him. They must have been spying on us. The captain told them that he'd come from Shanghai to check out his fleet. He had stopped by the embassy for a social call. He explained that he didn't get the orders to sink the fleet till noon yesterday, a day after he'd visited the embassy. But the police think that the captain came here to get orders from Rome via the embassy."

"That's impossible," I say. "The ambassador was going crazy because of Rome's silence."

"But the timing looks suspicious. And looks matter." Papà strokes Carolina's hair. "They say General Badoglio's new government betrayed the Axis powers. And it has to be so, because someone gave the orders to sink the ships. That was disloyal to Italy's pact with Germany and Japan."

Disloyal. At school, they say disloyalty is the worst crime of all. "If they think we're disloyal . . ."

"It's the ambassador. Not us. We're just servants."

"Do you really think they'll see it that way?"

Papà tucks Carolina's hair behind her ears. "It's the truth. We have no power. No knowledge."

We sit as the afternoon sun fades. It's as though we're fading, too.

Carolina finally crawls out of Papà's arms. "Want to play cards? Botan taught me. And Papà made Hitomi buy me my own deck. It's used and dirty, but it's a whole deck."

"Where is it?" I ask.

"I'll get it." Before Papà or I can stop her, she runs from the room. The policeman at the sliding partition lets her pass, but he blocks Papà and me.

I bite the side of my hand to keep from screaming. A moment later Carolina runs past the policeman again, and spreads the cards on the floor. Tears spring to my eyes.

"See?" she says. "That's a cherry blossom. And that's the moon. And that's a bush warbler. Look at them! You have to look, or I'll punch you."

"Punch me?" And I laugh. Laughing is the last thing I expected.

Carolina laughs, too.

I kneel and look. Italian playing cards are exciting, with swords and clubs and kings and horses. But Japanese cards are calm, all about nature. I've always loved the look of them. I put all my attention on the game.

At five o'clock a policeman herds us into the dining room, where the ambassador and Pessa are seated at the table.

Another man reads from a paper: "Excellency, I have the honor to inform Your Excellency that there has arisen a state of war between Your Excellency's country and Japan beginning today. I avail myself of this opportunity to renew to Your Excellency the assurances of my highest consideration." He reads in Japanese, then puts another paper on the table in front of the ambassador. It's in Italian.

The policeman says, "This letter is signed by Shigenori Togo, minister of foreign affairs."

The ambassador reads the letter. "This is tragic," he says in Italian. He looks at me.

The interpreter has disappeared. I translate into Japanese for the others in the room.

"Tragic," repeats the man in Japanese. "And my duty is most distasteful." He now reads another paper in Japanese. It's about what will happen next. I don't know some of the words he uses. He places a numbered list in Italian in front of the ambassador. He bows to the ambassador and to his wife, to the policemen, and he leaves.

A policeman says, "We have to do something about you. The evening newspapers have come out, so everyone will know about Italy's disloyalty. You'll be in danger. Whatever we do will be for your protection."

I translate.

The ambassador sits with his arms on the table and looks at the policeman. If there had been food on the table, his arms like that would have been rude. But there is no food, so I don't know what these policemen think. Still, I stare at his arms and hope he'll notice.

The policeman says we must collect our radios, cameras, binoculars, and weapons and put them on the table to be taken away. We can't leave the embassy. A decision will be made soon about what to do with us. We must prepare a room for all the policemen to stay in.

Then the policeman turns to Papà. "Make dinner. The others can collect your weapons for you."

Weapons? What do they think we do here?

9 SEPTEMBER 1943, TOKYO, JAPAN

The next morning, I hear, "Wake up."

Papà sits bolt upright. I wriggle out from under Carolina's arm and rub my eyes. A policeman stands over us.

The man kicks the bottom of Papà's foot. "Hurry." He looks at me. "You, too."

"I can't go anywhere without my little sister."

"Bring her." He leans over. "It's just breakfast. You're going to make us breakfast. *Shikata ga nai.*"

Papà looks at me for a translation. I say, "Life goes on." Our teacher says those words after every report of a battle that Japan has lost. We repeat it and go back to our work. Whatever happens, you still need to do your schoolwork. You still need to wash and sleep. You still need breakfast.

In the kitchen the policeman stays beside us. "You have no

pickled vegetables? But clams! Ah, wonderful in miso soup." Papà was going to serve them at the feast in the captain's honor. We make the soup.

None of the servants has shown up. Or if any did, the police turned them away. So Carolina and I are busy in the kitchen.

Captain Prelli, the injured naval captain, is there, at the dining table, with the ambassador and Pessa and the policemen. No one looks at me as I serve them. Pessa urges the ambassador to eat, but he doesn't touch his food. The captain hardly eats, either. His right arm is in a sling, and he's inept with his chopsticks in his left hand.

The ambassador's eyes meet mine. He glances toward a corner.

I go, sit on my heels, and listen. A policeman orders the ambassador to declare loyalty to Mussolini. Somehow they see Mussolini as leading another government somewhere in the north of Italy, alongside the new one led by Badoglio. I understand every word, but I can't make sense of it.

The ambassador seems to understand. He says, "Badoglio's government is the only legitimate one." He speaks quietly, in poor Japanese, but his voice is steady and firm, and the message is clear.

The policeman gets furious, but the ambassador sits tall. He's right: we have to be loyal to Italy's government, not to whatever mess Mussolini has made. I will serve the ambassador extra clams if I get a chance.

The policeman orders us to pack our bags—one suitcase

per person—and meet back at this table. Fast. The people of Japan hate us now. The emperor has declared that Italy is an enemy. We have to leave for our own protection.

We are the enemy.

Carolina runs off. But I stay to hear this policeman. The ambassador needs me. Carolina will be safe. No one pays her any mind. She has to be safe!

The ambassador asks where they're taking us.

The policeman says that for now the few Italians scattered across Japan are all being sent to an internment camp.

I don't know what that is.

The policeman frowns at me. "What are you waiting for? Go pack."

I throw all my clothes into my suitcase. I jam in my red lacquer box. I wear my school pants and white shirt.

Carolina is dressed just like me. She stands with her small suitcase in one hand and Lella in the other.

"Put Lella into your suitcase," Papà says to Carolina.

"I'm holding her."

"You'll hold your suitcase in one hand, and I'll have your other. How can you hold her if . . ."

"I'm holding her." She curls the hand with Lella against her chest.

"Put on your kimono sash," I say. "That way you can tuck Lella in."

"Someone might steal her from my back. She's safe in my arms."

Papà reaches for the rag doll.

"No!" shouts Carolina.

Papà takes Carolina by the upper arms and shakes her. "Listen to me. You do whatever I say, the instant I say it." He straightens up and passes Carolina's suitcase to me. "Simona will carry your suitcase. You hold Lella by one hand and me by the other."

"All right," says Carolina.

"Then I can't hold anyone's hand," I say, which is a stupid thing to say, since there is no one else to hold hands with.

"You don't need to hold hands. Nothing's going to happen," Papà says firmly. "When Japan bombed Pearl Harbor, the American ambassador was placed under house arrest in the American embassy. Then he was released to return to America. The same will happen to us. I'm holding Carolina's hand so she won't wander off. That's all."

"I'd never wander off," says Carolina.

I walk out of the room as straight-backed as Papà, a suitcase in each hand.

The captain is already there. He has nothing to pack. We wait in silence for the ambassador and Pessa. When they appear, Pessa has two suitcases.

"One suitcase per person," says the bossy policeman.

Pessa's face crumples. She leans the top of her head against the ambassador's chest.

"This way we can hold hands." The ambassador talks very gently. "You said you wanted that."

Pessa doesn't answer.

"I have no suitcase," says the captain. "I'll carry it." He reaches for one of Pessa's suitcases.

The lead policeman steps in front of him. "You're not going to the same place."

The captain looks at me. I translate.

The ambassador takes one of Pessa's suitcases. "Leave this one. It's smaller."

Pessa cries now. "That's the one the servant packed for me. I asked her to pack it with my special things."

"It's going to be all right." The ambassador holds the suitcase out to me. "You carry it."

Everyone wants me to carry everyone else's suitcases. But I don't have a third hand.

The ambassador yanks my suitcase out of my right hand and holds out Pessa's suitcase. "Take it!" He throws my suitcase aside.

I run to get my suitcase.

The ambassador grabs my arm and swings me around. He presses Pessa's hateful suitcase into my hand.

"Enough!" shouts the bossy policeman. "We're going!"

They herd us to the front door, and we put on wooden clogs. Our leather shoes disappeared weeks ago. They stuff us into police cars. I sit squished in the back with Carolina and Papà and a policeman.

"I'm sorry, Simona," whispers Papà.

I don't answer. He didn't offer to give up his suitcase. He

didn't tell the ambassador to throw away Carolina's suitcase instead of mine. It doesn't matter that it would have been just as unfair for Papà to lose his suitcase or for Carolina to lose hers. No one stood up for me. Someone needs to take care of me, too.

Now I have nothing in the world except the clothes on my back. The red lacquer box . . . Nonna's letters . . . lost. Tears press behind my eyes. But I'm too furious to cry.

The train station is crowded and dirty. It used to be spotless.

As I watch, a man puts his hand into another man's pocket and runs off with his wallet. The victim chases the thief, but no one else does. What's wrong with people?

When we climb onto our train, Papà takes off his clogs, to leave them in the entrance area, but a policeman says they'll be stolen. So he puts them back on.

The policemen push us inside the train car, fast, so that we trip over ourselves, but we get seats. People stand around us, smashed against each other. The three of us jam into two seats, with the suitcases on our laps. The ambassador and Pessa sit in front of us, with policemen in front of them. The captain sits behind us with two policemen squished against him. One is Our Policeman, the one who woke us this morning and allowed me to bring Carolina along to the kitchen. I look over my shoulder at him, but he's staring down at his hands.

The stink of the coal combines with the heat to make the press of everyone unbearable. Nausea rises in my throat. The seat is hard; the air is dusty. People glance here and there, watchful.

The train jerks. Screams and shrieks come from the end of our train car. Everyone talks at once. Oh no! A man fell from the gangway connection between our car and the next. He was lost under the wheels.

Pessa pulls on the ambassador's arm. "What happened? What are they saying?"

The ambassador looks back at Papà.

"I didn't catch the words," says Papà. But his eyes meet mine.

I press my face against the window so the ambassador can't ask me for a translation. A man dies, and we don't stop. Is his family on the train? Are they losing their minds now?

Carolina snakes her arm through mine. I pat it.

The train stops at Tamagawa Station, in a tiny village close to Tokyo.

"Get up!" A policeman pulls the ambassador's arm.

The ambassador stands and backs into the crowded aisle to let Pessa pass in front of them.

Papà stands and takes Carolina by the hand. "Come on."

"Sit down," says a policeman.

"We're getting off," says Papà.

"Not you. You're staying on. With the captain."

"We're not military." Papà shakes his head. "This is a mistake."

"Sit down."

"We should stay with the ambassador." Papà clutches the ambassador's shoulder from behind. "Tell them we should stay with you," he says in Italian.

The ambassador turns an ashen face to the policeman. "We're diplomats."

"You are," says the policeman in front of him. "He's a cook. We need cooks."

Papà's eyes flick back and forth between the policeman and the ambassador. "My daughters are not cooks. They'll go with the ambassador."

"No! We're staying with you," I say in Italian. "Together, all of us together."

"Hush, Simona," says Papà. "The captain will be in a prisoner-of-war camp. I'll never let you girls go there."

Our Policeman takes me by the upper arm. But I pull free.

"Sit down now!" The policeman in the aisle presses down on Papà's shoulder, forcing him to sit.

The ambassador and Pessa have already squirmed up the aisle. The crowd closes behind them.

Papà's face goes deathly pale.

Oh no! What have I done?

I press my forehead against the windowpane. A moment later Pessa appears on the platform. She mouths to me, "My suitcase!"

I still have her suitcase!

The train rolls on to Yokohama, then beyond. The next

time it stops, one of the policemen yanks Papà to his feet. "Hurry." He produces a club.

We are shoved up the aisle and fall off the steps onto the platform. The train leaves. I look at the sign: Ofuna Station.

"Move!" The policemen march us to a soldier.

"What are they doing here?" The soldier points at Carolina and me.

Our Policeman mumbles something to the soldier, and they argue.

Papà sets his suitcase down on the ground, puts one arm around Carolina, the other around me, and pulls us to him.

Now he'll scold me. I deserve it. "I'm sorry—" I say.

"Hush, Simona. What's done is done." He's breathing so hard, his body rocks. "No more mistakes. We pay attention. We listen to each other. We take care of each other."

A truck rolls up, with more soldiers standing on the flatbed. Two jump out and heave the captain up into the rear. They reach for Papà. He pulls away. "This is a mistake," he says to the officer in charge, bowing and bowing. "I'm diplomatic staff."

"You're a prisoner," says the officer.

The soldiers reach for Papà, but he swings his suitcase into the truck and climbs up. He extends an arm toward Carolina.

The policemen close around Carolina and me, cutting us off. I scream and claw at them. I can't see past the soldiers now, but I hear Papà's frantic shouts: "No! No! Simona! Carolina!" I hear him over the rumble of the truck taking him away. When the ocean of policemen parts, I see only the open mouth of the tunnel where the truck disappeared.

Carolina sobs.

Papà's gone.

I wipe my tears with the back of my hand. I pull Carolina to me and wrap both arms around her. "Hush," I say, just like Papà said before. "Hush so you can hear me." Her cries slow to gulps, then sniffs. "We're together, Carolina. We take care of each other."

She sucks on one of Lella's braids. Soon another truck comes.

Our Policeman puts a hand on my back. *"Ganbatte."*

Persevere? School kids say that before tests. Is he out of his mind? This is nothing like a school test. Papà is gone. Our Policeman actually thinks he's being kind. I hate him.

I boost Carolina up onto the truck. She turns and grabs at me. "Don't leave me."

"I won't."

"Ever!"

"Ever."

"I won't ever leave you, either, Simona."

I put the two suitcases, Carolina's and Pessa's, onto the truck and climb up.

CHAPTER

TWENTY-ONE

12 SEPTEMBER 1943, KAMAKURA, JAPAN

Carolina plucks a weevil from the rice. "Got another." She squats with the wooden bowl in front of her feet, like any Japanese girl. Good. When I told her we must avoid acting Italian, she said she didn't even know how to act Italian.

This is our third day in this empty house out in the countryside, and I am doing my best to be strong. Observation and strategy, those are the keys, as the ambassador advised. I'm determined to teach them to Carolina. I can feel Papà's presence. It's almost as though he's inside my head, watching me, being proud of me.

Carolina and I will find a way to join Papà. Sooner or later someone will say or do something that allows us to get to him. We have to stay alert. We have to win the trust of the guards.

We're already doing that. My favorite guard likes Carolina. He's an ordinary policeman from the nearest town, Kamakura, with a scraggly mustache and nicotine-stained fingers. He says Carolina acts right because she does what I say, not like spoiled foreigners. Carolina doesn't lick her fingers at meals, she says the proper Buddhist thanks before and after eating, and she holds her bowl under her chin to not make a mess. I call her Karo-chan, and she calls me Simo-chan. Even when no one is around, we behave as Japanese. That way we can't be overheard being Italian.

I promised Carolina she'll get a treat for all her good behavior soon. We haven't yet opened Pessa's suitcase. When we do, Carolina will get first pick of whatever is in it.

Carolina says she has a treat in her suitcase for me, too. I'll get my treat when she gets hers. She's trying to act like we're taking care of each other. Like Papà said. And maybe we really are, because I look forward to that treat.

"Another," crows Carolina in triumph as she flicks a weevil across the floor. "Another, another, another." She hates the idea that we might eat bugs.

I finish stitching up a rip in a shirtsleeve. I mend the clothes of the military guards at the Ofuna prisoner-of-war camp on the other side of the town. Papà is the cook there. My favorite guard told us, and he said we're never to tell anyone, because the prison is secret.

This house has broken windows and no furniture. We aren't allowed out. From the windows, we see farmers' fields.

We burn pine cones in the fireplace to boil rice and make miso soup. At night we lie in the bare upstairs with no bedding or mat. Carolina sleeps with Lella inside her shirt. She says, this way, if Lella wakes in the night, she won't feel lost. I fall asleep with my arms around Carolina.

A military guard always sleeps downstairs. The first night the guard on duty said he'd kill us if we tried to escape. I didn't believe he meant it. But the next morning my favorite guard said he did. He explained: "Being a prisoner is dishonorable. You should fight to the death. An honorable soldier would rather kill himself than get caught. So prisoners deserve death. If they try to escape, they get what they deserve."

I bowed and said, "We're not soldiers."

He looked at me. Then yesterday morning and again today at breakfast he brought us tea and rice cakes. Just one rice cake each, but they were wonderful.

We still wear the clothes we put on at the embassy. The grime makes me itchy. Once my favorite guard comes back, I'll ask him about a pot big enough for boiling laundry. I fold the mended shirt and set it neatly on the pile with the others. "What would you think of putting on fresh clothes?" I say to Carolina.

Carolina giggles. "You'll look funny in Pessa's clothes." She picks out one last weevil, then goes to the stairs and says over her shoulder as she climbs, "But putting on fresh clothes can't count as my treat."

I rush up the stairs behind her, then sit on my heels in

front of the suitcase I hate. Pessa is much larger than me, of course, but I hope there will be something I can wear. Carolina sits beside me, ready to pounce on her treat. I open the suitcase. It holds a single sheet of expensive embossed stationery, a tiara, and the fur coat that Pessa bragged is real fox fur. I take them out. On the bottom is Pessa's canary, dry and lifeless.

Carolina sucks in her breath, and her hands fly to her face.

Pessa said a servant packed this suitcase for her. What servant did such a thing? Cruel to Pessa, cruel to the bird.

"We'll bury him," I say quietly. "When the other guard comes back. The nice one."

"Wrap him in the white paper. He can be a mummy."

"Good idea," I say. "Do you want the tiara as your treat?"

"The guards would hate me if I wore a tiara. It's better not to have a treat at all."

I wrap the bird in the white paper and stuff the coat and tiara back into the suitcase. I go to close it, but see a cloth pocket glued inside the lid. I pull out newsprint. It's Mickey Mouse, "Great Adventures." Everyone loves Mickey Mouse. Papà read those stories aloud to us back in Italy. Even Nonna laughed. I remember this very issue.

Carolina puts her hand on the back of my neck. "Is it something else bad?"

I take deep breaths to keep from crying. "It's funny. We can read it later." I put the newsprint away. "Change your clothes."

"But you can't change yours. You don't have any."

"I don't feel dirty yet."

"Yes, you do. That's the real reason we opened Pessa's suitcase. You've always said being dirty is disgusting."

"I was wrong."

"If you don't have clean clothes, I don't want them, either."

I give a small smile. "All right."

"The bird is sad," says Carolina. "Sad enough that it's time for your treat." She smiles. How she can look so genuinely happy, I have no idea. I force a smile in return.

Carolina opens her suitcase. She lifts out her clothes. There on the bottom is a photo. Nonna.

I clutch it to my chest. "How . . ."

"I was afraid the red box wouldn't fit into your suitcase. So I took out the most important thing." She shrugs. "Then you fit the box in. . . ."

"You did good." I kiss her cheeks. "But promise me, Karo-chan, promise me that you won't keep other secrets from me."

"Even good ones?"

"You must tell me everything, Karo-chan. I mean it."

"I promise."

Footsteps click on the floor below. We hurry down the stairs. It's my favorite guard. "Please," I say, "we need to go outside. We need to bury someone."

"Who?" he asks in alarm.

I unwrap our mummy bird.

His face softens. "Go bury it in the farmer's field. I'll watch you from the doorway."

We bow, then walk out into the onion field and squat

between rows. The earth near the plants is soft. I pull out three onions to claw a hole big enough for the mummy. Carolina places the bird in. We cover it together. I set the onions in the path for the farmer to find.

"We should sing something," says Carolina. "My teachers say singing is a way to give someone else energy to help them on their way."

"You're right."

"Do you know 'Children's Greengrocer'?" she asks.

"I sang that in third grade, too."

So we sing about three children whose father has gone to war. They push a cart to market to buy the things they need to stock their family store. The cart is heavy, so they have to work together, and they are proud and happy to do it.

"And now," I say, "because this bird is so sad, you get another treat."

"Not my onions!"

I jump up. A bony farmer stands behind us. He threatens us with a long piece of wood. I bow to him. Carolina bows to him. "We are not bothering your onions, honorable farmer," I say. "We are singing."

"I heard you." The farmer picks up the three onions. "If you didn't mean to eat my onions, why did you pull them up?"

"We buried a bird," says Carolina.

"A bird?"

"It was dead," says Carolina. "Your onion field is a good place for a bird to rest."

"What kind of bird?"

"A yellow one."

"A pet?"

"It belonged to a rich woman," says Carolina. "She gave it to us."

"She gave you a dead bird? Not a nice gift." The edges of the farmer's mouth twitch. He's fighting a smile! "All right, my songbirds. You have a choice. Run back to where you came from. Empty-handed. Or sing to my wife and take these onions away in exchange."

I stare at him in astonishment.

Carolina bows. I quick bow, too.

"We prefer the second choice," I say.

I look back toward the house. The guard's not standing outside watching us. I look ahead. The farmhouse is really close. It won't take long to sing to the farmer's wife. And this guard never gets angry; that's why he's my favorite. But if he does, the farmer can explain. And Carolina wants to go, I can tell. I want to go, too. It will be so good to be with someone other than military people even for a little while. I calm myself. We'll be all right.

We follow the farmer to his house, and he calls his wife to the door. We sing to the clearly dumbfounded woman. The farmer tells her about the dead bird that someone gave us as a gift. And now he smiles freely.

The woman beckons us inside. She walks to a window where a bird sits in a cage. "A white-eyed warbler," she says.

Green and yellow, with black legs, and a white ring around each eye. It's lovely. The bird snaps. Insect wings stick out from its beak. Ha! That's why she can keep a pet—it doesn't cost anything to feed it.

As we walk back, Carolina swings the onions by the green stalks. "Do you think we can visit them again?"

"I'll ask our favorite guard."

He still isn't watching from the doorway. Good. He won't even realize we left the field.

Oh dear, there's a truck out front! I run inside. Our guard argues with a soldier who has Carolina's suitcase in his hand.

"Lella!" screams Carolina. She grabs her suitcase.

I don't see Pessa's suitcase anywhere.

"Get into the truck," says the soldier to Carolina. "Now!" He looks at me. "You, too."

"See? They came back," says our guard.

The soldier glares at us. "Go!"

TWENTY-TWO

3 FEBRUARY 1944, NAGOYA, JAPAN

We stand in line, shivering. February snow flurries cloud the windows. They come faster and thicker by the minute.

"Attention!" shouts the guard.

"Good morning, honorable soldier," we murmur in Japanese, bowing from the waist.

The guard wears black boots, a tan uniform, and a helmet. He calls out the roster. We listen carefully because his pronunciation of Western names is garbled. When he says my name, I answer, "Yes," loud and fast. Since Carolina and I were brought to this internment camp, the number of people has grown to nearly fifty, all Italians with the misfortune of living in Japan at this horrible time. Italy surrendered last September, and in October declared war on Germany. At least Italy hasn't declared war on Japan—yet.

The guard counts us, but this morning, he counts only the adults. That feels ominous. Maybe he's overlooking the children because we can't escape. We're too hungry, too cold. Besides, where would we go? It can't be that he's overlooking us because he assumes we'll die.

"At ease." The guard announces today's job assignments.

I put my white arms around Carolina from behind. They look like bones. Carolina hugs herself. Her arms are nearly blue. Inside her shirt, Lella makes an extra layer against the cold. It's not enough. The other children's arms are hidden—not by long sleeves but by the fact that they wear multiple shirts and at least one shirt is large enough that they can keep their arms inside it. This morning they look like a waddle of penguins.

Each person came with a suitcase, except Carolina and me. We have only hers, and when we arrived here, we found it had been ransacked. The only things left were her deck of cards, Lella, and the photograph of Nonna. And someone had thrown in the newsprint of Mickey Mouse from Pessa's suitcase. Anything that anyone else could use was gone.

No one here acknowledges that we have nothing. We're outsiders. The other Italians band together in the groups they've traveled with since being taken. The ambassador and Pessa looked alert when we first appeared. I thought they might band together with us, and maybe the ambassador could help us find Papà. But after I told Pessa her suitcase had been stolen, she didn't come near us. The ambassador sometimes looks at us almost apologetically, but he stays right by Pessa's side. I don't care. They sleep in a different building anyway.

At first, not having extra clothes didn't matter; the weather was warm. Sure, we were dirty because we couldn't wash our only outfits, and being filthy mortified me. Our hair smelled sour, moldy. But after a while, filth was nothing compared to hunger. Then the rains came, hard and long. The air inside our houses dripped. The guards insisted that we do all chores in the central building. So we dashed from our building through the rain to the central building, then went all day in wet clothes with teeth chattering. Others changed out of their wet clothes. Carolina and I couldn't. The others said they had nothing to spare. No one had packed for winter. Somehow, they had thought they'd be sent home to Italy before winter. After all, no one is military. Some people are diplomats from the Kyoto consulate; many are scholars. They expected to be treated with traditional Japanese courtesy. When they weren't, they closed in on themselves.

These days, they won't look at Carolina and me—the have-nots.

I think about Papà a lot. We are somewhere near Nagoya. I overheard that from the guards. In school we studied the history of Nagoya, but all I know about it today is that it was bombed last year by the Americans at the same time Tokyo was bombed, and it's far from Tokyo: four hundred kilometers.

The prisoner-of-war camp where Papà is cook is close to Tokyo. It's the next train stop after Yokohama. So Papà is far away.

But I still feel him. I sense him working all the time, but unable to sleep because of worry about us. I see his face as he looks at my bare arms now. I hear him scolding me for being stubborn and not putting my arms inside my shirt.

I can't obey the Papà in my head, though. Not about this. That's because I always hold to the ambassador's words about strategy. My bare arms are strategy. I insist on touching Carolina constantly. That means that one arm needs to be out in the air. Oh, I could take turns nestling one arm at a time inside my shirt. But I want everyone to see my cold arms. Let them relent and give up a shirt.

Carolina has become more stubborn than me. She keeps her arms out in the air, too, though she's so skinny now that both arms fit inside her shirt. Even when she's napping, she leaves her arms open to the air, and she naps a lot. She just lies down on the ground and sleeps.

As the guard's eyes pass over us now, Carolina says something under her breath to Lella. At the same time, she reaches one hand under the hem of her shirt, and I know she's caressing the rag doll's foot. This is a habit. We've all developed habits. At night people open their suitcases, and their chests relax as they fondle a familiar object. Owning something helps.

So when the stealing began, it felt inevitable. As things disappear from suitcases, people blame the guards. But they look at each other with narrowed eyes. Since the first thefts, people wear all their clothes. And layers help against the cold.

The guard says, "Dismissed."

A few adults gather for calisthenics before breakfast, though most go wait in line at the toilets. Men first, then women, then children. That's the order for weekly baths, too. If we need a toilet before our allotted time, we have to wake up earlier.

I'm in the toilet line. When it's my turn, I place my feet in marked spots and squat over a pit. The spots are farther apart than at school, too far for Carolina, so she uses the chamber pot. When we first came, I wanted to use it, too, but the guard said no.

I'm weak today. The weaker I grow, the more I'm sure I'll fall in.

The girl next in line whispers, "Don't look down."

I know she's trying to be nice, and I don't look down now, but I will have to look down later. That's because it's my job to empty Carolina's chamber pot into the pit. Big white worms writhe in the dark down there.

Now I join Carolina in the line for "coffee," made from roasted corn. A man, Antonio, is in front of us in line. He coughs and brushes stray fallen hairs off his shoulder, and that one slight action makes him sway. The fingers of his left hand trill the air. He looks down at his hand, and I see him move his lips, as though he's talking to himself. He puts his hand behind him and trills the fingers more. He lifts his hand to the side of his face and pulls on his fingers.

A woman, Virginia, stands in front of him, and jerks his hand back down to his side, then faces forward again.

"I can't feel my fingers," he says in Italian.

"Hush, Antonio," says Virginia, without looking back.

Antonio swings his head to both sides. Terror twists his face, but he keeps quiet. No one wants to attract a guard's attention.

He's a big man, but he's sick.

I look at Carolina's blue arms. No one here has a calendar, so it's easy to lose track of time. But the radios were loud on the second anniversary of the bombing of Pearl Harbor. Carolina's birthday is 7 December, the day before the bombing. So we know she has turned nine. My birthday is at the end of February, and if I've kept time correctly, it's now 3 February. I'm almost twelve. I should have a lot more strength than she has, yet I'm so tired. How much worse it must be for her. "Carolina," I say into her ear in Italian. We always use it to remind the others that we're Italian just like them. "Put your arms inside your shirt." She doesn't do it. "Now," I say fiercely. "Or else. Why won't you do what I say?"

"I do what you do."

"That's stupid."

"No, it's not. You know things."

My heart stops. My little sister thinks I know how to get through this. She counts on me. Where did all that talk about the two of us taking care of each other go? Doesn't she listen to Papà in her head the way I do? "I know nothing, Carolina."

She punches me in the belly. "Don't say that. Say the right things, or don't talk."

I want to punch her back. But the guard will notice.

After "coffee," we help make the rice gruel for breakfast. Then all of us eat in a circle on the floor. Some adults used to stand, but they got too weak. And no one is allowed to lean on the wall. So everyone sits, and the weakest lean on other people.

After breakfast Carolina threads needles while I huddle with the women and darn socks. Japanese soldiers hate holes in socks. So boxes of holey socks appear each day. We sew fast, pausing only to exhale onto our frigid fingers; the amount of food for dinner depends on the number of socks we darn.

A Japanese boy passes by, sweeping with his long broom. "Want thistle?" he whispers to me in Japanese. "Mugwort? Chickweed?"

"We got diarrhea the last time we ate that stuff," I say, and keep stitching.

"I know what you want. A kimono."

A kimono with big sleeves. A boy's kimono would be big enough that I could fold Carolina inside with me. "I have nothing to trade."

"Your sister has cards."

Carolina jerks her head up from her task of threading

needles. She looks at me and mouths, "NO." She fingers her cards every night. My eyes plead with her. She looks away. Stubborn.

"All right," I say to the boy.

"Bring them tomorrow morning."

In the late afternoon we all go to our houses. As we walk, I look for ways to escape so we can go find Papà. I do this every day.

Carolina and I live in a house that holds sixteen people. The downstairs has a room for the police in the daytime, a corridor with a storeroom and toilet pits, and a room with a table and benches, where we eat the evening meal. Then there's the kitchen with an oven, the only warm place. The second floor consists of a large room that would take eight tatami to cover the floor. We sleep in rows burrowed under futons to keep warm; the windows don't shut well.

The best place in the house is the room behind the kitchen, where the couple whose last name is Nishino lives. They guard us at night—a strange idea, for they're old. They walk bent like cupped hands, and they don't have the heart to be harsh. They talk with Carolina and me at night. I would have thought they liked us, except I don't count on anyone liking us anymore.

When we get to our house today, the water in the bottles to use at dinner is frozen. We set them by the fire to melt. The food basket holds four eggs and a can of sardines, for sixteen of us. We boil the eggs, then scoop them out to make rice in the same water.

Rita is using the handle of a spoon to cut the eggs into quarters when her husband, Xeno, comes up behind her. "Adults should get bigger portions," he says.

Rita stands with the spoon in her hand. I stop stirring the rice so I can hear every word. Finally she says, "We always divide it equally."

"Adults need more."

Rita puts the spoon down. "Do you want the children to starve?"

"Children need less."

Rita stares at the eggs. My stomach squeezes so hard, I nearly yelp.

"Shame," calls out Silvia. "Shame, shame, shame on us for even discussing this."

We finish cooking in silence. But when Rita fills everyone's bowls, Carolina's and mine hold less. Even less than Mariella's, the only other child in our house. She's older than me by a couple of years—but still. At least Carolina's and mine are equal. At least I don't have to fight myself over whether or not to give her some of mine. At least that.

At dinner people talk about the smell of jasmine, the taste of grapes. About walking along the shore, standing on a dock, holding a warm stone. Italy memories. Papà sometimes did that. I pretend it's him talking.

"Is there almond between my teeth?" asks Bernardo.

"The last time you had almonds was Christmas 1941," says Valeria.

"I had them for dinner!"

"You're confusing dreams with life."

A look passes among some of us. Valeria sees it. "Don't you dare think that." She faces each of us in turn. "He's just hungry."

"A man was sick today," says Patrizia.

"Priulli. His name is Antonio Priulli," says Xeno. "We'll all be sick if we don't get something more to eat than rice."

After dinner, the others go upstairs. Carolina and I go into the back room to see the old couple. We sit on our heels against the wall. The woman, Nishino-san, sits near us. The old man whittles on bamboo while Nishino-san tells us what she did today—work with the silk farmers—and we tell her what we did. I don't know why Nishino-san permits us these conversations, but I love them. When we first started, I did it as strategy, so that the old man and the old woman would think of us as Japanese children, at least partially. In case that became useful. Now I love these conversations because it's a chance for us to be the girls we used to be for a little while— the girls who spoke Japanese with their friends all day long. And I love the conversations because the old couple is kind. Kindness is rare.

Tonight, as Carolina tells about her day, Nishino-san shuts her eyes. When Carolina stops, Nishino-san says, "With my eyes closed, I can believe you are my daughter when she was little. You sound like Yuki did. Simona sounds like she's from Tokyo. But you have changed your talk since you came here. Now you sound like a child from here."

This is good. Carolina is like a chameleon.

Now I tell Nishino-san about the man Antonio, who can't feel his fingers.

Nishino-san's face snaps to attention. She reaches out and yanks my hair.

"*Aiii!*" I yelp.

Nishino-san looks surprised. I should have said *itai*, like a Japanese child. But the Italian popped out. I want to bite my tongue. After a second, though, Nishino-san nods with satisfaction. She yanks Carolina's hair. Carolina doesn't say a word, though I know how much it hurts. Nishino-san opens her palm and blanches in dismay; strands of hair lie there.

Oh, Lord. No. Please, please, no.

Nishino-san walks to a basket in the corner. Her toes point inward, because from the time she was little, she has spent the better part of the day sitting on her upturned feet. She told me that country women her age are all like this. She leans over the basket, and a moment later stands in front of us holding out a boiled white radish with both hands. "Do not speak, girls." Her eyes dart toward the sliding partition that separates this room from the kitchen. "Let me talk awhile."

I bow and take the radish, and open my mouth to thank her.

"Do not speak!" She puts her finger to her lips.

The radish smells like old water, not quite rotten. Still, I salivate. I take a bite and pass it to Carolina. We pass it back and forth. Meanwhile Nishino-san talks about silkworms. About picking mulberry leaves to feed those worms, and gathering their droppings for fertilizer. When we swallow the last bite of radish, she says, "Go to bed. Don't talk tonight. Go to bed, and tomorrow"—she mimics eating—"I will tell you more about silk."

It's rude not to allow us to thank her, and Nishino-san would never be rude, so I'm sure now that she knows someone was listening through the rice-paper partitions. The others must wonder what Carolina and I do with the old couple in the evenings. When we first started this habit, they asked, and I told them the truth. But they said we could practice Japanese with Mariella. She speaks as well as we do. Mariella doesn't want to speak to us, though. Like everyone else, she doesn't trust us. We aren't part of her original group.

The others might be spying on us. They'd be outraged to know we've shared a radish without saving any for them. That would make them feel justified in how they treat us. They talk as much about loyalty as our teachers did. They would call us disloyal. And we are. But the portions at dinner make me think again. From now on, we'll get smaller portions, I just know it. So it isn't evil of us not to share the radish. We bow our thanks and climb the stairs.

People sit on futons and talk softly in the dark. Carolina walks ahead of me to our futon. We hide under it and take off our clothes, turn them inside out, and put them back on. That way one side airs out overnight and we don't feel so grimy. Then we crawl out and sit on the futon. Carolina opens her suitcase and takes out the deck of cards. She fingers it. I take out Nonna's photograph. I can't see it in the dark, but I know every detail of it, and I recite those details to Carolina now. Then I tuck the photograph into the side of my underwear. I tell Carolina that it helps me sleep safely. But really I do it just in case anyone might try to steal it in the night. All sorts of things have disappeared out of people's suitcases in the night.

Carolina stacks the cards into a neat deck and kisses the top. "Goodbye, Botan, my friend," she whispers in Japanese. She hands me the deck.

I won't feel sorry for her. I won't feel sorry for myself. We need a kimono. To keep us warm. Alive.

I touch Carolina's cheek. It's rice dry. Like mine.

CHAPTER

TWENTY-THREE

25 February 1944, Nagoya, Japan

My belly cramps so bad that I curl into a ball under the futon. This shouldn't be happening. Not to me.

Almost everyone else has gotten sick in the last few weeks. They can't see well. They're faint and weak. Hair falls out. Gums bleed. They're dizzy.

And they have cramps.

Carolina and I are skinny, but Nishino-san has kept us from getting sick. She feeds us sweet potatoes and taro, both harvested back in November but still good. As we eat, Nishino-san describes the boxes she and her husband set up for silkworms to form their cocoons in, and how long it takes the cocoons to be ready for harvesting. She talks about spinning thread off the cocoon. She talks and talks, and we eat. Twice she's given us each an egg—a whole egg! And sometimes onions and bitter mandarins and dried wild greens. Once, even a fish skin.

The rations the guards supply go up and down. Rice is scarce, and a guard grumbled about it being a travesty that we get any at all when the people of Japan have so little. Sometimes they give us bread. It's so good that if someone looks at you while you're eating, you turn your back and curl over the bread like a dog with a bone. And if you happen to get a little extra, you bury it in a hole you dug somewhere between your sleeping quarters and the central building, to save for later.

Usually they give us fish at dinner. But so little that people are slowly starving. Some sit listless in a heap all day.

Not long ago, International Red Cross representatives inspected our conditions. I listened to every snatch of conversation I could. The American government claimed that the Japanese were cruel to prisoners of war. The International Red Cross came to make sure we were treated fairly. They noted that we had futons. Many toilet pits. That we got fish almost daily. They didn't talk to us; they questioned the guards. When the ambassador protested in his nearly unintelligible Japanese at the small amount of food, the lack of jackets, and the chores all day long, the head guard said that Europeans were lazy pigs. The International Red Cross left. Everyone is getting sicker.

Except Carolina and me—until now. Our portions at dinner have been cut, but not as much as I feared they would be.

And that one extra shared sweet potato a day from the hands of Nishino-san makes all the difference. Carolina's hair isn't falling out anymore. Her eyes are clear. So why am I cramping now? No!

"Get up." Mariella reaches under the futon and yanks on my foot. "Everyone else is already downstairs."

"I can't." I clutch the futon to my chin. "I have cramps. Really bad."

"You're sick like the rest of us." Mariella's face softens. "We all thought you . . ." She shakes her head. "You have to come get breakfast anyway. No one will make you work. It's better than being alone."

I shake my head. "I'll throw up if I move."

"All right; stay here. If they ask about you, I'll explain that you're sick."

Carolina sits up and peeks out from under the futon. "Don't be sick, Simona."

"You know she can't help it," says Mariella. "Come with me and see if they'll let you bring back rice gruel for Simona."

Carolina shakes her head. "I won't leave her."

"Don't be stupid," says Mariella. "If they don't let you bring Simona food, at least this way you'll eat something."

"We stay together."

Mariella presses her hand against her mouth. But then she drops her shoulders and nods. "Breakfast is hardly anything anyway. You won't die if you skip it, and your sister needs you." She goes to the top of the stairs and looks back. "If they'll let me, I'll bring you food."

"They won't let you," I say. "But thank you. Truly."

Mariella gives me a smile and disappears down the stairs.

Carolina pokes my shoulder. "You're not supposed to get sick."

"I know."

"I have to use the toilet," Carolina says. "Don't you? Come down with me." Carolina climbs out from under the futon. She has the kimono on—the one that cost us her deck of cards. We alternate days wearing it.

I manage to follow her downstairs without retching. Since no one's around to stop me, we both use the chamber pot.

Maybe Nishino-san knows a remedy for cramps. We go into the old couple's family room. They aren't there; their day starts even earlier than ours.

The urge to get clean overwhelms me. I take the communal cooking pot and slide open the rear door. No one's about. It snowed two days ago, and the snow hasn't melted yet. I pile snow into the pot, high above the top rim. Then I go back to the kitchen and light the fire. Every move hurts. I want to double over this pain in my belly, but I have to keep moving. As the snow melts, I fill a bucket with snow and add more. When the water in the pot finally reaches halfway to the top, I add the last bucket of snow. Then I take the pot off the fire, and we strip. We're naked without having to rush, for the first time in almost half a year. It feels strange to look at our pale ribby bodies. I laugh. Carolina puts her hand to her mouth and peers around. Then she laughs, too.

"Someone is going to see the smoke from the fire soon," I say. "We have to hurry."

We dip our shirts into the water and use them to scrub ourselves. It would be so lovely to actually bathe, but this is the best we can do, and this is wonderful. The water still holds ice crystals; it's bracing. It cuts the cramp pain. We dunk our heads and scrub more. Why isn't anyone coming to yell at us?

I open a cupboard. A bit of lye and some seed pods that I recognize for cleaning. If I use them, Nishino-san will go without. Ashes alone are enough: I rub our clothes with ashes on the worst stains while Carolina scrubs Lella. Then I boil the clothes. We fish them out onto the floor. As soon as they're cool enough, we wring them hard.

It's midmorning by now, so this fantastically peaceful time with just the two of us together can't last. Someone will burst in soon. I pull on my wet underwear and school pants and shirt. Then I stand in front of the fire, holding out the kimono with both hands and flapping it. I turn slowly as I do that, so that I toast myself. Carolina does the same. Now she swings Lella near the flames. It takes a long time to dry out. Really long. It feels like forever. It's surely well into the afternoon by now.

The cramping in my belly has totally gone. We're ravenous now. Daily breakfast is a tiny puddle in a bowl, but we rely on it. I won't steal food from Nishino-san and her husband, though. They already sacrifice to give us food at night. I look out the back window. There's a kingfisher perched on a dry stick of a near-dead bush. Flashes of orange and white, sharp against the vivid blue. I think of Aiko, and our signal of her saying she'd seen a bird outside her window when she had an issue of *Chikakiyori* to pass to me.

Beyond the bird, I spy a horse-drawn wagon standing by the house down the hill. The back of it is filled with branches and dried leaves. And there's a sign attached to the side: KATAKURA INDUSTRIES COMPANY.

Katakura. I know that name. The interpreter said it to the ambassador. When he talked about the groups that wanted revolution, he mentioned the Katakura silk workers. Maybe that wagon will go to a factory where the workers are against this war. I check every direction. No one is about even now. But people might be looking from windows, just like we're doing.

"See that wagon?" I ask Carolina.

"The one with the horse?"

"Who knows where it's going," I say slowly.

Carolina comes close, and her arm presses against mine. "Maybe," she whispers, "maybe somewhere near Papà."

My words rush out, "Do you think you could make it to the wagon fast?"

"I can run in wooden clogs."

"It's through snow. Our feet will freeze."

"Not if we run fast."

"If they see us . . ."

"Then we have to run even faster, so they don't." Carolina tucks Lella inside her shirt. "Let's get our shoes and I'm ready."

"You wear the kimono."

"It's your turn, Simona."

"You'll get cold faster than me."

"You have cramps."

"They stopped. Today you wear the kimono. No arguments."

Carolina puts on the kimono. We get our shoes and run.

We leave prints in the soft snow. But I can't take the time to sweep them away. Besides, my hands will freeze. We run and run and run. We climb into the wagon and burrow deep under sticks and leaves. I can't hear or feel or think anything till my heart slows enough for my breath to catch up with it. Now I feel the dried stems poking us everywhere. A smell comes, all wheaty, like cut grass, like Nishino-san's hands. Mulberry leaves! Of course. For the silkworms. We're really in this wagon. No one shouted. No one saw.

Unless they're coming silently.

Moments later, the horse whinnies and someone clumps around at the front of the wagon, and then we're moving. Away from here. Go. Go, go, go, go, go. Fast, before anyone sees our prints in the snow.

Wagons don't go fast, though. This wagon bumps and sways. It's so slow that my whole body stiffens with tension.

The cramps come back. But that's good—they keep me from screaming in fright. Because we'll be stopped any second. What have I done to Carolina? And I don't even know why I did it. I saw that sign on the wagon, and everything tumbled apart inside me. This wagon can't be going to the Katakura factory. The interpreter said the factory was in Tokyo. No one would take a horse and wagon all the way to Tokyo. The local mulberry producers must dump their loads into a rail car that carries the mulberry to Tokyo. When the driver of the wagon dumps this load, he'll find us—there, in front of everyone at the train station . . . not in some factory where the workers want revolution, but in front of people who hate us.

I'd give anything to undo this—to be back in the internment camp. This is as bad as when I insisted we stay with Papà on the train.

Papà talks inside my head now. What's done is done. Calm down.

But I can't calm down. The guards will catch us now.

Or now.

Or now.

We roll slow, slow, slow over that bumpy road.

I'm practically crazed by the time the wagon stops. I peek out. We're in a town, but not at a train station. Across the street is a flatbed truck with sides. I can't see into the back of it. I can't tell if we'll be able to hide there. But we can't stay in this wagon; someone has to be on their way after us right now.

"Carolina?"

"My feet are cold."

I touch them. "Like fish on ice. Do you think you can run?"

Carolina pops up. We crawl out, race across the street, and climb into the back of the truck. It's half-full of bamboo poles. I try to dig grooves for us, but each time I roll a pole aside, others shift to take its place. So I lie on top of the poles, in the open. Carolina lies beside me. "Stay close, so you don't get too cold," I whisper.

"I'm a fish. Fish don't get cold."

Come, someone. Please come. Soon.

And someone somewhere must be looking out for us, because the truck starts up and goes fast. But a moment later it slows, and I peek over the side. We're going through a city now. Not like Tokyo, but big. We pass the train station. The sign says NAGOYA. We haven't gone very far at all yet.

I lie back as the truck goes faster. The wind rushes over us, blowing away the snow as fast as it falls. But the wind is colder than the snow. We'll freeze if this keeps up. I tuck my arms inside my shirt and roll to lie on Carolina, face to face, to give her more protection. The truck keeps going for what feels like hours. Finally I peek again. We're in the countryside. The sun is setting on our left, so we're headed north. In the not-too-far distance a snow-covered mountain rises high. Mount Fuji! We're only a hundred kilometers from Tokyo. And much closer to the prisoner-of-war camp at Ofuna. It's the end of February. In three days, I turn twelve. Maybe I can spend my birthday with Papà!

The truck turns up a road through a forest. The engine stops and the driver gets out. Footsteps clump away. I sit up. "Come on, Carolina."

She doesn't stir.

I shake her shoulder. No response. I pull on her hands, on her feet. I listen to her chest; I put my hand under her nostrils. Nothing. But that's because it's too cold to feel anything. That's the reason. That has to be the reason. I pound on her chest, and I hear Lella crack, the doll has frozen so hard. This can't be happening. No! "Carolina!" I scream. "Get up!" I scream and scream.

Hands pull me out of the truck. I can't stop screaming. A hand slaps over my mouth.

"Who is she?" says an old man.

"I have no idea," says the man who holds me from behind and nearly suffocates me. "But she's foreign. And there's another girl in the truck—maybe dead."

"What did you do, you idiot!"

"Nothing! It's not my fault. Look at you, blaming me. I could as easily blame you."

"This is horrible. If we call the police, then they'll blame us both. We'll get in trouble, and we've done nothing bad. No!" He shakes his head. "We have to get rid of them."

"I have an idea. Those women up the road. We'll dump them out front of their place."

"Right! I've always suspected they're up to no good. If they get in trouble, they'll deserve it."

The man throws me back into the truck and runs to get into the front. The truck bounces wildly. I'm screaming, "Carolina," holding her, rubbing her.

Moments later, we're tossed onto the ground.

The truck honks and drives away.

TWENTY-FOUR

25 FEBRUARY 1944, MOUNT FUJI, JAPAN

A woman undresses Carolina and lays her blue body on a futon by the fire. She strips off her own clothes and lies beside Carolina, rolls my sister gently onto her own belly and chest, tucks Carolina's hands into her armpits, folds Carolina's feet between her legs, and closes her arms around Carolina's back. My sister is enclosed in that woman's body.

A second woman spreads a blanket over them, then a second blanket.

"This one's shivering hard," says the woman who's holding me from behind. I am no longer screaming or struggling. We stand by the fire, near Carolina's head. The woman strokes my hair and hugs me tighter.

Carolina has not moved. I know. My eyes never stray from her.

"She'll get frightened if you try to take her clothes off," says the blanket woman. "And fear is a strain on an already weakened heart." She brings another blanket from a corner stack and wraps it around me, looking into my face. "It'll get better," she says quietly.

I fix on her a moment and take a deep breath. My eyes turn again to Carolina.

The blanket woman runs out the door. A while later, she comes back with a flurry of white. She slides the door shut and brushes the snow from her shoulders and shakes it from her hair. "It was just the two of them. I walked all the way out to the main road. I'm sure."

"That's good," murmurs the woman hugging me. I feel her words on the back of my neck, warm and puffy.

"I'll make broth. You keep her snug, Fujiko." The blanket woman scurries around.

Carolina still does not move. Please, oh, please, please.

The room is quiet except for the cracks and pops of the fire. A wave of confusion makes my eyes blur. I know where I am—a little house in the woods—with three women—but it seems I am nowhere, in no time. Where is Carolina? Is she still inside that body? She'd better be! She'd better not leave me! The pressure in my ears hurts. I can't tell if it comes from outside or inside my head. My hands and feet and arms and legs and all parts of me ache.

The woman who was hugging me—Fujiko—lets go and

takes my hands to her face. She exhales on them. "Let's move closer to the fire." She hugs me again, and we sidle closer.

And Carolina moves! I gasp.

Fujiko follows my eyes. She shakes her head. "That was just Sanae's hand, moving up and down the girl's back." She lets go of me and walks over to Carolina. She lifts the blankets a little so I can see. Carolina lies still as a rock. "I'm sorry," Fujiko says, quiet as snow.

My throat is raw from screaming; my eardrums threaten to explode.

The blanket woman hands Fujiko a bowl. She holds it to my lips and tilts it. I don't want to drink. I don't want to be so hungry and love the smell of that miso so much. I don't want to be here, to be alive, if Carolina isn't. But I can't stop myself. The soup is warm on my lips, on my tongue. It flows down my throat, sending warmth everywhere. It burns all the way to my stomach.

"Slow," says Fujiko. "It's all yours. No one's going to steal it."

I didn't even realize I'd taken the bowl from her hands. I press it to my lips. I drink again. And again.

"You're half-starved." Fujiko shakes her head. "Just like a Japanese child."

"Where do you think they came from?" The blanket woman tugs on my legs to make me sit. "Look how stained the little one's kimono is. We'll have to replace it."

"Who knows what these children have been through." Fujiko gets a pot. "I'll fill the tub. She can bathe."

"What if she doesn't understand?" says the blanket woman. "She could panic."

"She's not a panicky sort," says the woman wrapped around Carolina—the woman called Sanae. "She's watching everything we do. She'll figure it out."

Fujiko sings. She starts quietly, like a whisper. "In the morning as I wandered on the seashore . . ." I know this song. It's one of the most beautiful songs we sing at school. Her voice gains strength, and the others join in. If my throat didn't hurt so much, I would, too. Carolina needs a song.

Fujiko pulls a tub over to the fire, and she and the blanket woman heat water from buckets, to fill the tub with water. They make a bath that's deep and warm and smells like heaven. I dip my hand into the camphor water and twist inside with guilt. I'm alive. I can eat. I can bathe. It shouldn't be true. Not without Carolina. I shouldn't want to get into that water.

Fujiko helps me undress and looks over my body. "Good!" she calls out in relief. "She has no bruises." She puts a small basin of water on the floor beside the tub and magically produces a bar of soap. Real soap. "Wash yourself." She hands it to me and mimics scrubbing.

I clean off in the basin, then climb into the tub. The ache in my body eases. I slide underwater.

Fujiko pulls me up. "Sit tall. You will be all right. Under-

200

stand?" She leans her head forward. "I am Fujiko." She taps her chest. "Fujiko. What's your name?"

"Ah, little one, I saw that eyelid move. Can you hear me?" It's Sanae who's speaking—the woman cradling Carolina.

I stand up in the tub.

"Bring the soup, Kotsuru," says Fujiko.

The blanket woman quickly brings over a bowl.

The blanket woman is Kotsuru.

Sanae sits up slowly and moves Carolina ever so carefully so that my sister is sitting on her lap. Carolina hangs limp, but her skin has turned pinkish gray.

"You feed her, Fujiko. You did good with the big girl." Kotsuru hands the bowl to Fujiko.

Fujiko holds the bowl under Carolina's nose. "Breathe it in, little one. It tastes good. The big girl liked it. She ate all of hers. You can eat, too. Please, little one. A sip."

And Carolina lifts her head. She opens her eyes.

"Carolina," I call, my voice raspy.

Fujiko touches the bowl to Carolina's mouth and tips it. Soup dribbles down Carolina's chin.

"Maybe that's her name: Carolina. I think they're sisters," says Sanae. "The curls on the big girl make them seem different. But their faces are similar."

Kotsuru comes over to me. "Sit down. Stay in the water. Carolina's getting better. Let us take care of you both."

I squeeze my hands together. I'm chilled again. I lower myself back into the tub, but I keep my eyes on Carolina.

Kotsuru looks around. "Who would like a bowl of noodles with eel?"

"You have the best ideas," says Fujiko.

Kotsuru goes to work cooking noodles with eel. I watch Carolina. Did she hear? Noodles. Noodles disappeared from the embassy meals way before rice; we haven't had them in months and months. Carolina loves them. The vagueness in her eyes gives way now to a fierce intensity. She looks at me as though to send a message; then, anxious, her eyes search the room. Panicked. She's right. We have to watch for clues, stay ready. Who are these women here in the middle of nowhere?

I look around the room, too. A large low table stands against one wall. Ink jars are lined up at the rear of it. Pencils and paintbrushes are arranged neatly beside a stack of paper. A packed bookshelf goes clear to the ceiling. Stacks of books rise from the floor here and there. A couple of sets of drawers, a basket of pots and pans and cooking utensils, bowls, cups, folded futons, and blankets. The ordinary things of life. A good home, even if strange, with so many books and art materials.

Now I think, these women call each other by their first names. I've never heard adults do that except to a servant. These women aren't servants. They act like sisters, but they look nothing alike. Fujiko wanted even me, a child, to address her by her first name. It's odd, but friendly. Intimate.

I look back at Carolina. Her face now shows open fear.

Kotsuru said that fear could make us worse. Oh no! What's

scaring her? Nothing here seems threatening; nothing seems awful.

Carolina's face crumples. She whimpers. I twist my neck this way and that, searching for the answer. And then I know! I reach for the towel hanging by the fire.

"Don't you want to enjoy the bath longer?" says Fujiko.

I wrap the towel around myself and go to the heap of Carolina's clothes, hidden from her sight by Sanae's body. I pick up Lella and bring the doll to Carolina. She snatches it and holds it to her face. Then she hugs Lella and rocks her like a baby. "I want noodles," she says in a husky whisper of Japanese. She clears her throat. "And eel."

The women laugh.

I cry. My sister is all right. I sob.

Fujiko touches me on the cheek. "So you speak Japanese. That will make it all much easier. Come back into the tub now. Your sister can join you."

Carolina cleans off; then the two of us soak while we smell the eel cooking and listen to the noodle water bubbling. Lella sits by the fire. I watch Carolina's face pinch in pain, and I know that her body hurts much worse than mine did as I thawed, yet she doesn't cry. Not one tear. I love her fiercely.

"The little one is Carolina," says Sanae, who has dressed and is now smoothing the front of her kimono. "If you tell us your name"—she looks at me—"we will tell you ours."

"You are Sanae. And you"—I wave my hand—"are Fujiko. And you"—I wave again—"are Kotsuru."

"A clever one," says Kotsuru. "I could tell from your eyes right away."

"You could be a spy with those skills," says Sanae. "I bet you've figured out a lot about us."

"At least one of you is an artist," I say. "At least one, a scholar." My face grows hot, but I won't back away from the challenge. "Someone is rich, to be able to buy noodles and eel on the black market."

"A spy indeed," says Fujiko. "But we didn't buy the noodles. We bought wheat, and Kotsuru made noodles. It was the last wheat available."

"We know something about you, too." Kotsuru lifts the rice pot from the fire and sets it on a flat stone. "You have not eaten enough in a long time. You have not enjoyed a bath in a long time. Is that all you want us to know about you? Really?"

"I am Simona."

Kotsuru smiles and bows. "It is a pleasure to meet you. Our time in this cabin has been good until this moment. But things have changed." She hesitates. I hold my breath. "We were missing children. You have filled that gap. Now our time in this cabin feels just right."

I breathe out with a smile.

"Your arrival is auspicious," says Sanae. "We were three before; now we are five. Five is a good number. A handful."

"Where are your parents?" asks Sanae.

I can feel Carolina's eyes. I don't look at her. We never mention Papà except in our prayers. It's a silent pact. But I have to answer the question. "Our father is a cook at the prisoner-of-war camp at Ofuna."

"Is there a prisoner-of-war camp there?" says Sanae. "I never heard of one. So you came here from there?"

I shake my head. "We left Ofuna. They took us to another place—an internment camp near Nagoya—where there are other . . . Italians." Does she hate Italians?

Sanae nods. "I know about it." She fills bowls with noodles. Kotsuru adds strips of eel. They hand out the bowls and chopsticks. "Do you want to come out of the tub to eat properly?" asks Sanae.

I want to shovel that food down my throat as fast as I can. But I want us to be polite. So I put my hands on the side of the tub to stand. Carolina kicks me under the water. "I want to eat now," she says. "In the tub."

Kotsuru smiles.

The women sit on their heels on the floor beside our tub and murmur thanks. I do, too. I pull on Carolina's toe. She murmurs thanks. We eat, slurping loudly. The eel is a miracle. These noodles are a dream.

"So," says Kotsuru. "You were at the Tempaku internment camp in Nagoya. And you ran away." She tilts her head toward me in question. I nod. "How did you get here?"

"We climbed into the back of a truck—and when the drivers stopped and saw us, they got scared and dumped us here."

"What about your mother? Where is she?"

"She died. In Ostia, near Rome. Four years ago."

Kotsuru nods. "I'm sorry to hear that." She takes Carolina's and my empty bowls. "Do you think you'd get a stomachache if you had seconds?"

"No!" says Carolina.

So we have a second bowl of noodles and eel.

Five is the best number in the world.

TWENTY-FIVE

17 MARCH 1944, MOUNT FUJI, JAPAN

"Blue," says Carolina. She smooths the paper with both hands, then reaches for the ink.

I wrinkle my nose. Carolina has been working hard drawing the decorative border, so she deserves the right to choose how to paint it now. But . . . "Blue onions?"

"They're in the shade. Look outside."

I slide the door open a tiny bit. The chill of the mid-March morning makes my face tingle. We planted the onion sets right after my birthday. I can't tell if they've grown any yet. But they're in partial shade now, and they do not look blue.

Fujiko comes up behind me and puts her mouth to my ear. "Often the edges of the paper are cut off by the printing press anyway." She goes back to her "thinking chair," where she thinks up new manga—comics.

I go back to the art table, ready to humor Carolina, but she didn't wait; half the onions are blue. I laugh and bury my face in her hair. Nonna always told us to count our blessings. The smell of Carolina's sun-warmed, clean hair feels like a blessing.

I reach for the red ink and color in the pilot in the first of three airplanes. This pilot is a pig. The other two airplanes are piloted by a goose and a hound dog. We're helping Fujiko and Kotsuru and Sanae to make anti-war manga.

Kotsuru pulls the last of the laundry from the line over our heads and folds carefully. She pats the top of the pile and comes to lean over the table between Carolina and me. "Good work."

Fujiko comes near and peeks, too. "Maybe one of you girls will become a professional cartoonist."

"Like you," says Carolina.

"I'm not professional," says Fujiko. "Not anymore. I was. Before the war. But when the government demanded that all cartoonists join the New Cartoonists Association of Japan, I refused. So I lost my job."

"Why did you refuse?" asks Carolina.

"They wanted me to make jokes about things that weren't funny. Like mothers sewing colorful patches on their husband's clothes because there are no new clothes to buy. They want everyone to think the sacrifices of war are trivial, nothing to complain about."

"Papà calls that propaganda," says Carolina.

A chill shoots up my back. Ever since I told these women

that Papà is in the prisoner-of-war camp, Carolina has managed to bring him up several times a day. It's as though she's been holding all her memories inside, and now she feels she's allowed to let them out. But what chills me is the nature of what she says. I didn't know she listened so closely to the secret things Papà said to me. I didn't know how much she understood.

"I'm sorry you lost your job," I say to Fujiko. My voice trembles.

"If you're thinking she went hungry, you're wrong," says Kotsuru. "Fujiko's family is rich. They own this cabin. Fujiko was born here—under the shadow of Mount Fuji. That's where her name comes from. No, no, it's Sanae who went hungry. She's from a poor family. She was a teacher at the best school for girls in the Surugadai district of Tokyo. When she got fired, she had nothing."

I know about that! Last fall a girls' school in Surugadai was closed because the teachers spoke out against the war. Their students reported them. That's why Sanae said I had spy skills the first day we met them! She knows about child spies.

"Papà didn't get fired," says Carolina. "He got stolen."

Kotsuru tilts her head. "Yes. That's the right word. Many men and boys get stolen by this war."

"Did you lose your job, too?" I ask Kotsuru.

"Not exactly." Kotsuru looks hard at me, then at Carolina. "It's a long story. Ugly. But you told us your story, so if you want to know mine, I'll tell you."

Maybe I don't want to know.

"Please tell us," says Carolina.

"You may be right, little bird. Knowing another's story can help you through your own. Come."

We squat in a circle, the three of us.

"My husband and I ran a bakery in the Fukagawa district of Tokyo. Our son, Toshio, played at our feet as we worked." Kotsuru smiles. "We made *kasutera*."

"What's that?" asks Carolina.

"Sweet, eggy bread. It was our specialty. Everyone loved it. Some mornings the line went all the way to the corner. But the military needed cooks—as you girls know too well—and bakers were prized. My husband, Daishi, somehow wound up in battle instead of in a kitchen. He was killed at Attu."

"I'm so sorry, Kotsuru," I say.

"Poor Toshio," says Carolina. "Poor you. It's good to sleep when you're sad. You must have wanted to sleep for a month."

"I'm Buddhist," says Kotsuru.

"Everyone is Shintoist and Buddhist," says Carolina.

"Yes, but I am a Chinese-style Buddhist. The Buddha has a saying that everyone needs to understand: *Satori-no ato-ni-mo sentaku-o.* Do you understand?"

Satori-no ato-ni-mo sentaku-o. After enlightenment, laundry. Maybe I understand that.

"No," says Carolina.

"It means that no matter what happens to your mind and soul, you still have to do the necessary things of daily life. So

I went right back to work the next day." Kotsuru looks away a moment, then back at us. "But things were different for a widow—a woman without a man. Military police came to the bakery, picked up food, and left without paying. Over time, there was less sugar, then none. Less flour, then none. Then the military police took away my iron oven. They said everyone must make sacrifices. *Okuni no tame ni.*"

For the sake of the country. How many times have I heard that? I've come to hate that saying. "That's what Keiko's mother said when her brother was killed." I don't add that Riku died at Attu, too.

"The military police said there were no more iron chains on the graveyards because every bit of iron went to fight this war . . . so how could I complain about losing an oven? I revere my ancestors. But . . ." Kotsuru shakes her head. "The dead don't need those chains; the living do need bread. I took Toshio to live with my mother."

"Family should be together," says Carolina.

I cup the top of her foot with my palm.

"Except, my mother had a cough. It turned out to be tuberculosis. Toshio caught it and died quickly, even before my mother died."

Kotsuru's face is dry, but tears roll down my cheeks.

"You couldn't have known," says Carolina. "It's not your fault."

Kotsuru smiles. "Thank you, Carolina. You think clearly. But at the time I couldn't think clearly. I couldn't think about laundry. I couldn't think about the Buddha. I couldn't think at all."

"That's when she met us," says Fujiko. "None of us could think straight alone. But together we found a path."

The sound of Sanae's noisy old truck makes us look up. The house door slides open and Sanae comes inside.

"School time," I say. Sanae gives Carolina and me daily lessons. She's a far better teacher than my teachers in Tokyo. Carolina and I stand and go to the drawing table to put away our manga materials.

"No school right now," says Sanae. "I heard news. Something you two should know."

"Us?" I go on the alert. "Something bad?"

"Italy's Mount Fuji erupted earlier today."

Italy's Mount Fuji? Oh. I can hear Papà in my head, equating Mount Fuji with a volcano in Italy. "Vesuvius?"

Sanae nods. "The Allied troops are evacuating everyone. A whole village will burn from the lava flow, for sure. But maybe no one will die."

"What village?" asks Carolina. Her face has gone pale. I realize she doesn't know where Mount Vesuvius is.

"San Sebastiano. Do you have family there?"

"No," I say. "Lido di Ostia is far from there."

"Good," says Sanae. "Let's celebrate that your grandmother is safe."

"We can write her an extra page tonight," says Carolina.

212

Now that we have paper and ink again, we write in our on-going letter to Nonna every night, even though no mail goes from Japan to Italy anymore. We'll hand her the letter when we're finally with her again. Just like we'll hand Papà the letter we're writing to him, once we're with him again. I still have to figure out a good plan to get us back with him. I will. Soon.

"Good idea," says Sanae. "And I have another idea. Last week I bought seedling potatoes for planting on the first good day. Today is bright and getting warm, a perfect mid-March day. Everyone's planting in the countryside, so we should, too. Who's going to help me?"

"Me!" Carolina's hands fly wide. I catch her ink jar before it can spill and ruin our work. She skips once around the room, then pulls on her heavy kimono and runs out the door.

Everything could have gone so wrong. Nonna could have been in danger. But she's not. And Carolina skips. My sister skips, like she did before all of this. I wish I could feel like I did before the war.

I go over to the clothes shelf. Carolina and I have stacks of clothes now. Fujiko bought reams of silk, and in the evenings we sit in a circle sewing. We each have two new pairs of school pants now, and two new shirts and a warm kimono. In my stack are also two long strips of material that I have secret plans for. In Carolina's stack is a lightweight summer kimono. We haven't yet made me a summer kimono. I pull on my warm kimono and follow Carolina outside.

Sanae hands me the hoe. "You're the expert," she says. "You showed us that when we planted onions."

I feel Carolina's envious eyes on me. "But Carolina can put in the potatoes," I add quickly. "And mound them into hills. She's expert at that."

"You'll never guess what I got at the market today," says Sanae.

"Let me guess," says Carolina. She squats in front of the seed potatoes and touches them, one by one, as though counting inside her head. "Hmmm. You were gone a long time, so you drove far. That means it's got to be really good. Hmmm."

I hope she won't guess something too extravagant. We want Sanae to be proud of what she managed to find. Last week Fujiko asked everyone what their favorite foods are. She's decided that we all need to fatten up. She gave Sanae extra money for shopping at the local black market, and some beautiful handpainted bowls to barter with, too, all so that Kotsuru can cook lovely things. Sanae has been managing to bring home the right ingredients.

"Fresh eggs," guesses Carolina.

Sanae grins. "How many?"

"Five," says Carolina.

"Double that," says Sanae.

Carolina's eyes widen. "Ten eggs!"

I work the ground even harder. Ten fresh eggs. It's like the best holiday ever.

"All wrapped in wisps of rice straw. And guess what else."

Fresh eggs. That's more than enough. We mustn't be greedy. "Vegetables," I say.

"Of course. A whole box. But guess something more. A delight."

"Sugar," says Carolina.

"Right!"

My jaw drops. "Sugar disappeared a year ago!"

"Our little cabin in the woods is better stocked than the best hotels in Tokyo," says Sanae. "But you guess now, Simona. There's still something more. Guess what your mouth most wants."

I laugh. "I don't know."

"We do. We watched you eating that first meal here. Your face spoke."

I blink. Could she really mean it? "Wheat flour?"

"A big bag." Sanae touches the tip of my nose. "Kotsuru can make enough noodles to satisfy even you."

"And she can make *kasutera*," says Carolina. "Her specialty."

I get an idea. "What vegetables did you buy?"

"Spicy leaves and lotus root and bamboo shoots and soybeans—from Nagasaki."

I look at Carolina. "After Kotsuru makes noodles and *kasutera*, there might be some eggs left over," I say. "Fresh eggs—eggs that will froth up just right. We can cook something, too, Carolina."

Carolina looks at me. A smile comes. She beams. "Something that was Papà's specialty. It can be our specialty for now. Frittata."

"What's that?" asks Sanae.

"Italian omelette," says Carolina. "You'll love it. Everyone does."

TWENTY-SIX

24 MARCH 1944, MOUNT FUJI, JAPAN

I fold a manga into a small square and hand it to Carolina. She tucks it into the package. I fold another. She tucks that one in. "We've finished the whole pile." A month's worth of work.

Sanae seals the package and addresses it.

"Sweden?" says Carolina. "Why are you mailing them to Sweden?"

"My cousin lives there." Sanae's face colors a little. "He moved there early in the war. I miss him."

"But what will he do with all these manga?"

"He'll unfold them and iron them flat. Then he'll send them to anti-war newspapers in Sweden and Spain and any-place else where there are people brave enough to publish them."

"Can we send our letter to Nonna, too?" asks Carolina.

"No one can mail letters to Italy now. We talked about that. Sweden is neutral in this war, so letters go there. Italy is Japan's enemy."

"But can we put it inside your package, with the manga, so your cousin can mail it to Italy?"

Sanae looks astonished. Then she smiles. "How smart you are! Go get the letter. And, Simona . . ." She hands me an envelope. "Address this."

Sanae unseals the package, and we put Nonna's letter inside and reseal it.

"Be careful," I say. "Come back fast."

"Oh, I won't be home soon. I'm going to Nagoya."

"Nagoya?" I say, confused. "That's so far."

"And my brother's truck is old and rickety," says Sanae. "But it's best this way." Sanae shows no emotion as she talks of her brother. He died in the Battle of the Santa Cruz Islands a year and a half ago. Maybe she misses him less now. I miss Papà as much as ever. But that's different; Papà is alive and we're going to find him again.

"Why not go to the village post office?" I ask.

"Think about it," says Kotsuru. "It wouldn't be safe to mail them from a post office in a small town, because if the package gets opened by the censors, it will be easy to track down where it came from. Postal workers in small towns remember faces. The police would be waiting the next time Sanae appeared."

"Then why not go to Tokyo?"

"Tokyo mail is the most likely to be opened," says Kotsuru.

"We considered Yokohama," says Sanae. "It's the closest big city, but the Special Higher Police Section is there. They're the strictest in all Japan, and the cruelest."

"So Nagoya it is," says Kotsuru. "Nagoya is big enough to have several post offices. Sanae hasn't yet had to return to any of them more than once, even though we mail manga every month."

"Don't forget the ingredients for my birthday celebration," calls Fujiko. She's already at the drawing table, starting in on a new set of manga.

"Fresh eggs and milk and a citrus fruit," I say. I don't have to list wheat flour and sugar because there's still plenty left. Carolina and I are going to make custard baked in a crust. Just like Papà did for our birthdays. This cabin will smell like everything good.

Sanae goes out the door with the package clutched to her chest. We hear the truck rev up and drive off. I wish it were evening already and we could hear it returning.

"I'll fold the laundry," says Kotsuru.

"You girls and I need to check the clothes piles," says Fujiko.

Our clothes are clean and stacked neatly on the shelf. Like always. "You make me think of Hitomi," I say as I go over to Fujiko, who now stands by the clothes shelf.

"Who is this Hitomi?"

"She was one of the servants at the embassy. Her son,

Naoki, was my first friend in Japan. Hitomi would hate your political views, but she'd approve completely of your habits. She always kept everyone's clothes perfect."

"I bet keeping the clothes perfect wasn't part of an emergency plan." Fujiko raises her eyebrows.

"Emergency plan?" I feel a bit sick to my stomach.

"Since you've been here, one of us has always been with you. But it's getting warmer every day. In a week, when April starts, we'll have lots more activity."

"What kind of activity?" asks Carolina.

"You don't need to know that unless it turns out we think you'd be so good at something that we enlist you to help us. Ignorance can protect you. But from now on, we might all be off and away somewhere during the day. So the two of you could find yourselves alone at home." Fujiko puts her hand on top of her own clothes pile. "That means you need to know the emergency plan."

Carolina picks Lella off the top of her clothes pile and hugs her.

"Nothing awful has happened to us here," says Fujiko. "The emergency plan is intended to keep it that way. Please tell me you understand. Tell me you are ready for this."

I grabbed her hand and squeezed it. "We're ready."

"Good. Because you have to be. There is nowhere we could hide you girls that wouldn't be dangerous, to you and to us."

"We brought you danger?" But of course we did. I

never thought of that. I've been so happy to be here that I haven't thought of the risk to them at all.

Fujiko shakes her head. "We accepted that. Our lives are dangerous in so many ways. The Economic Police make regular rounds among wealthy homes, not just in Tokyo, but in all cities, and lately even out in the countryside. Usually they confiscate goods bought on the black market. Or they impose a big fine. But sometimes they arrest people."

Kotsuru brings over the fresh folded laundry. We place the clothes carefully into the stacks—all tops together, all bottoms together. "Every visit to the black market puts us in danger," says Kotsuru. "And every manga mailing puts us in even more."

"But we want a free life. We insist on a free life," says Fujiko. "So we choose the risk."

Carolina and I didn't choose danger. It happened to us. But we chose to work on the manga. And I'm glad; I want to keep working on them and end this war. "What do we do if the police come for us?"

"You'll hear them way down at the foot of the incline long before you see them. And they won't honk, like the men who dropped you on the road did. So, first, you ring the bell that hangs by the window," says Fujiko. "Ring it hard. Then put on all your clothing, one piece on top of the other, and run into the woods. We will run in separate directions. But you and Carolina can decide whether to separate or not."

"We'll run together," says Carolina.

I tighten my arm around her shoulder.

"Make a clear mental plan of where you will go. Choose a direction. We've all done that already, but you must do that now. Never tell anyone. That way none of us can give anyone away if we're caught and tortured."

I tighten my arm around Carolina's shoulder even more.

"Whatever you decide, don't go to the prisoner-of-war camp where your father is."

Carolina stiffens. "But—"

"Little girls don't belong there. Especially little foreign girls. Believe me on this. Your father will find you when he can. Trust in that."

I can feel Carolina fighting Fujiko's words. But I'm grateful. Now I see that I haven't made a plan to meet up with Papà yet because the whole idea of going anywhere near the prisoner-of-war camp terrifies me. I've worked hard to forget what Papà said when we were on the train together, because the hope of getting back to him has kept us going. But now his words ring in my ears: "I'll never let you girls go there."

"Most important," says Fujiko, "do not come back to the cabin. Even if it looks deserted. For sure, there will be some-one here, waiting to catch whoever comes back." Fujiko hands me a pair of scissors. "Put these on your pile. Scissors are an important emergency tool." She looks at Carolina. "So long as you two are together, one pair of scissors is enough." Then she hands me a small drawstring purse. "This has money. Enough, I hope. For train tickets, for food."

I thank her and put the scissors and the money purse on top of my clothes pile.

"This is for you," says Kotsuru. She hands Carolina a larger drawstring purse.

Carolina looks inside. "It's empty."

"I hope it stays that way. But it's just the right size for Lella. In case she should want a hiding place."

Carolina throws her arms around Kotsuru. Kotsuru holds Carolina tight for a moment, then steps away. "I can never concentrate on work when Sanae is dropping off a package," says Kotsuru. "And all this talk of danger is oppressive. Would anyone like to go on a mountain hike with me?"

"I would," says Carolina.

"Me too," I say.

We look at Fujiko. She smiles. "Oh, all right. A walk in this light chill will be lovely. Much lovelier than when it turns warm. When we get back, let's all sew together on Simona's new summer kimono."

We walk outside into the brilliant sun and a chorus of birdsong.

"So many birds," says Carolina.

"Around one hundred species of birds nest at the foot of Mount Fuji," says Kotsuru.

"You sound as much like a teacher as Sanae," I say.

Kotsuru laughs. "Sanae taught me."

I remember my school lessons. The study of Mount Fuji is important. Not just birds but lots of reptiles and insects, and even many mammals, live here. Foxes and squirrels and black bears. But what Japan is most proud of is the *kamoshika*. It's sort of a goat and sort of an antelope, and it lives nowhere else on earth except the islands of Japan. I hope we'll see one.

But I don't say that. I don't want Carolina to be disappointed if we don't see one. Today is happy. Even with the emergency plan, nothing feels dangerous here. It feels like heaven. As if there's no war anywhere, now or ever.

"Do you know how to forage?" asks Fujiko. "To feed yourself from the forest?"

"A man once taught us about giant mushrooms," I say.

"Mushrooms are dangerous unless you can identify them precisely. But plenty of other plants are edible and easy to recognize."

We spend the morning learning to find bracken, angelica, and royal ferns. Butterbur, wild licorice, and wild sesame. Today, fiddlehead ferns make me laugh.

CHAPTER
TWENTY-SEVEN

It's April first, and like Fujiko warned us last week, the women have grown suddenly very busy. Kotsuru and Fujiko left in the truck early this morning. Probably to the local black market. Carolina is doing a history lesson with Sanae.

"I'm going for a walk," I say.

Sanae looks up at me and gives a brief nod. "I have a chore this afternoon, so come back by lunch." She bends over Carolina again.

I pull on my heavy kimono and walk up the hill, alone for a moment. I don't really remember the last time I was alone. Certainly not since the police came to the embassy and took us all away. It's a delight to walk with no one watching.

I go quickly, and finally come out on a clearing where I can see the top of Mount Fuji. Steam rises out of fissures in the volcano's sides, and the bushes and trees around those fissures are stained yellow. The steamy mountain makes me think of Mount Nantai, near the ambassador's summer villa. I hope the ambassador and Pessa are all right, even though they were awful not to adopt Carolina and me into their group at the internment camp. But it's hard not to act awful in an internment camp.

Most of all, I hope Papà is all right. I breathe deep and close my eyes and say a prayer.

The stories of Kotsuru and Fujiko and Sanae are dreadful, but they comfort me. These women have made it through terrible things, against terrible odds. When we find Papà, maybe he'll tell us his stories. But I won't press him. And I might not tell him all of our stories, either. It wouldn't help him to learn Carolina almost froze to death.

I know now how these women met. They were in line waiting for rations. No one in line talks to anyone anymore. No one knows who to trust. But Kotsuru broke the silence. She looked at the ink stains on Fujiko's fingers and told her that her son, Toshio, used to love drawing. He wanted to be a *mangaka* cartoonist when he grew up. But he died. Kotsuru swayed on her feet, and the two other women quickly took her arms. They whispered. Little words of sympathy. Then of anger. They took a streetcar to Fujiko's home.

It didn't take long to form a plan, because all of them were ready for a change.

Fujiko was afraid of staying at home because her neighborhood association watched her all the time after she'd refused to join the new association of *mangaka* cartoonists. She figured they'd report her to the police.

Sanae had been fired from her teaching job because she'd spoken out against the war. And she missed her brother, who'd been killed. Her family didn't need her brother's truck, so she took it before the military could confiscate it, and left without saying goodbye. It would only have endangered her family if she'd told them anything.

And Kotsuru had no one left to say goodbye to.

So here they are, working together. What crazy luck Carolina and I had to wind up here. I breathe deep. The air smells of rotten eggs. That's how volcanos are.

I'm heading back when I hear something. So faint. It can't be . . . Our warning bell! We're supposed to scatter. But I'm here, and Carolina isn't.

I race through the brush toward the cabin. It's so far! I stumble, get up, race again. I stop short. Noises come from inside our cabin. Crashes. People inside are throwing things about. I squat, half behind a tree. Men shout. But no women. No child.

The men come outside now. They're young—like overgrown boys, in dirty shirts and ragged school pants. They must be the Economic Police. Buying on the black market has done us in! The men carry things from the cabin—cooking pots, bedding, paper and ink, food. Then they destroy the cabin with axes. At last, they get into two trucks and drive away.

I wait. The woods are quiet.

I get up and walk through the debris, looking every which way, staying alert. The men took everything that could be sold, except the books. All those wonderful books. Those they ripped and scattered. No one is here—no wounded person.

Where would Carolina go without me? Probably Sanae took her with her. Where? I make a pile of broken wood and sit on it so I don't have to sit on the damp earth. I need to stop shaking and think. The closest town is Hakone. Fujiko talked about a Shinto shrine nearby, too. But Shinto priests are loyal to the Japanese government—I know that from Hitomi. They won't help a foreigner, even a child.

The sun fades and the air chills and my heart shrinks with dread. I know I'm not supposed to, but I must. I stand and shout for my sister as loud as I can.

She comes clomping out of the woods. "Carolina!" We run to each other. My eyes blur and my nose runs.

Carolina hits me. "Where were you!" she says in Italian.

"I went on a walk. I told you. It was just bad luck."

"You weren't here and Sanae said I couldn't go off alone and she dragged me with her and I had to punch her to make her let me go."

I wipe my face. "You punched her?"

"You left me!"

"I didn't leave you. I took a walk."

"I punched Sanae."

I nod. I remember when Carolina punched me in the line for "coffee" at the internment camp. It hurt. "Sometimes people have to punch."

Carolina squeezes my hand. "I have our clothes."

"You grabbed our clothes? How could you manage that?"

"It was hard. You weren't here!"

"I'm sorry. I'm sorry, I'm so, so sorry."

"I used my summer kimono. I dumped our stuff onto it and folded up the top and bottom and tied the arms and dragged it into the woods."

"That was smart."

"But then Sanae came and pulled me away, so I had to leave it. She said to run with her because I'd get caught on my own, but I wanted you. So after I punched her, I ran as far away as I could and stayed there till I got cold and came back and heard you calling me."

"You did good."

"It was hard."

"I know. You did really good. Do you know where you left it all?"

"Of course. Lella's there."

"Let's go rescue her."

We walk into the woods and find our things exactly where Carolina left them. We strip and put on our two new pairs of school pants and our two new shirts. We put on our old school pants and old shirts on top, so we look tattered, like everyone else. We put on our summer kimonos, then our heavy kimonos on the very top. We walk downhill through the woods. I won't let myself think about how alone we are. We have each other; that has to be enough. I won't let myself think about how we don't have a plan. We're observant. Strategic. Stubborn. That has to be enough.

We walk till we see a town. It's evening, so we make a little nest in the brush under a tree and lie down to sleep.

"We'll travel tomorrow," I say.

"Where?"

I put my arms tighter around Carolina and try not to think about how black the night is. "Tokyo."

"Are the others in Tokyo?"

"Who knows? We're not supposed to look for each other. That just puts us all in danger, if anyone is following us."

"Then why Tokyo?"

"We know Tokyo. Or some of it, at least."

"Is Papà in Tokyo?"

"You know he's not, Carolina. He's in the prisoner-of-war camp at Ofuna."

"He might have gotten free. We got free."

I don't answer.

"We should go to Ofuna," says Carolina.

"Remember what Fujiko said."

"Fujiko doesn't know everything," says Carolina.

"For now, Carolina, we go to Tokyo," I say firmly.

Carolina squirms. "Don't leave me again."

"I won't."

"I was scared."

"So was I."

"I was more scared than you."

"I'm sorry, Carolina."

"Do we have to leave?"

"You know the rule. Besides, you saw what the men did to the cabin."

"Will those men come back?"

"I don't know."

"Tell me the men won't come back, Simona."

"They won't come back, Carolina."

Carolina relaxes against me. She actually believes, even though she told me what to say. I wish I had an older sister to trust like that.

"It's warmer this time," she says. "If we get into a truck, we won't freeze. We won't die."

I feel for her hand. "We'll take a train. Fujiko gave us money."

Carolina makes a little slurpy sound, and I figure she's sucking on Lella's braids. "Tell me this train will be better than the last one."

"It will be better than the last one."

"Good." Carolina is quiet a moment. "Simona?"

"What?"

"Don't leave me again."

"I won't. I'll never leave you." I gulp. I'm all she has. It's my job to save Carolina.

"Say it again."

"I'll never leave you."

"Pray now."

We pray for Papà to be safe. We pray for Zio Piero to keep Nonna safe. That's how we end every day.

TWENTY-EIGHT

2 APRIL 1944, HAKONE, JAPAN

I cut my hair off. It's nearly black, so I don't think people will look twice at the ragged edges left behind. The telltale curls are gone. That's what matters. "Should I cut yours?" I ask in Italian.

"My hair is straight," Carolina says. "Like Japanese girls'. Like Mamma's."

"We can leave it be." I stretch both arms, still working the kinks out from sleeping under this tree. Then I smooth a strip of white cloth across my thighs. "Lean your head this way."

"Put the scissors away first."

I put the scissors in the small money purse. "Come on." Carolina leans toward me, and I tie the cloth around her forehead and knot it at the rear. "When I tell you, you pull that down and cover your eyes. I'll only do that if I'm afraid someone suspects we're foreign. That way they'll think we're blind instead. Understand?"

"Of course."

I switch to Japanese. "From this moment on, nothing but Japanese, understand?"

"Of course I understand," she answers in Japanese.

"You are now Karo-chan all the time, understand?"

"I'm not dumb," says Karo-chan. "But . . . will I ever be able to be Carolina again?"

"Yes." And before she can ask, I add, "I promise."

I smooth the other strip of cloth and tie it around my own head. We can't both have our eyes covered at the same time. One of us needs to lead the other, even if only through partly closed eyes, but I think we should look alike. Farmers have cloths like that, to catch sweat. I had planned for us to use the strips in summertime as we worked the garden at the cabin. It isn't nearly hot enough yet to sweat, but the cloth is practically like a uniform. We look like good farm children. I hope.

Karo-chan gasps. "I didn't take our letters to Papà and our new one to Nonna. I wasn't thinking fast enough."

"You thought plenty fast enough, Karo-chan. And having those letters on us could have been dangerous. From now on you can recite letters to me. And I can pretend to be Papà and Nonna, and recite letters back to you. We won't write them on paper."

"But they'll never get them."

"That's all right, Karo-chan. You know they're thinking

about us, right? So they know we're thinking about them. We have to get moving now."

Karo-chan points. A small cluster of fiddlehead ferns. We pick them and chew the welcome bitterness. We missed both lunch and supper yesterday, and our stomachs have become accustomed to regular meals, so this won't satisfy us for long, but it works for the moment. Moment by moment. That's all we need.

Karo-chan tucks Lella inside her innermost shirt and ties her empty cloth bag to her kimono sash. I tuck my money purse with the scissors inside my shirt. We hold hands and walk along the outskirts of the town till we find railroad tracks. *"Ganbatte,"* I say, as though we're about to take a test.

"Ganbatte," says Karo-chan.

I do an assessment. Our winter kimonos are too obviously new. I take mine off. Without a word, Karo-chan takes hers off. We still have our summer kimonos on, so our arms aren't chilled. Karo-chan's summer kimono is dirty up the back from being dragged when she used it as a *furoshiki.* I lie on the ground and squiggle around. Karo-chan watches me and nods. She's so smart. I tuck our winter kimonos inside my summer kimono. My front is puffed up now, but plenty of children carry stuff inside their shirts or kimonos this way. Now it isn't so obvious that we aren't starving like other people.

We follow the train tracks into town. "Chin to chest," I say to Karo-chan. We both look down as hard as we can. Town is busy even though it's Sunday. Last week the government announced that all loyal Japanese would take no break in the workweek anymore. There aren't enough workers left, so everyone is needed in fields or ammunition factories.

Close to the station a boy sits on a step in a doorway, selling flowers. He's barefoot, and the flowers are nothing but the earliest weeds of spring. A bowl of boiled bamboo shoots balances on his lap.

"I'll buy your bamboo shoots," I say.

"You look funny."

"I'm from Tokyo." I hold up my smallest coin in his face. "Do you have rice?"

"I already ate my rice bran pudding." The boy's eyes stay on the coin. "I have old peanuts, for planting. They're raw, but if you chew on them a long time, they get better."

I nod.

The boy goes inside the house and comes out a moment later with his hands brimming. "Karo-chan," I say, "hold your bag out." Karo-chan extends her bag.

The boy dumps in peanuts. Then the bamboo shoots.

I give the boy the coin and take a bamboo shoot in each hand. So does Karo-chan. Karo-chan and I search desperately for a place to eat. It's rude to eat while we walk, and we can't run the risk of someone scolding us and taking a good look at us.

"Let's go behind a building," says Karo-chan.

We scramble behind the closest building and eat. The bamboo shoots are tender, fresh out of the ground. The nuts are dry and almost woody. But the boy didn't lie; chewing helps. A train whistle cuts the air. Clouds billow from the engine. We run across the street to the station and stand in the ticket line. Prices are posted. Good. I won't have to lift my face to the man. I take out the right amount and tuck my purse away.

The woman in front of us exchanges greetings with the ticket salesman. "Takayama," she says. That city is way to the northwest. The boy beside her moves closer.

"Documents," says the ticket seller. "Name card."

The woman digs around in her bag.

Documents? Is this a new rule? I clutch the money in my hand. We have to get on this train; trains are the safest way. I step up to the window and hold my handful of money on the ledge. "Good day, kind sir. I seem to have misplaced our documents." I keep my eyes practically shut, but I can see his neck through my lashes.

"Where are you going?"

"Tokyo. Two for Tokyo, please. Third class."

"That's ninety kilometers. You only need documents for trips over a hundred kilometers."

I open my hand and let the money fall onto the counter.

"Not so fast." He hesitates.

I lean against the counter to keep myself from falling.

"Where are your calluses?"

"What?"

He gives a small laugh. "Just teasing. You're a good girl to quit school and help in the fields. Keep your arms tight over whatever you've got inside your kimono. There are thieves everywhere now. Make sure you change trains at Odawara." He lays down two tickets.

My hand shakes as I take them. Amazing. No one expects to see Western children here—so no one does. As long as we talk right and behave right, people think we are who we pretend to be. Language matters more than the shape of eyes. But if anyone looks too hard, we'll get caught.

On the train, Karo-chan sits near the window, me on the aisle. We slump against each other and pretend to sleep. It turns out to be easy to know when to get off at Odawara, because nearly everyone gets off there. And they all head to another train, so I know that's the one going to Tokyo.

The next train is filthy and crowded. The seats are threadbare. Karo-chan and I sit together in one window seat with a woman squashed against us in the aisle seat. We look out on flat rice paddies and streams and thatched houses. We pass a Shinto shrine with white ribbons tied to a tree out front. Each ribbon wishes luck to a soldier. There are so many, the tree looks snow-covered. All the other trees along the railroad tracks have been cut down. The stumps stand like ugly scars.

The train stops frequently, and at one stop I see the sign: OFUNA. Papà. I can smell his coffee breath, his garlic hands. Karo-chan looks at me. Her face begs. I close my eyes. Maybe she's right? By the time I get to my feet, the train's going again. It's better this way. It is.

The train stops in bigger stations now. I catch the name

Shinagawa; that's closer to the embassy than the Tokyo main station. I grab Karo-chan's hand, and we try to fight our way up the jammed aisle. It's impossible. But hands push us into a seat. Then they push us right out the window. We fall onto the platform. We're lucky; neither of us is hurt. It's easy to follow the signs for the local train that will take us to the Tamachi Station.

Finally we arrive on the streets of Tokyo. I've never walked home from this station before, but I'm afraid to get on a bus. People here might be more wary than people in the country-side. They might take a second look at us and decide to call the police. I lead us north along the big road. I pray we'll see something I recognize soon, because all I know is that the embassy is northwest of the station.

As we walk, my chest tightens. I don't recognize any of these stores.

Karo-chan stops dead. "I won't go."

"What?"

"I won't go back to the embassy."

"What makes you think we're going there?"

"That's the shop where Papà bought coffee beans."

"Oh!" I kiss her cheek. "Good! Which way is the embassy? I just need to get my bearings so I can find the way from there."

"The way where?"

And I know where. The idea has been forming all along. It might work. "To the washerwoman's."

"The one who folds paper?"

"Yes."

"She's blind." Karo-chan smiles. "She won't see our eyes. She won't know who we are. Good idea, Simo-chan."

Karo-chan leads us through the streets till I recognize where we are. Then I take the lead. We part the curtain to the chiming of the bells. The washerwoman comes slowly, offering a polite greeting and bow. We greet her back, and her smile fades. "Where is your mother?"

"We are alone," I say.

"Alone? Whose laundry did you bring?"

"We didn't bring laundry. We came to work for you."

"These days everyone does their own laundry except rich people. I don't have enough work to keep myself busy."

"You would have more business if you repaired clothes as well. Rich people don't like to sew."

The washerwoman pats her caved chest softly. "You can sew?"

"I'm excellent at it."

"Excellent? Your sister is too young to be excellent at it."

"You'd be surprised," says Karo-chan. "And I can plant potatoes in extra high mounds. I'm good in a garden. We both are."

"The neighbor's boy helped me in the garden last summer and fall. But he was conscripted into the army a month ago. He can't help me this year."

"We'll make everything grow," I say.

"He guarded it for me so no one stole my vegetables."

"I can bark like a dog," says Karo-chan.

"The weather is just right for planting a new garden," I say.

"He checked my laundry for stains and moved my hands to the ones that needed more scrubbing."

"We're very good at finding stains," I say.

The washerwoman pats her chest faster. Then she drops her hands and her mouth tightens into a pucker. "I can't pay you. I'm barely managing. Go back home."

"We don't want pay. We want a place to sleep."

"And something to eat," says Karo-chan.

"We'll do anything you say."

The woman goes to the stool by her counter and sits. "I recognize your voice. I know everyone's voice. Where's your mother?"

She must mean Hitomi. We used to come with Hitomi. "Gone," I say.

"And your father?"

"I don't know," I say.

"You're orphans."

"We're not orphans." Karo-chan's voice is sharp.

"There are many war orphans. There's no shame in that. They are skinnier than me. With legs like sticks and extended bellies. Naked boys with shaved heads."

"You don't know!" says Karo-chan. "You can't even see us. You can't see them. How do you know those things? We're not orphans! Don't say that! Don't ever say that!"

I put my arm around her. "We're not orphans," I say quietly. "We just need help. And we will help you."

"I had three sons," the washerwoman says. "The last one left home over a year ago. That's why I needed the neighbor's boy to help out." She presses her lips together for a moment. "My sons died in this war. One, two, three, like that. One, two, three."

Tears spring to my eyes. "I'm sorry." My voice is broken with tears. "Very sorry."

"*Morainaki* is a good thing. Maybe *morainaki* is the only thing holding Japan together these days. The only thing that makes us feel we are still a community. It helps."

Morainaki. Crying at the sight of someone else's misery. "Everyone needs help," I say.

"Yes."

CHAPTER

TWENTY-NINE

17 April 1944, Tokyo, Japan

The rain beats a steady rhythm on the roof. Karo-chan and I sing in time to it. Tanaka-san loves singing. That's what we call the washerwoman. Her first name is Natsu; I overheard her answer questions when an official came to the shop. Tanaka-san has taught us so many traditional songs over these past two weeks that we could now sing a different song every day for a month. She leans her head side to side and claps as she sings. I love the plover's song—where the little birds sing *chi-yo, chi-yo* so sadly. Most of the time, Tanaka-san sings with us, but right now she's out waiting in a ration line.

This is Tanaka-san's home. The front part on the street serves as the laundry shop. Sliding partitions separate off the living space behind that. Karo-chan and I are now in the shop part, sitting behind a bamboo screen. The wonderful thing about a bamboo screen is that you can peer through it and still remain unseen. People on the other side view only your outline, not your face, your eyes. This way Karo-chan and I can watch for customers. If any come, we tell them to leave their laundry on the counter. There are several pairs of origami animals there. The customer puts one animal on their pile of laundry and takes the identical animal away as their receipt. All customers know the routine, of course. But Tanaka-san likes having her customers realize that someone behind the screen is watching, in case they have sticky-finger inclinations.

I sit on the mat and sew. What I told Tanaka-san turned out to be true. There are still rich people in Tokyo, and they are grateful to find reliable workers who won't overcharge them. But they are so rich, they don't want their old clothes repaired. They want new clothes, and the stores in town have an ever-dwindling selection. So they come with material and we make clothing. Tanaka-san takes orders only for traditional pajamas, with a loose jacket top that overlaps at the front and ties in place, and short, drawstring pants that come down to the knees. Everyone wears them at home, and sometimes for quick errands. If we do a good job on the pajamas, Tanaka-san will consider taking orders for other clothing.

The pajamas I'm sewing now are dark green silk. We're making four pairs, for the mother and father and two small sons. I imagine them snuggling together at night in their matching pajamas, and I make very small stitches, to be sure nothing will come apart if they toss and turn in their sleep. Anyone would be proud to wear such pajamas. Papà would be proud of me for making them.

I wonder about this pajama family. Why is the father not off being a soldier? But maybe the father isn't at home—maybe he's away at war. Maybe he's in prison. Who knows what the mother doesn't talk about?

I don't let Karo-chan help a lot. Too much depends on this work. If the pajamas come out right, Tanaka-san will keep employing us. I have to do everything perfect. Karo-chan sews decorative Xs across the ties on the jacket.

Right now, though, she's playing with rocks and leaves she gathered from Tanaka-san's garden, where we work part of every day. The leaves are people while the rocks are animals. They seem to have a lot of disagreements over food. Karo-chan names the nicest leaf-person Botan. Karo-chan used to play like this in the internment camp, using any little bits of trash she could find. Rocks and leaves are better.

At night Karo-chan plays with Lella. She sleeps with Lella tied to her chest. During the day she keeps the doll in the drawstring bag Kotsuru made, folded up in the futon we share. For safety, she says.

The little bells on the curtain chime. I peek through the bamboo of the screen. Two policemen! They call out a greeting, and one of them lifts a sheet of paper from a hook by the door while the other scans the room. His eyes stop at our screen. "Who's there?"

I put down my sewing and kiss my finger, then touch Karo-chan's lips with it. That's our signal. We both wear white sashes around our foreheads. Now we pull them down over our eyes. These are different from the sweat sashes we came here with. They're strips of gauze that Tanaka-san uses in cooking chicken. She hasn't had a chicken to cook in a long time, though, and who knows when she next will, so she won't miss them. We can see decently through them without revealing to others the shape of our eyes. I come out from behind the screen and bow from the waist as deep as I can.

"What's this? Covered eyes? So the blind washerwoman has a blind daughter." The policeman's face looks doubtful. "She never talked of a daughter before. And who's that child behind the screen?"

"Relatives help in time of need," I say in my most respectful Japanese. I bow. But I'm clever. I bow facing the way I'm standing, not facing the policeman. That's how Tanaka-san does it. "How can I serve you?"

"This is an official inspection. Where's your air-defense equipment?" He looks at the other policeman.

That policeman reads off the sheet of paper. "It says here that you have two fire hoses, two helmets, one ladder, three fire extinguishers, two boxes of sand, three buckets, and two shovels. Where are they?"

I stand very still. I don't know where half those things are.

"The shovels are in the garden." Karo-chan comes out from

behind the screen and bows. "I forgot to bring them in." She feels her way dramatically along the room partition, slides it open, and disappears into the inner room. She looks phony, fumbling like that. The policemen must have noticed. My mouth goes sour.

"Another blind relative?" the first policeman says incredulously.

I bow and hold my hands behind my back to keep them from flying out. My whole body wants to fly away. Living with Tanaka-san has been too good. Nothing good can last.

The second policeman says, "I heard that in Hayama many people eat only the rations; they have no money to buy anything else. Night blindness has become common. I didn't know it had become so bad that it was total blindness. You're from Hayama, aren't you?"

I bow.

"They sound like Tokyo children to me," says the first policeman.

"Easy mistake," says the second policeman. "Hayama is so close. But I have a good ear for accents."

Karo-chan comes in, soaked to the bone and dragging the shovels, which the rain cleaned at least. She brings them forward, then veers to the side and plops them down. "Here." She addresses the wall. She's the worst phony blind person I've ever seen. "I can bring the buckets, too." Her hair drips pathetically.

"Forget it," says the first policeman. "Just tell the

washerwoman to get one more helmet. There are three of you, not two. Everyone needs a helmet. If we are bombed, they will save you."

I bow. "I will relate this important information. Thank you very much."

"And be smarter than the washerwoman," says the first policeman. "Give massages or wash hair. Good jobs for a blind person. I don't know how the washerwoman gets out stains without seeing them. I wouldn't trust her."

"Blind people know things," says the second policeman. "They feel things you can't feel. They hear things differently, too."

"Maybe," says the first policeman. "But you listen to me, girl. Don't expect people to keep bringing you their laundry. Give massages."

"Thank you for this important advice." I bow repeatedly. "Thank you. Thank you."

The policemen leave.

I drop onto the floor on my bottom and wrap my arms around my knees. I shake all over.

"We did good, Simo-chan. They're gone."

"You overdid the blind part. Don't bump along the wall like that."

She hits me on the head. "I brought the shovels. And I knew where the buckets were. Tell me I did good."

"You're right."

"Say it!"

"You did good."

"Call me Karo-chan."

"You did good, Karo-chan. We're a good team."

Karo-chan collapses beside me.

We sit there a long while, limp. Then Karo-chan changes into dry clothes while I hang her wet ones to dry. We go behind the screen again, me to my sewing and Karo-chan to her game. I watch the edges of her hair curl a little as they dry. Oh no! Maybe her hair will turn curly like mine and Papà's. She'll hate it if we need to cut it off. "Flatten the bottoms of your hair, Karo-chan."

Karo-chan presses her hair against her neck. Then she jumps to her feet. "I have an idea." She runs into the back of the house and comes back wearing an air-defense helmet. It's padded with cotton and it holds her hair in place, so it will dry flat.

"A perfect idea. You have many perfect ideas, Karo-chan."

Tanaka-san finally comes home.

"You were gone a long time." Karo-chan takes her *furoshiki* from her.

"Thank you, child. The ground was so slippery, I decided to wait for the rain to let up." We follow her into the cooking area, and she unties the *furoshiki* and sets the few vegetables in a basket. "The price of rations has gone up again. It costs six sen for one person's daily share now. And all they give are taro and bean sprouts and green onion. They say the farmers can't produce enough crops."

"We'll have lots in the garden soon," I say. "The first potatoes are already planted. As soon as the rain stops, Karo-chan and I will plant the seeds you bought—pumpkin and spinach and beets."

"We'll need more than that. We'll have to buy seeds on the black market. And the ration distributors say there are no more seedling potatoes for the next planting. The woman in front of me in line complained of hunger, and the official told her to practice self-control. What's she supposed to eat—the air?"

"The rain is coming often now," I say. "There will be more food, and the rations will increase. The garden will grow. It will get better." When she doesn't respond, I say, "What else can we do, anyway?"

Tanaka-san makes a little humming noise and sways as she prepares tea. The knot of gray hair twisted at the back of her neck bobs along. She kneels and sits back on her heels. "Sit with me, girls. You have the right attitude, Simo-chan. *Shikata ga nai.*" My teacher used to say that, and the policeman said that in the embassy when he told us to make breakfast before they arrested us. Life goes on. We have to keep doing our jobs.

Karo-chan settles on one side of Tanaka-san, and I settle on the other. "The police were here," says Karo-chan.

Tanaka-san stiffens. "What did they want?"

"It was an air-defense inspection," I say.

"We need another helmet," says Karo-chan.

Tanaka-san reaches out and touches Karo-chan's head.

How does she aim so well, on nothing but sound? "Ah, you're wearing one."

"I like it. But I'll take it off now."

"No, no. You can wear it inside whenever you want."

I gesture to Karo-chan to take it off now. "How much does a helmet cost?"

"I can borrow one from the neighbor till her son comes home from war." Tanaka-san stands a moment in thought. "Help me fill the pot, Simo-chan. I have laundry to do."

I lift the big pot, and *clank!* The bottom of the pot falls out. It clangs against the firestone! It's old and tired and ruined now.

"Disaster." Tanaka-san touches the pot sides. Her face looks utterly hopeless.

"I'll get another," I blurt out. "Karo-chan, play behind the screen while I'm gone."

"No!" Karo-chan runs into the inner room where we sleep.

"What are you talking about?" Tanaka-san reaches for me, but I'm already sliding the door open. "There are no pots," she says. "There are no metal goods anymore."

"I'll get one on the black market."

"Even if you can find one, how will you pay for it?"

"I have a little money. And when the money is gone, it's gone. I was saving it for an emergency. This is an emergency. I'll be back."

"I'm coming with you." Karo-chan is at my side again, stuffing Lella inside her shirt.

"Stay with me, Karo-chan," says Tanaka-san.

"I stay with Simo-chan." Karo-chan lifts an angry face to me. "You promised you'd never leave me again."

"You'll be safer here with Tanaka-san."

"I'm coming with you."

"Don't talk to anyone you don't know except the merchant." Tanaka-san pats her chest. "And offer less money than the merchant asks for."

"I'm good at this," I lie.

We slip our gauze sashes over our eyes and step out the door just as an old man comes up the walk.

The man holds out his hands. "Wait. Give me something to eat." So many beggars line the streets, but I've never seen one go door-to-door.

"We have nothing," I say.

"Is that so?" His mouth falls open, as though the effort of keeping it shut is too much. He walks sadly toward the neighbor's.

Karo-chan and I bow our heads and set off for the black market Papà took us to. We turn down a street, and a boy no bigger than Karo-chan runs out of a house and walks behind us. We walk faster. The boy walks faster. We turn at the next corner. The boy turns at the next corner.

"What do you want, boy?" I call without looking back at him.

"What do you want?" he echoes.

"Nothing you can give."

"Then you want nothing."

I stop. The boy catches up to us. I lean toward him. "What do you mean?"

"Tell me what you need. I'll get it."

"A big pot."

"Old or new?"

I can't believe the question. "Old. But still strong."

"Wait here." He runs down the block.

"It's for Tanaka-san," I call after him. "The blind washerwoman. So it better be good. You better not cheat us."

The boy stops. "Tanaka-san?" He crosses the street and runs in the other direction.

"That was smart," says Karo-chan. "He was going to cheat us."

"Yes, I think so." We wait.

A woman peeks out of a window. "Go away, beggars."

"We're not beggars."

"Then you're thieves. The police take away thieves."

"Let's go home," I say to Karo-chan.

"But the boy will come looking for us here."

"He knows Tanaka-san's shop. If he really has a pot for us, he'll come there. And if he doesn't, we can go to the market, like I planned."

We walk home slowly, trying to act like blind people.

The boy intercepts us on the last block. "Here." He holds

out a large iron rice pot, and his face radiates hope. He's counting on us; he needs our money badly. I hope it's a good pot, so
we can buy it and he'll smile.

"Put it on the ground."

He sets it on the ground, but he keeps one hand tight
around the handle.

"Help me inspect it, Karo-chan." So the two of us squat
and feel that pot everywhere, like good blind girls. "It seems
strong. Why would someone give up such a strong pot?"

The boy puts his other hand around the handle, too. "The
sellers are moving. Evacuating Tokyo, like lots of people.
They have family down in Kyūshū. Everything grows good in
Kyūshū. No one there is hungry. So this family is selling stuff."

Kyūshū is the big southern island of Japan. Its farms are
famous. Still, this boy knows too much about it, as though he's
making it up. And even when moving, people take their good
stuff. "Why sell this pot?"

"It's too heavy to carry. There's only the mother and three
little kids."

"How little?"

"Two and four. The oldest is my age."

"You stole this pot, didn't you?"

"No!"

"I don't believe you."

"Well, I don't believe you're blind. Tanaka-san never used
to take in sewing. But ever since you came, she has. I bet you're
the ones who sew."

"We have a secret sewer," says Karo-chan. "So we can't tell you who she is."

"I don't believe you. Anyway, you knew I was a boy right off. So that proves you're not blind."

He speaks awfully loud. But I don't dare look around for eavesdroppers. "Boys' footsteps sound different from girls' footsteps," I say. "Come on, Karo-chan. Let's go."

"You're a liar," says Karo-chan. She stands up. My sister is crazy. I grab her arm. She pulls free. "That mother with the three little kids you just talked about—you lied. The oldest boy is you."

The boy pushes his face close to Karo-chan's. "How do you know?"

"Blind people know things. Even the police say that."

The boy looks frightened. He bows. "I'm sorry. Don't tell. My mother said Tanaka-san could have the pot for free." He walks away, hanging his head.

Stunned, I watch the boy leave. We carry the pot home, but I stop out front of Tanaka-san's door. "How did you know he was talking about his own family?"

"I didn't." Karo-chan shrugs. "I don't know how to say it in Japanese." She pulls me down so she can whisper into my ear. "I bluffed," she says in Italian.

I give a laugh. Karo-chan is smart and brave. Tanaka-san is sensible and kind. And the people we come in contact with seem to believe us. Maybe this life with Tanaka-san will work out. Maybe this good thing will last until we're back with Papà.

We go in and put the pot on the floor. Tanaka-san runs her fingers all over it. "It's a fine pot. How much did you pay for it?"

"A boy gave it to us for free," I say.

"No one gives anything for free."

"They're moving to Kyūshū, and he said his mother wanted you to have it."

"But only after I told him that blind people like us"—Karo-chan slaps a hand over her mouth; she realizes she slipped—"I mean, like you, know things. I scared him because he was trying to scare us. And I don't care if it was a lie."

Tanaka-san waits. Is she wondering what Karo-chan means by talking about blind people like us? Tanaka-san has no idea that we pretend to be blind to others. Please, please, don't let Karo-chan have given us away.

When we don't say anything else, Tanaka-san finally fills the pot and puts it to boil. "I'm blind and I know things," she says. "The boy learned a good lesson."

CHAPTER
THIRTY

28 MAY 1944, TOKYO, JAPAN

It's nearly June, and the strawberries in the bowl in front of us are the first of the season. We're enjoying them with the satisfaction that only a farmer can have.

A man shows up at the shop door. It's early Sunday morning, and even though Sunday is a workday now, usually work starts later. But we don't panic. We bow our heads and go quickly behind the screen. I pick up the pajamas we're making and stitch a seam while Karo-chan works on decorating a sleeve edge.

The man hands Tanaka-san a letter. It isn't a true letter, because it didn't come by the postal service. The postal service no longer delivers regular letters. This is a message passed from one friend's hand to another's, from her brother in Sapporo to

Tanaka-san here in Tokyo. The man reads the date on the outside of it: 12 May 1944. It took over two weeks for it to arrive here. The man and Tanaka-san share tea and chat.

After the man leaves, Tanaka-san flaps the envelope over her head. "Read it to me, Simo-chan. It's bound to be a poem."

This is the first letter we've seen Tanaka-san receive our whole time here. I open it quickly and read:

> *"Trees have been stripped raw*
> *Sharp savage empty despair*
> *How can we write poems?"*

My hands shake. "This is not a safe poem to keep, Tanaka-san. If an official came inspecting for air-defense equipment and he saw this . . ."

"Read it again. Read it over and over."

I read the poem four times, and my voice grows sharp. This poem is the way Aiko feels, and Papà feels, and Sanae, and Fujiko, and Kotsuru. It says what Karo-chan and I know too well.

Tanaka-san puts her hand on my wrist. "Shut your eyes and say it now."

I close my eyes and recite the poem.

"You, Karo-chan, you say it."

Karo-chan recites the poem perfectly. Her voice shakes.

"Can you recite it now?" I ask Tanaka-san.

"I could have recited it after the first time you read it. But I wanted to make sure it was yours, too. My brother is a very good poet. He is famous throughout Japan. He works at the Hokkaido Imperial University."

Hokkaido. That's the northernmost island of Japan. "Have you ever gone all the way there to visit him?" I ask Tanaka-san.

"I grew up there. My brother says I should come back, now that our parents are dead. His poems are just like him: angry." Tanaka-san sounds disapproving.

"Aren't you angry, too?" I dare to whisper.

"About the war, yes. But I used to be much angrier and about so many more things. When I was a child, my mother pampered me, convinced that a blind girl was useless. So I came to Tokyo, alone, and set up this shop."

"I've never heard of a girl leaving her family."

"Nearly none do. Especially not blind girls. And rich girls don't become washerwomen." Tanaka-san laughs. "My poor mother. No wonder she disowned me. I was proud in those days. And furious. But my anger was never like my brother's—then or now. He blames everyone. Everyone outside Japan. He can't admit that we might have brought some of this misery onto ourselves. Now burn his poem in the fire. Then get a piece of paper for my answer."

"You have writing paper?"

"Of course," says Tanaka-san. "Look on the kitchen shelves."

Karo-chan rips up the letter and feeds the pieces to the fire while I search for a brush and ink and paper. I've never seen Tanaka-san write before; there's so much about her I don't know. Ah! There they are, under a piece of cloth. A stack of white paper, and jars and jars of ink. In different colors. What does a blind woman do with colored inks? Or any ink at all? I put a brush, one sheet of paper, and a jar of black ink on a low side table and carry it all to her, ready to be amazed.

"You're my scribe." Tanaka-san lets her hands fall onto her thighs, and she leans forward as she speaks.

> *"Soybeans, long beans, rain*
> *Plum blossoms spread generous*
> *Calm your heart with green."*

I pick up the brush, eager to transcribe this haiku. It matches our strawberries perfectly. Yes, Tanaka-san's famous brother is right in what he says in that first haiku. But Tanaka-san's answer is right, too. We had a rainy spring. Welcome rain. But when it kept on, incessantly, we feared the crops would rot in the ground. Then the sun played its marvelous game, and everything grew strong and sure. Far better than we could have hoped. We will have plenty of food this spring and summer. "I love your haiku. How do we send it?"

"I'll get the professor. He was a childhood friend of ours. He's the one who helped me set up this laundry when I first arrived in Tokyo. He always makes sure my letters arrive quick and safe."

And so Tanaka-san goes outside to tell a neighbor girl to fetch him. Karo-chan and I have never seen the professor. But Tanaka-san talks about him often; she says he knows everything. He usually visits her regularly, but he's been ill all spring, and we only got word that he's well again a few days ago. Karo-chan and I retreat behind the screen.

When the professor arrives, Tanaka-san greets him with deference. He puts a pile of laundry on the counter, and she promises to scrub it extra clean, which means, of course, that Karo-chan and I will examine it for stains extra carefully. I don't understand; they were childhood friends. Equals. Does being blind change things? Tanaka-san hands him her haiku. The professor bows and slips it inside his kimono.

"Do you have time to talk today?" asks the professor. "I have missed talking freely to you. It is always consoling to visit with you."

"And I am always honored to learn truth about the world," says Tanaka-san.

"Oh, you have helpers," says the professor. "In two sizes." His voice grows louder and I realize he's approaching our screen. I kiss my fingertip and touch Karo-chan's lips, and we both slip the gauze sashes over our eyes and stay still as death.

"Please don't interrupt your chores because of me." The professor's footsteps make wispy noises on the tatami mats as he walks back toward Tanaka-san. "Do you trust these girls not to run to the neighborhood association?"

Members of the neighborhood association watch each other for suspicious behavior. Every household belongs. As far as I can tell, no one pays any attention to a home with three blind females.

"I trust them totally."

"That's old-fashioned of you. Delightfully so." The professor settles himself on the mat. "Tōjō is an idiot. He likes to appear where he does not have to be, even now, as he ruins everything. The show-off."

I've never heard anyone criticize Premier Tōjō before. He's the general of the imperial army—no one should dare. My arms go all gooseflesh. But Papà and I hate show-offs, too. I like this professor.

The professor lights a cigarette, and the sweet smell of the tobacco snakes around the room. "Tōjō surrounds himself with a cabinet of old businessmen who understand nothing. So he gets the advice he deserves—rubbish. We'll have a revolution if we aren't all killed first."

"Has something new happened?" asks Tanaka-san.

"You haven't heard? Yesterday the Americans landed on Biak, Dutch New Guinea, a key Japanese air base near Papua. And Tōjō will surely send as many troops to defend it as he can, which means we'll divert forces from India. After all the past fighting, we'll lose India anyway."

"Should we want India?" asks Tanaka-san.

"Exactly. I love how you say things so simply." The professor rubs his chin. "We have no business wanting any of it when everything is going wrong among the ordinary people right here in Japan. No food, so babies are born deformed. Many too weak to suckle. University students hunted down for labor.

No one can study. Soon Japan will have no educated people." He falls silent.

Tanaka-san gets up and makes a second pot of tea.

"Thank you. But tea is not enough," says the professor. "I am hungry. You must be, too. Let's have a treat. May I take all of you to Fuji Ice for lunch?"

Fuji Ice is wonderful; I went there once with Aiko and her mother. Many eating places have closed, but not Fuji Ice. Still, Karo-chan and I can't come out from behind the screen and show our faces. The professor is clearly too smart to be fooled by our eye sashes.

But Tanaka-san says, "What a pity we cannot accept your generous offer. We must finish our work, or customers will complain."

"Customers have no one else to turn to. Most laundries have closed."

"A blind woman has to be extra careful, extra conscientious. It doesn't take much to tarnish one's reputation, especially when most people tend to avoid the blind."

"You're not fooling me with that talk, Tanaka-san. Something's on your mind. But think about the girls, listening with disappointment. They deserve a treat after having had to endure my ugly words."

"Perhaps I can take them to Fuji Ice one day when there is less work," says Tanaka-san. "They can know it was your idea and be grateful to you."

"May I please leave money for that treat, at least?" He stands up and goes to the counter. "I'll come back next week. Sunday again. It's my best day."

"Thank you for such kindness."

"Thank you for allowing me the relief of our talk."

"Thank you for sending my message. Thank you. Thank you."

The professor leaves. I remember Aiko telling me I was only one of two people she could be completely honest with. Maybe that's how the professor feels about Tanaka-san. Does everyone in Japan have a person they can tell their doubts to, someone they can grumble to without fear?

Tanaka-san stands a moment facing the door. Then she goes to the counter and folds the money into a purse. "Come, girls. We're going to Fuji Ice for lunch."

Karo-chan and I emerge from behind the screen. Tanaka-san just refused to go to Fuji Ice with the professor, and now she's taking us there herself. There's only one way to make sense out of all this.

I bow to Tanaka-san, even though she can't see me. "I was afraid you had figured out that we pretend to be blind. Karo-chan gave us away when she talked about telling the boy that blind people like us know things."

"I would have figured it out anyway. The neighbors asked me about your eye sashes the day you brought home the pot. You didn't move like me, so they suspected you. It's a good thing Karo-chan tipped me off, in fact, because I didn't hesitate. I explained that you had my same syndrome, which worsens over time. You weren't entirely blind yet, but you wore sashes so people would help you if you asked."

I bow low and know that Tanaka-san senses how low I go. "Do you know why we pretend?"

She pets my head softly. "What springy curls are growing here." She puts a finger through one of my newly grown curls. "How many Japanese girls do you know with curly hair? And when you first came, I recognized your voices. You used to come with a servant who worked at the Italian embassy. When your short hair started to grow longer, I put it together." She sighs. "In fact, it's time to trim your curls again. I wish I could use your scissors and help."

"You know about my scissors?"

"This is my home, Simo-chan. It's important that I know everything that's in it." She reaches for her kerchief. "From now on call me Obasan."

Obasan. What children call their aunts or very close family friends. "Thank you, Obasan."

We go to Fuji Ice and stand in a long line. If Aiko is still living just with her mother, if her father or her brother hasn't returned yet, she has no money to go to Fuji Ice. But I look up and down the line at every girl about my size anyway. I can see well enough through this gauze.

Everyone wears khaki-colored caps—war caps. I notice someone ahead in the line, about a dozen people away. A boy. Barefoot, and his clothes are filthy and ragged. But just seeing the back of him, he seems familiar. The people around us say that in the Ginza area even the food shops have lines of a hundred people. But everyone has to sacrifice for the good of the emperor.

My eyes keep returning to that ragged boy. He scratches his neck and looks back at the line behind him. Naoki! He's thinner and so much more grown-up. But it's Naoki. I search the line around him for Hitomi. I don't see her.

Karo-chan presses against my side. "Don't stare," she whispers.

"Don't you see who that is?"

"Don't stare! People will know you're not blind."

She's right. But Naoki has noticed me. He looks from me to Karo-chan and back. The way he feels about the war . . . No, I can't let him know it's us. I can't take that risk.

Naoki steps out of line and walks toward us hesitantly.

I squeeze my hands together and turn my back on him. But I want to talk to him so much. I have to! I turn again.

But something has happened; the whole line is breaking up. The shop ran out of food. So we scurry with Obasan and most of the people around us to the Matsuya department store nearby. I tell myself not to look back, but I do. Naoki's gone.

At Matsuya the line also gets cut off before we're served. By this time all I want is our radish greens at home. And a chance to think about Naoki. But Obasan takes us to Fujiya, and we finally have lunch. Noodles! In a broth with a suspicious-looking seaweed and costing eighty sen, a fortune. But noodles! We slurp them down.

When we get home, the neighbor is in our yard. She has chopped down the camphor tree. She stands over it with an axe, puffing hard. Obasan smells the oily air and sighs. The neighbor lifts her head defiantly. "Your tree threw morning shade on our vegetables, and morning is the most important time. It's our right to make a neighbor take down trees or walls. Everyone has to have a garden. That's our patriotic duty. It was my right to fell this tree."

I loved the camphor tree. I loved how we put its leaves in our bath to make the water smell fresh and strong and good. I loved how it made me think of Aiko. And somehow of Nonna. But food is food. The neighbor woman is as skinny as we are.

The neighbor looks around. "That plum tree has to go, too."

I think of Obasan's haiku. "We could give you plums," I say. "They will make up for the small shade that tree throws. And plums can be dried for use all winter."

"Dried and salted . . . or pickled and rolled in a rice ball." The neighbor swallows, and through the gauze I watch the knob of her throat rise and fall. "I get half the plums."

"All right," Obasan says.

"Half. Not one less."

"Half. And leave the tree you cut down. It is mine."

"You can't cut it up. You can't use an axe without seeing."

"I'll get help. It's my tree. Leave it."

"It will cost you to get help." The neighbor woman stands tall. "I'll chop it into pieces for you, if you give me half the wood."

"Next time you want to do something to my home—to any part of it, the land or the building or my family . . ." Obasan puts one arm around me and one around Karo-chan. "Next time, ask first. We are neighbors. That is the courtesy neighbors give one another."

The woman drops her head. "I'm sorry. You went out, all three of you, and I thought it was an opportunity to do it without a disagreement. I'm sorry."

"Chop the tree up. But take only one quarter of the wood."

"Agreed."

We go inside.

"We're your family," says Karo-chan. "You said so. You stood with your arms around us, just like Papà did the last time we were with him. This is your home. And this is our home. And when Papà joins us, it will be his home. Right?"

Obasan puts a hand on Karo-chan's arm. "We do what we can."

"But it will be his home, too. We can do that. Right?"

"We can try."

I kiss Karo-chan's cheeks. "Family is family."

Karo-chan goes to our bedding, takes out Lella, and doesn't ask again.

THIRTY-ONE

The professor stomps into our laundry. "My villa," he says to Obasan, "it's been vandalized by the intellectual thieves." He places his dirty laundry on the counter. "Forgive me. I am beside myself today." He bows.

Obasan bows. "Tea?"

The professor walks in a circle, like an animal tethered to a stake. I worry he will wear a ring in the old tatami mats. "At least a dozen villas were sacked. Those stupid, stupid boys."

"They are uneducated," says Obasan as she prepares the tea. "Perhaps not stupid, just uneducated."

"They stole food," says the professor. "And the police couldn't care less. One policeman asked me if this vandalism meant I wouldn't be able to eat waffles anymore. The snide fellow! I haven't had waffles in over a year. They broke my Western records—all my jazz. And they destroyed my books!"

Obasan gasps. "Your beloved books." She sighs. "Those boys have been forced into factory labor. All day long. Every day. Is it any surprise they hate scholars and anyone who makes a living from something other than working with their hands?"

It dawns on me: that's what happened to us in Fujiko's family cabin at the foot of Mount Fuji. The intellectual thieves must have noticed Fujiko's big spending at the black market in Hakone and her refined language, and decided she was a scholar. It wasn't the police at all.

"Tokyo is disintegrating," says the professor. "So many children work in factories that schools have more teachers than children."

"Please sit," says Obasan, bowing.

He sits. "That's the worst part—what's happening to the children. When the government turned all the golf courses into public gardens, I hired neighbor children to plant potatoes and cabbages and rhubarb on a small section of it. They tend the plot for me. It's appalling to hire children, but I do it because they're so poor. And you know what?"

Obasan pours the tea for the professor and then for herself. She doesn't answer.

"They know everything about gardening. Children younger than the younger of your two girls behind the screen over there."

Karo-chan and I know all about gardening, too. And we love it.

"Their days are spent gardening instead of studying. It's wrong."

Obasan sits, waiting for the professor to bow and thank her and take his teacup in both hands and sip.

"Your girls shouldn't be sewing all day. They should be in school." The professor jumps to his feet again. This is awful behavior—the tea is already poured. "It's wrong that any children should even live in Tokyo now." He's walking in that circle again. "Children were supposed to have been evacuated last August, and here it is June of 1944 and they're still here. There's no food in Tokyo. They should be in the countryside, with farming relatives. Farmers are the only fat people left. Why are your two girls still here?"

Will he come over to us? Karo-chan and I pull the gauze sashes down over our eyes. My heart beats like crazy.

"Your clean laundry is ready, Sensei." Obasan is on her feet now, too. She bows. "Please find it on the shelf."

The professor stops short. He folds his arms one over the other. "You must have many reasons why the girls are here. It's not my concern." He bows. "I'm sure your tea is delightful. I wish my worries would settle and allow me to enjoy it properly."

"I understand." Obasan bows. "These are not trivial worries."

"I have behaved this morning in a way unusual for me. I have no excuse. But perhaps I have an explanation. The ration of only six cigarettes a day for men is fewer than half what I

271

need. I waste time searching for a decent smoke and pay absurd sums on the black market. I am not myself."

"I need no excuse. No explanation," says Obasan. "We know each other too well for that."

"Thank you for the laundry. Thank you for listening. If there's anything left from this money"—he puts a handful on the counter—"please consider using it to allow the girls a day off from work."

"You are most generous." Obasan bows.

"The next time, I will bring you a box of tea, to help make up for my failure to enjoy this fine tea you prepared today. Tea from the Kumamoto prefecture. I remember how you loved it as a girl. You said it tasted like mountains."

Obasan gasps. "You'll never find it in Tokyo. Not these days."

"Yes, I will." The professor bows again and leaves.

Karo-chan counts the money. "What will we spend it on?"

Obasan feels the money and puts some into her money box. "The rest is yours. You decide."

"I want to go back to Fuji Ice," says Karo-chan.

"But I get to decide the route we walk," I say.

So Karo-Chan and I pull the gauze sashes over our eyes again, and the three of us walk the route I've been thinking about all week. It isn't far, and my memory serves me well, because soon we pass the little home I recognize, even though I was there only once.

We walk a few steps beyond, and I pretend to trip. I squat. "Please, may we rest awhile here?"

Obasan and Karo-chan squat as well. We huddle, like cats.

The house is like any other: wood and paper. There's a large vegetable garden out front. Greens I don't know. But I recognize sweet potato leaves. Children are tending it. All of that is normal. But what's odd—what's so totally different—is the number of children. There are so many. Closer to the house is a pile of old bicycles. Children sit there, guarding it and chattering.

My eyes examine them one by one. They are small, so it's silly to search. But I do anyway. No one is Naoki.

"That's a new language," says Karo-chan.

"Korean," says Obasan. "They come here to work in the factories."

"Don't they have factories in Korea?" asks Karo-chan.

"They don't come here by choice."

Karo-chan doesn't ask what that means. "It sounds funny. The air smells funny, too."

"They make different food," says Obasan.

"Their cooks must be awful."

Obasan laughs. "I wouldn't know. I never tasted it. I stand in the ration lines and listen to them whisper to each other, but I don't speak Korean, so I can't ask how they prepare things. I know they have different spices."

A child in the garden shouts. A few go running into the

house. I want to stand to see what the fuss is all about. But I'm supposed to be blind. I stay in my squat. Children come out of the house with jars. They pick things from the garden dirt and put them into the jars.

"Beetles," says Karo-chan. "They're collecting beetles."

"To eat," says Obasan.

"Koreans eat beetles?"

"So do Japanese now. We will, too, if it comes to that. We will mash them and roast them. Maybe I'll add some ginger." Obasan laughs and stands. "Can we go now, Simo-chan? Have you seen what you needed to see?"

"What were you looking for?" asks Karo-chan.

"An old friend."

"Naoki?"

Could she actually remember that this used to be Naoki's home? "Yes."

"I saw him."

"What? Where?"

"Three boys crossed the street up there and went down the block. That way. I think one was him. But it was when you first tripped. So they're gone by now."

"Can we go that way, Obasan?"

"This is your treat. You decide. But I need to be back at the laundry by early afternoon."

We turn the corner where Karo-chan says. Up ahead three boys are painting on a postbox. When they see us, two run off. But one is Naoki. My Naoki. My cheeks heat. He walks backward away from us for a few steps, looking keenly at us. Then he turns on his heel and follows the others. He's barefoot, and the bottoms of his feet are caked with dirt.

We walk past the postbox, but we cannot stop and linger. Still, I see enough. Big, fast strokes in red paint of skinny children. Naked. Starving. A boy with the flag wrapped around his belly and a woman glowering down at him. She holds a gun.

"What is it?" asks Obasan. "What do you see?"

I've stopped asking her how she always knows when I'm upset. I describe what we saw.

"We must walk quickly," says Obasan. "*Rakugaki* is an offense. Someone is bound to have seen the boys doing those scribbles. Someone will tell someone, who will tell someone, and soon the police will come."

But we're too late; a policeman runs toward us in high black boots. "Stop!" he shouts. He points at the postbox. I don't turn my head. Neither does Karo-chan. We are professional liars by now. "Who did that?"

Obasan bows. "Did what?" she asks, and her voice sounds weak and old. She is also a professional liar.

"That." He points. "That *rakugaki.*"

"We cannot see it," says Obasan.

"Did you hear them talking? Do you know the scribblers?"

"We heard only each other," says Obasan.

"You must have heard them run away. Which direction did they go?"

"My nieces were chattering," says Obasan. "Loudly. As young girls do."

"This sort of criminal behavior is bad for public morale," says the policeman.

"Ah," says Obasan. "Do you want to describe the *rakugaki* to us?"

"No!" The policeman bows. "You may leave."

We walk another block.

"Do you still want to go to Fuji Ice?" I ask Karo-chan.

"The food is still good there. And we still have money," she says.

So we walk the rest of the way in silence.

CHAPTER
THIRTY-TWO

18 June 1944, Tokyo, Japan

Two weeks later, the sirens sound; I'm half-awake. They wail as I sit up and shake Karo-chan awake. Obasan is already putting on her day clothes. We strap on our helmets without talking. Air-raid alerts happen a few times a week.

Tokyo has concrete shelters—maybe in the rich neighborhoods. Other people use cave-like shelters dug into one of Tokyo's many hills. A few go to basements in the rare Western-style buildings that have them. But most people can't go into those places.

The government recommends that ordinary people gather in clothes cupboards within our homes. But people say they are frightened of being aboveground. And who has cupboards big enough to fit a family? They trudge to a *bokugo*—an open-pit shelter, nearly two meters deep. Some people have dug a *bokugo* beside their home, so they just step outside and into the pit. But we don't have enough land for both a *bokugo* and a garden—and we need the garden. So we go to a *bokugo* down the block, beside the street.

Two women and three small children are already there when we arrive. We climb in and squat, heads bent over; that's what the radio tells everyone to do. Two more women come, supporting an old man between them. This *bokugo* is already full. Another woman comes with a baby. We squish together so that the woman and her baby can fit. Karo-chan sleeps crammed between Obasan and me.

Finally the sirens sound again, and everyone trudges home. As we walk, dawn comes sweetly over the horizon, as though this could be any peaceful day, anywhere. It feels unreal, that anything can still be so pretty.

Once inside, we fall onto our futons. By the time we wake again, it's nearly noon.

"Ha," says Karo-chan. "The professor hasn't come yet. He's later than us." She's right; it's Sunday, and the professor is as regular as a calendar. "He must have spent all night in a shelter, too."

"It wasn't all night. It was just a few hours before dawn," I say. "And I'm grateful he hasn't arrived yet. His complaints tire me."

"Look who's grumpy," says Karo-chan.

"I'm not grumpy. What's the point of complaining when there's nothing anyone can do to make things better?"

Obasan rubs her palm on her forehead. "You're giving me a headache."

Karo-chan whispers into my ear, "Some people do things to make life better. Have you forgotten making manga?"

Fujiko and Kotsuru and Sanae.

And Naoki. He scribbles on postboxes. The woman pointing a gun at the boy. A shiver shoots up me. Naoki has changed. Making *rakugaki* out on the street is even more dangerous than making manga in a cabin.

I hear the ambassador: *Resistance matters.* I know, I know. But I'm not brave like that. I never want to run in fear again.

The professor finally shows up and drinks tea with Obasan. He really did bring her that special tea last week, and he refuses to let her make it for him. So they drink ordinary tea.

Karo-chan and I are behind the screen. She calls out to the professor, "Were you in a *bokugo?*" She gives me a challenging look, daring me to scold her for being so rude. "Is that why you're late?"

"I don't go to a shelter when the siren sounds," he says.

"Where do you go?"

"I stay in bed." He sips his tea. "I'm late today because I got tangled in a crowd out in front of a hotel. They're training for air raids. They think training will save them from firebombs." He takes another sip. "Nothing can save us from firebombs."

Obasan pours him a second cup of tea as he says, "Can we turn the radio on, please?"

The radio says we should sharpen our bamboo spears.

American bomber planes are coming soon, and Japan will blast them out of the sky. But some American soldiers will drop over Japan in parachutes. It's everyone's duty to kill them before they kill us.

"Nonsense." The professor turns off the radio. "I was wrong. It's a mistake to listen. After what happened on Friday, how can they expect anyone to believe them?"

"We have not received news for a few days," says Obasan. "What happened on Friday?"

"A disaster. Forty-seven American planes attacked Yawata in Kyūshū and only two were shot down."

Kyūshū. The boy who gave us his family's pot said they were moving to Kyūshū because the farmers there had food. That poor boy, that poor family. "Did anyone die?" I ask.

The professor turns his head quickly to face our screen. "Do you have family in Kyūshū?"

"Neighbors here moved there."

"Yawata had little damage. The Americans targeted the steelworks. So your neighbors are still alive. But they won't be for long. Kyūshū is the most southern big island; it's easy to reach. And it's Japan's breadbasket, as they say. The Americans will destroy it soon enough."

When the professor leaves, he puts extra money on the counter, like always.

Obasan takes her price for the laundry and hands the remainder to Karo-chan. She takes out her button box. "Here," she says, holding out the wooden box.

Karo-chan takes the box. "Buttons?"

"I found another home for my buttons," says Obasan. "You and Simo-chan can use that if you want."

"For what?" I ask.

"The professor is not a fool. We may need to get out of Tokyo soon."

"How?"

"Trains. You can have treats each week, or you can save the money the professor gives you. In that box."

"I hate trains," says Karo-chan.

I just look at her.

"I hate traveling," says Karo-chan.

I look away.

I hear Karo-chan go into the inner room and slide the partition shut.

The button box still sits on the counter. I look inside it. Karo-chan left the remaining money there.

THIRTY-THREE

21 JULY 1944, TOKYO, JAPAN

I wake to the radio. Obasan keeps it on constantly now, and all last week it talked about how the Americans captured the island of Saipan and the people there killed themselves rather than be taken prisoner. The radio played traditional songs praising honorable suicide.

Right now the radio is talking about what a fine start Premier Koiso is off to. But we know that the government is a mess. Premier Tōjō's cabinet resigned. Then the premier resigned.

And it's not just Japan. Everything is falling apart. Yesterday in Germany an explosion plot to kill Hitler failed. We're supposed to celebrate his survival. But how can he lead when his own officers have turned against him?

There's no news about Italy. No one here cares what happens there.

I wish Obasan would turn the radio off.

I wish someone would turn this war off.

And I wish I could turn on my brain. We got here at the beginning of April, and now it's late July and I haven't come up with a plan to reunite us with Papà. Ever since Obasan's declaration that we are family, I have allowed myself to rock in her warmth. Papà is close by, but both Fujiko and Papà warned against going to the prison camp. Karo-chan and I are all right without Papà for now. But sometimes I wonder—I swallow—what if Papà is not all right without us? He wouldn't want me to ask myself this; he'd say it was absurd. We are children. What can we do?

I go to the front door and look out. It's raining. For over a month it was dry. No one could plant. People entered the laundry with haunted faces. The rains finally came, and now they won't stop. There are lots of floods.

A man comes hurrying along the walk carrying a package under his arm. He holds his umbrella high so that I see his face. I recognize him; he's the one who brought the haiku from Obasan's brother. I run into the inner room, where Karo-chan still sleeps.

I hear the messenger come in and talk to Obasan. Then he's gone.

"Did you get a present, Obasan?"

"Open it and let's find out."

I open the package. "It's stuffed with dried-up leaves."

Obasan runs her fingers through them.

I take a deep whiff. "Is it more tea?"

"It's just dead leaves," says Obasan. "Junk."

Karo-chan comes from behind me, wiping sleep from her eyes. "What could it mean?"

"My brother is telling me to come to Hokkaido or I will be nothing more than dead leaves."

Karo-chan grabs my hand. "Will you go, Obasan?" My sister's hand squeezes mine. I squeeze back.

"No. We have our garden. We have our work," says Obasan. "And both are thanks to you. We are surviving here."

I rush and get the ink and brush and paper. "I'm ready to write your message back to him."

"Who needs to receive more packages of leaves?" says Obasan. "Messages are over. Put the ink away."

We spend the morning at work. No customers come.

"Obasan." I fold up my sewing. "I'd like to go for a walk."

"It's still raining," says Karo-chan.

"So I bet there's no one out and about today. It's a chance to be outside without worry."

Obasan stays silent.

"Where are we going, Simo-chan?" asks Karo-chan.

"You don't have to come," I say quickly.

"If you're getting drenched, I am, too."

"My umbrella is strong," says Obasan. "Karo-chan, please go fetch it."

Karo-chan runs into the inner room.

I tiptoe to the kitchen shelf where the writing tools are and grab a jar of ink. I slip it inside my shirt. When I turn around, Karo-chan is there, staring at me. "Are you ready?" I ask, as though everything is normal.

We pull the gauze sashes over our eyes and step outside. Rain thrums on the umbrella.

The streets are empty, so we can keep our heads up and go fast. I twist in and out of blocks. It feels safer that way. No one who sees us can point out to a policeman where we went except to say we turned at the corner.

"Slow down a bit," says Karo-chan. "Look at the gardens." Vegetables rot in the ground. Some plots are huge puddles. "Soon they'll have nothing at all to eat. What will Papà cook for the prisoners then?"

"Papà's smart, Karo-chan." I speed up again. "He tends the prison garden properly."

"How do you know he works in the garden?"

"Of course he does. He mounded the dirt properly. He staked the vines. It's a better garden than even ours with Obasan."

We turn the corner onto a street full of shops. On the other side from us is a restaurant we went to long ago with Papà. People used to say it made the best dumpling soup, and Papà took us there so he could learn how to make them. The line goes halfway down the block.

An air-raid warning siren goes off; these days there are warnings day and night.

No one gets out of the restaurant line. Hunger wins over fear.

Karo-chan and I don't rush to a *bokugo*, either. Last week there were three warnings in a single night. We just listened to the sirens at home and waited for them to stop.

We turn another corner. And another. We stop in front of the postbox. Someone painted over Naoki's *rakugaki*.

"We can't paint in the rain," shouts Karo-chan above the sirens. "Besides, you didn't steal a brush."

"We were never going to paint."

"So what are we doing here?"

"Looking for Naoki," I shout.

"He's probably hiding somewhere."

The sirens end, and the sudden silence makes everything feel slow, even the rain. Up the road, people are climbing out of a *bokugo*.

Karo-chan and I get the same idea at the same time. We walk toward those people. A woman, two small children, two old women. That's all.

We turn to leave, but one of the old women goes back to the *bokugo* and calls down, "Come out!"

After she leaves, we walk up and peer in. Someone is curled

over his knees. The rain pelts his back. "Is anyone there?" I ask, like a blind person would.

Silence. Then, "Simona? Is that you?"

Hearing my name out in the open turns me cold. *Simona* is strange for a Japanese name, but possible. *Carolina*, though, is definitely Western. I must stop him from saying her Italian name. "Karo-chan is with me," I say quickly.

Naoki uncurls his neck. He looks through the rain at us. "Come down."

Karo-chan and I go into the *bokugo*. We squat. Naoki doesn't join us under our umbrella. He's already soaked through. I turn so my back is to him. Karo-chan does the same. If anyone looks down into this *bokugo*, they won't know we're friends. That's safer. No one will be able to report they saw us talking with him here. After all, what Naoki does is illegal. I must protect Karo-chan.

"Welcome to my home," says Naoki.

"You live here?"

"Here and other places."

I want so much to look him in the eyes. "It's good to see you," I say.

"Can you see me? Really?"

"Not behind us," says Karo-chan.

Naoki laughs.

"Where's your mother?" asks Karo-chan.

"One day she didn't come home."

"What happened?" asks Karo-chan.

"If I asked you that, would you want to answer?"

"I'm sorry," I say. "Oh, Naoki, I'm so sorry." It's all I can do to keep myself from turning around to face him. But I mustn't. No one can know we're friends. "I brought you something." I reach inside my shirt and put the jar of ink on the ground behind me.

"Is this something to eat?" His voice is closer.

"It's ink."

"Next time we'll bring something to eat," says Karo-chan.

"Ink is better than food."

"We'll bring both," I say.

"You can't. It's enough that you brought me ink. If anyone sees. . ."

"Where will we meet you? And when?" It's been so long. I stretch my hand backward.

He holds it.

20 AUGUST 1944, TOKYO, JAPAN

"I was right," says the professor. "Back in June, I told you they'd destroy Kyūshū. They bombed our breadbasket three times—to starve us."

The radio is on. It says we should all stand tall, ready for the coming victory of the Japanese air command forces.

"Turn that thing off, please," says the professor. "Is there really anyone left who believes that nonsense?"

Obasan turns off the radio and goes about preparing tea.

He says, "You know there isn't, my good friend. You don't answer me when you agree with me. You help me know I'm right." The professor puts his laundry on the counter. He's holding something else in the other arm, wrapped in newsprint. He puts that package on the floor and slaps his hands together. "Guess the latest, my mysterious little girls behind

289

the screen. They tapped my telephone lines. They listen in on all dissidents now."

Obasan kneels. The professor sits on the mat. She pours him tea.

"After the theft, I had the remainder of my things packed up and sent for safety to good friends in Karuizawa. Way in the west."

"You are preparing to leave Tokyo, then?" asks Obasan.

"I'm preparing to flee. Most of my friends have already." He leans forward. "Listen to me, please. Tokyo will be bombed. Go to Hokkaido with your girls. Your brother wants you. Hokkaido isn't a target in this war, not yet. That's where I'd go if I still had family there."

"We are managing."

"You will starve."

"Ah, how foolish I am," says Obasan suddenly. "I should have offered you a treat before the tea. Let me prepare one." She goes to the kitchen cupboard and brings back a cucumber, a knife, and a board. "Will you cut it, please?"

"Where did you get this? Not the ration lines. It isn't even shriveled."

"We have a kitchen garden. The cucumbers came in early. We've been eating them all week. The eggplants are now ready."

The professor slices the cucumber. "Your vegetables will die off when autumn weather starts."

"Our plums and peaches will be ready then."

"And in winter?"

"We'll face winter when it comes."

"Maybe it won't be starvation for you three, then. Maybe it will be fire from bombs."

Karo-chan stops sewing and sits like a statue.

The professor eats a slice of cucumber. Then he picks up his package again and waves it around in the air. "Can you smell this?" The pungent, spicy odor of cedar saturates the room. "Do you know what it is?"

"I think I do," says Obasan.

"Please do me the honor of accepting it and teaching these two girls the finer things in life."

Obasan sets the package on the counter and opens it. Mushrooms tumble free. They have light, bell-shaped caps and thick stems. Obasan feels them, then holds her hands to her nose. Delight fills her face. *Matsutake.*

"They're early this year because of the rains. I hope you will enjoy them."

A man comes to the door with a basket, selling candy. When the professor asks the price and the man answers, I put my hand over my mouth to hold in the gasp. Fifty times what candy cost the last time Papà bought us some—only a year ago. But the professor buys a packet. "Girls like sweets." He holds the candy packet high, like he did the mushrooms. "Please, come sit with Tanaka-san and me and enjoy it."

Karo-chan and I slip the gauze sashes over our eyes. My forehead breaks out in a cold sweat. Please don't let him insist.

Obasan stands. "You are immensely generous." She bows. "But I regret that I cannot permit such an extravagance. Mushrooms are enough." She bows again. "The girls have work to finish now. They mustn't be disturbed."

The professor is silent for many minutes. "Children work. No time for sweets." He crawls toward us. Karo-chan and I grab each other's hand. He puts the bag of candy on the mat in front of our screen. Then he stands and leaves. Without a bow.

I set the candy on the counter. The newspaper that held the mushrooms lies crumpled there. Newspapers are rare now because there are no trees left to make paper from. Most people get only radio news. I spread out this unexpected treasure and read to Obasan.

But I don't read everything. And I don't let Karo-chan look on with me. I don't want them to know. There on the front page is a photo of an American office girl. On her desk is the skull of a Japanese soldier. The look on her face is triumphant. The article says she is a typical American. I know better than to believe newspapers; maybe that isn't even a Japanese skull. Maybe in America that girl is considered hideous because she is so full of hate.

But I still hope I never meet an American.

That night we cut mushrooms and garden eggplant in long slices, Papà's way, but cook them spicy, Obasan's way. When

Karo-chan and Obasan are asleep, I burn the newspaper, and I go out in back of our home with a bowl of dinner for our guest.

I sit in the dark and wait for his visit—my Naoki. Really, though, he's our Naoki. It's just that he comes so late that the others rarely get to see him.

Naoki walks on silent feet. He sits beside me, takes the bowl, and eats fast.

"Naoki, do you ever see Aiko?"

"After her brother died, her mother took her to live with relatives in Shiga prefecture."

My heart hurts. I remember promising Aiko that Gen would not die. How foolish I was. "It's good to know she's safe."

"If she were here, she'd tell you not to say stupid things. No one is safe."

"We felt safe," I say quietly, "only five months ago, in a cabin, at the foot of Mount Fuji."

"Tell me about it," Naoki says.

I tell him everything, every detail I can remember. Fujiko, Sanae, Kotsuru. Like angels, like a fantasy. But, oh, they were so real.

We sit in silence a long while

"I wish I had met them," says Naoki. "If I had enough talent, I would draw manga, not *rakugaki*."

"You are talented. It's not talent you lack," I say. "But—no studio and paper and paints. You're a good artist. You could be a *mangaka* cartoonist."

"Thank you for the meal," says Naoki.

I will ask him about his day now, and he won't answer. He never does. "What happened to you today?" That is his cue to leave.

He hands me a rolled-up cloth. "Careful."

I cradle it in both hands. "Should I open it now?"

"No, no. Put her inside a box with a lid."

"Her?" I bring the cloth up close to my face. It smells of nothing but the hemp it's made of. "What's in here?"

"A gecko."

I push my hands toward Naoki. "We won't eat her."

He laughs. "I knew you wouldn't. I remember. Don't pick her up. But you can touch the back of her, just soft. Like this." He touches my cheek, soft as a feather. "Put lots of dirty leaves in the box. Full of bugs. And soon—two or three days—take off the lid. The box will be a gecko home."

"Animals don't get tame that fast."

"She won't be tame. And it won't be her home."

"But you said . . ."

"She will lay an egg or two. I felt her belly. I think it's two. Little white eggs. It will take a while for them to hatch."

I can't think of a box to use. But, oh, that old pot that the bottom fell out of—we still have it. Obasan hid it so no one would take the metal for the war effort. I can put it on the floor, and it will make a cozy home. I'm grinning into the night. "How long?"

"More than a month, less than two. If you hold the babies

right away, they will be pets. One for you, one for Karo-chan. They will keep your home bug-free."

I hold the cloth to my chest and curl around it ever so gently. "Thank you, Naoki-kun."

But he's already gone.

THIRTY-FIVE

3 November 1944, Tokyo, Japan

Obasan coughs. "Maybe I won't go with you."

"But it's sunny today," says Karo-chan.

"My chest says it's still October."

October was a rainy month, as bad as July. Obasan's cough won't go away. "We can do it without you," I say. "You stay warm."

We search for our geckos, Kaede and Masaki. *Kaede* means maple tree and *Masaki* means great timber. We named them that because Naoki's name means honest timber, and he's their father.

"Here they are," calls Karo-chan.

They're not in their favorite corner. Instead they're nestled inside the clothes cupboard. Maybe they followed a moth in the night. We cup our hands around them and scoop them away. They crawl up our arms. It tickles. We set them into the pot full of leaves that is their daytime home, safe from laundry customers. Our geckos will never wind up in anyone's belly.

I put the last peach, the last plum, on a dish on the counter, hidden under a cloth. Obasan's nose and fingers will tell her they are there. They are shriveled, but still good.

We didn't dry any fruit to preserve for later. They were so delicious fresh, and then, we had to give the neighbor half our plums, and Naoki thanked us so profusely every time we gave him some, so how could we set any aside for winter? We ate them, juice dripping down our chins, and listened to the radio and to the professor, and everything ugly they said was terrifying . . . but somehow unreal. We haven't seen bombs or bullets. But we've eaten fruits. Fruits sealed us away, safe.

As of today, the fruits are gone. We spent summer and autumn so far standing in line for our rations. We didn't need anything else because our vegetables and fruits were enough. Now, though, we have to go to the black market again, just like everyone else. That's where we're going today. There will be hardly any rice or fish—but we'll find something.

We put on our gauze sashes and walk, at the same pace we'd go with Obasan, a blind pace.

"Obasan is sick," whispers Karo-chan. "The professor is sick, too."

"It's just coughs. They'll both get better soon."

"Good."

It surprises me that Karo-chan is still comforted by what I say. Nothing feels sure to me.

An old woman comes out of her home and walks ahead of us. An old man, wearing only pants in this November chill, comes from the other direction. He asks her, loudly, "What's the news?"

The old woman shakes her head and keeps walking.

The old man shouts behind her. "What's happening in the war?" He crosses the street and wanders off.

There's a postbox ahead.

"Slow down," I whisper to Karo-chan. "Let's take a good look as we pass."

Lots of *rakugaki* in blue ink. That's the color of the last jar I gave to Naoki. We have only two jars left now. This scribble shows three people. I can't tell if they are children. I can't tell if they are male or female. They wear shirts and long pants, and their arms and legs peek out like bones. They are on their hands and knees, eating from a garbage heap. A woman stands beside them, smiling—lips closed, like a modest Japanese woman.

We keep moving. My heart hammers. It's against the law to even look at *rakugaki*. But I saw enough. I'm nearly sure Naoki did these, alone. His two friends from before are gone. One was picked up by the police, and Naoki didn't tell me what happened to the other. Just like he never told me what happened to his uncle. Or to his mother, Hitomi.

Up ahead a few people gather on a corner. They're looking up.

"Don't look up," says Karo-chan.

I don't think I would have, but I'm grateful she reminded me. We walk to the edge of the group, and I bump into a woman. I apologize over and over.

"You poor blind children," says the woman. "You can't see it."

"See what?"

"A giant jellyfish. It's drifting in the sky."

Is she insane?

"It's a balloon," says another woman. "I heard it on the radio just a moment ago. There will be many more. Rubberized silk balloons."

"What for?" I ask.

"A surprise weapon. Against the Americans. The radio promised to explain it all later."

Karo-chan and I bump our way around the people, which now form a small crowd, and continue in the direction of the black market.

"I want to see," says Karo-chan.

"Let's find a *bokugo*."

In the next block, there are two, end to end. We stumble getting in, like blind people would. But now we can turn our faces upward. No one will see us unless they come up to the edge and look down into this *bokugo*.

We wait. Soon enough a balloon sails over us. Enormous.

Lots of things dangle from the bottom. They do seem like jellyfish tentacles. We squat there a long while. It must be nearly an hour before another balloon sails over us.

Karo-chan climbs out. I follow her. It seems all of Tokyo has taken to the streets, looking up, wondrous.

The market is abuzz with rumors. People say the balloons have bombs inside, with little gadgets that will set the bombs off when they land. But they won't land in Japan. The wind will carry them to America, where they'll kill everyone.

Karo-chan and I buy a small bit of fish and go home under a sky now littered with balloons, all carrying the hope of death.

THIRTY-SIX

27 DECEMBER 1944, TOKYO, JAPAN

Karo-chan ties a knot in the end of her thread and sews. "My birthday was pitiful."

I don't know why she's talking about that now. Her birthday was three weeks ago. She's ten; she should make more sense. But I can't argue with what she said. That day a huge earthquake near Nagoya shook the east coast of Japan. It caused a tsunami, and lots of people died. The internment camp that we escaped from is in Nagoya. I think of Mariella and how nice she was that last morning, when I lay under the futon all cramped up. Is Mariella safe now? And the ambassador and Pessa, and all of those captured Italians?

Karo-chan says, "Pitiful, and everything has gotten worse since then."

That's true, too. After the earthquake, Americans dropped

bombs on Nagoya. The radio didn't say how many died, and the professor didn't know this time. Then America targeted Tokyo. Their planes come every night. The Japanese air force chases them away and their anti-aircraft guns make showers of metal fragments that rattle our houses.

The winter has turned hideously cold. Winds chill us no matter how many layers of clothing we put on. Karo-chan and I shiver in the ration lines as people cough and talk about relatives in the hospital with pneumonia. They complain that farmers outside Tokyo are cutting down orchards for firewood. That's crazy, because they won't have any fruit to sell next year, but I believe it. Each household was rationed a single bag of charcoal for the winter.

"Christmas was the worst ever," says Karo-chan.

Ah, so that's it. "I told you, we'll have some kind of treat soon. Something that will make all three of us happy."

"Promise."

I haven't yet figured out our treat. Still, I'm opening my mouth to promise, when a girl comes into the laundry. Even from our hiding place, I hear her teeth chatter.

She bows. "I have an important basket," she announces as though standing in front of a crowd. "It's full of materials for making dolls. We need volunteers to sew them. Oh! Are you . . ." She takes a few steps more into the laundry. "You're blind. I didn't know." She bows and turns to leave.

"Wait," I call. I know that girl. It's my old classmate Noriko. I sewed stitches in the sash that her brother wore into battle.

Her brother, Oto, was Aiko's sweetheart. "Obasan, please. We can help."

Noriko hesitates.

"What is this all about?" says Obasan.

"The special attack pilots," says Noriko. "Kamikaze."

"Kamikaze." Obasan sighs loudly. "Those new forces."

"They started in October, and they're very successful."

"The kamikaze pilots fly a plane directly into an enemy ship," says Obasan.

"They never miss their target," says Noriko.

"It's a suicide mission."

Noriko walks closer to Obasan. "It's patriotic."

"What are the dolls for?"

"The pilots need dolls with them in their planes."

"So these pilots are really boys," says Obasan.

"They're loyal citizens, defending our country." Noriko steps even closer to Obasan. "They're young and brave. Some are orphans. Some come from the countryside. They gather here in Tokyo, and they need . . . comfort in the airplane."

"A doll," says Obasan, pressing her hands against her chest. "A doll to die with."

"Think about it, old lady. There's no more metal to make new planes or bombs. So these pilots fly beat-up planes into targets—planes that are useless in battle but that make the best bombs. These pilots are heroes. The dolls are not to die with; they are to win with."

Obasan shakes her head.

"Would you rather we lose the war?" Noriko's voice threatens.

"Leave us the materials," I call out. "We'll make the dolls."

Noriko doesn't seem to recognize my voice. Of course not—we were barely friends. She puts the basket on the counter. "It's good to see you understand. I'll come back tomorrow to fetch the finished dolls. There are materials here for three dolls. Make them as big as you can." She bows toward our screen, but not toward Obasan. I'm glad Obasan can't see her.

After she leaves, I spread the squares of cloth out with care. Karo-chan draws a doll, and we figure out together how to make them. I cut the cloth, we blow on our fingers to warm them, and we sew like mad.

"I don't think Obasan is really old," says Karo-chan.

"You know that's just how you speak to women who live alone."

"I know. But she isn't old. Is she?"

"No. It's just her gray hair."

"Good," says Karo-chan. "I want her to live forever."

We're both so fast now that we finish the dolls by late afternoon.

Karo-chan peeks into the basket. "There's nothing to stuff them with."

I grab the scissors and cut off all my hair. The pile is pathetic, because I keep my hair short. I look at Karo-chan. Hers is long.

She meets my eyes. "No."

I look down.

"Wait here." Karo-chan gets up and runs outside. She comes back with a small basket full of fruit pits.

We stuff the dolls, and Karo-chan presses one of the dolls against her cheek. "They're lumpy," she says, and picks up the scissors. She holds a lock of hair straight out, shuts her eyes, and cuts it off. She blinks rapidly and hands me the scissors. "You finish."

We stuff the hair all around the pits, till the dolls are properly thick and soft. "They're lovely now," I say. I kiss her cheeks.

She paints plum pits black and shiny with ink from our last jar, and we sew them on, arranged in big circles as eyes. The dolls don't need a nose or mouth, but they need eyes to watch over the kamikaze boys—the divine wind boys.

I secretly save the scraps of material and a small bit of Karo-chan's hair. I have a plan.

After dinner the air-raid sirens sound. We keep talking; then we go to sleep.

Pop-pop-pop-pop! Pop-pop-pop-pop-pop!

I wake and jump up to sitting.

"Hurry." Obasan stands over us.

We're already dressed because we sleep in our ordinary clothes for warmth, so we put on our wooden clogs and run outside. A plane bursts into flames and streaks red through the black night, and falls in the middle of the city. Karo-chan and I stand, horrified. I describe the whole thing to Obasan. We wait, but nothing else happens. So we go back inside.

There are no more sirens, no more anti-aircraft fire. But I lie there and see red streaks cross the ceiling. They're not real, but I see them even with my eyes closed.

As dawn creeps into the room, I get up and take out the scraps left from making the dolls, and sew carefully.

When Obasan and Karo-chan finally wake, I turn on the radio. It says fifty American planes were shot down over Tokyo.

"Fifty?" says Karo-chan. "We saw only one."

"What does it matter?" I say. "No one believes the radio."

We hear shouting. People stand in the street and cheer, "*Banzai!*"

We shut the door against the icy wind.

"Idiots," says Obasan.

"Maybe not," says Karo-chan. "No one is smiling."

"We need smiles," I say, and I hand Karo-chan the present I sewed.

She examines it, and beams. "A toy gecko." She hands it to Obasan.

Obasan feels it, and her face lights up. "We can all play with it."

Karo-chan hugs herself in happiness. "Even Lella."

CHAPTER
THIRTY-SEVEN

24 FEBRUARY 1945, TOKYO, JAPAN

Obasan stands at the sink, preparing breakfast. "Oh no!"

Karo-chan hurries over. "There's no water!"

"It froze." Obasan sinks to the floor and sits on her heels. "That means our pipe burst. Last night was just too cold."

I pull the gauze sash down over my eyes. "I'll find someone to fix it."

"Who?" says Obasan. "Everyone is dead or in the military. How would we pay them anyway?" She slaps her chest. "What am I saying? There are no pipes to replace it with. Simo-chan, come crawl under here. Turn the shut-off valve, so we don't have a flood when the water in the pipe thaws and leaks out the crack."

I'm on my knees turning the valve when someone comes into the laundry. My back is to the person, and I'm covered by the sink. But where is Karo-chan? I pull the gauze sash over my eyes and wait under the sink.

"Aha! I've caught one of the mysterious girls out in the open." It's the professor. I don't know whether to be relieved or frightened. "Let me see you, lovely one."

"Forgive my rudeness, honorable professor," I say, "but I prefer not. Please turn your back while I go behind the screen."

He doesn't speak. But I don't hear him move, either.

"I beseech you, Sensei," I say.

I hear his feet on the mat. I peek. His back is to me. I run behind the screen, where Karo-chan hugs me. Her gauze sash is also in place.

"Modesty is a virtue." The professor turns and bows, then places his laundry on the counter.

"I didn't expect you," says Obasan. "It's Saturday."

"True," says the professor. "But something has come up, so I cannot come tomorrow." He sits on the mat.

"I apologize profusely," says Obasan, "but I cannot offer you tea. Our pipe froze."

"Do you really think I come for the tea, perfect though it may be? I can't miss a week with you. You allow me to speak. My only freedom."

Obasan bows and sits on her heels across from the professor. "I am humbled to be able to offer anything."

"Have you heard from your brother lately? New poems?"

"Nothing," says Obasan.

"I received a message from him."

Obasan waits.

"Open this once I am gone." The professor holds out a thick envelope.

"I don't want it."

How does she know what's in it?

The professor puts the envelope on the floor in front of Obasan. "You know that Americans firebombed Kobe three weeks ago?" he says. "And that American bombers hit Tokyo last Monday?"

"The port," says Obasan.

"And some areas of the city." The professor rubs his chin. "Go to Hokkaido. Do your brother a favor. Do me a favor."

"Perhaps when you leave Tokyo, I will leave Tokyo."

The professor laughs. "Your cleverness is a joy. In the midst of misery." He sighs. "You know that the imperial forces sank an American battleship on Wednesday?"

"I am blind, not deaf."

"Two kamikaze pilots hit the ship."

"Maybe they had our dolls," Karo-chan blurts out, leaning close to me.

"What's that?" asks the professor.

"We made them dolls," says Karo-chan. "Three."

"Those boys are duped," the professor says, almost in a shout. He stands and walks in that circle. "There's no point to their sacrifice. Japan cannot possibly win. Our government is

309

murdering the people." He crumples to his knees. "Mere boys. And deep inside those boys know it's futile. Imagine what that's like." He cries.

Karo-chan starts to get to her feet. I grab her and prevent her from going to him. He might still be a danger to us. But I know how Karo-chan feels. We're all crying.

The professor sits. "Everyone's suffering. The German city of Dresden was burned out ten days ago. Germany is lost. France presses from the west. Italy from the south."

My Italy! I go on alert. But the professor falls silent. I clench my fists and press them against my mouth to keep from asking.

The professor says, "After the bombing of the aircraft factory at Ōta, the government said there must be spies in Japan. Otherwise the Americans could never have known where that factory was."

"I heard this on the radio," says Obasan. "The government makes sure we get broadcasts, whether or not we have heat or water."

"Now every resident of Tokyo is ready to denounce everyone else. You can't feel those accusing eyes, my friend. Your blindness protects you. But we're all afraid of being reported for any little thing. Our society, our sense of community—ruined."

I've felt this. Now, when Karo-chan and I go to get rations, strangers' eyes examine us closely. I'm rigid with the fear of being discovered.

"It snowed yesterday," says Obasan at last. "And it's snowing now."

The professor goes to the door and peeks out. "How did you know?"

"Blind people know things," says Obasan with a smile. "Even if we can't feel eyes watching us."

"I am delighted to see that pride glimmering inside you, Tanaka-san. I apologize if I offended you."

"I still have a small bit of coal. But better than that, I have firewood from our old camphor tree," says Obasan. "If you gather enough fresh snow, I can make tea while the room fills with the lovely perfume of the wood."

"Will you girls help me?" asks the professor. "It will take lots of snow, even for just a pot of tea. We could play in the snow. I haven't played in the snow since I was a boy. We could dig tunnels. Make snow monsters. Throw snowballs. Come on, girls."

"Were you a stubborn boy?" asks Obasan.

The professor laughs. "You know I was. Your cleverness is a gem in the midst of misery. Give me all your buckets. I'll fill them so you have drinking water and laundry water for today. And I'll find more charcoal for you, and someone to fix that pipe."

The professor stays for tea, then for miso soup. Then he sits silent while Obasan does laundry and Karo-chan and I sew. Finally he puts money on the counter—ever generous— and leaves.

Obasan picks up the thick envelope the professor left behind on the floor, and slips it inside her clothes.

Karo-chan and I peek outside. It's still snowing. "We always wanted to play in the snow," I say to Karo-chan.

She smiles. "Why not now?"

We put on every bit of clothing we have. Obasan does, too. "Are you really coming with us?" I ask in surprise.

"I was a girl once." She ties a *furoshiki* around her head like a scarf. "It is a true crime to pass up rare joys."

The snow is up to our thighs. We play in the glorious and brilliant white until we're so cold that we can barely move. By this time the snow is as high as Karo-chan's bottom. People on the street exclaim, "Tokyo has never had such a snow!"

"I have a treat for dinner," says Obasan once we're inside. She boils kidney beans over the camphor-wood fire. "I was saving the beans for Simo-chan's thirteenth birthday in four days. But today has been good. Today is to celebrate."

We eat, then go to sleep exhausted and happy, truly happy.

That night, sirens wake us, and the roar of airplanes fills the sky. Bombs drop with deafening thuds. We run to our *bokugo,* squat, and curl over our knees, cold and helpless. I can't guess how many planes or explosions.

The sky is ablaze, and parts of buildings fly up with shafts of flame under them. I hear crackling as the heart of Tokyo burns, and I rock back and forth, my arms circled around Karo-chan from behind, my head buried in the back of her neck.

No. No. No.

CHAPTER

THIRTY-EIGHT

9 MARCH 1945, TOKYO, JAPAN

I jolt awake in the night. "The air-raid sirens."

"What time is it?" asks Obasan.

I light a candle. "Ten-thirty."

"Let's wait. I'll make . . ." Obasan goes silent midsentence.

I know she wants to make tea. But even the professor couldn't get our pipe fixed. We have no water unless we melt snow. We haven't been able to take in laundry for two weeks. It doesn't matter, though; no one brings laundry.

Karo-chan and Obasan and I hold hands.

Five days ago, the Americans bombed Tokyo again. If they do it tonight, that will be three times in two weeks.

A wind's been blowing since noon. Telegraph wires dance like crazy things, and boxes and trash go flying by under an overcast sky. If they bomb us, maybe this harsh wind will put out the flames. Or maybe snow will put out the flames. We had another heavy snowfall three days ago. Firefighters in their black judo-like robes tramp through the streets often now, and tell us this snow is our friend, this bitter cold is our friend. They say that if a bomb hits, we should break whatever ice we see, chop at it with axes, and throw the broken pieces onto the fire. That will put out the flames. They warn us not to wear rubber-soled shoes, because they'll melt if a firebomb hits our street.

But won't our wooden shoes catch fire?

The sirens stop. Obasan pats my hand. I blow out the candle, and lie staring up into the black air for a long time. Waiting.

The sound of planes—inevitable. I wake Obasan and Karo-chan. We go out the door, and Karo-chan and I look up. A plane roars, then another, then more. They come one by one. We stand in the doorway and listen and watch. Each plane's lights show the target below for the next plane. The approach begins as a raspy whisper. Then there's a high-pitched whine, then the roar. On and on. A never-ending line of planes.

But we don't run.

There are so many bombs, the air is hot. The snow melts around us, and I scoop water from the ground and throw it onto us to cool us. In minutes, our clothes are dry again.

Flames leap from place to place, carried by the winds.

Those harsh winds are disastrous! People run through the streets, and I see the terror on their faces because the flames are bright as daylight. A boy pulls a handcart by the handles in front, and his mother and sister push from behind. The cart is loaded with tatami mats and pots and pans. A bicycle rolls past, the front basket piled high with bowls. A woman runs with part of a futon tied around her. A boy in a helmet races past; pairs and pairs of wooden shoes hang from a rope at his waist. Has everyone lost their minds?

"What's happening?" calls Obasan to the passing crowd.

"Run, old lady," says an old man. "Avoid the bridges. They'll collapse. Go to the railway lines. Run along the tracks. Run!"

Obasan grabs my arm. "Where are the fires, Simo-chan?"

"Everywhere," the old man yells.

"So which way do we run?" cries Obasan.

The planes are still coming. Whisper, whine, roar.

"Let's head for water," says Karo-chan.

We link elbows and push through the crowds. Sparks rain down on our heads; we swat as if they're bees. We pass people in many open *bokugo* pits, curled over in hope, and people lying flat on the ground close to walls, facedown. We run with the wind behind, pushing us.

"There you are!" Naoki-kun sprints up. "I was scared when you weren't at home."

He and I hold on to Obasan and Karo-chan as we run. I think of Kaede and Masaki, our geckos. If our house burns, what will become of them? At least Lella is safe, tied to

Karo-chan's chest, inside her clothes. What stupid thoughts. Like everyone else, I've lost my mind.

Obasan falls. Naoki-kun lifts her from one side, and another boy appears and lifts her from the other. He's wearing an air-raid hood and a khaki civilian uniform. The night sky is so bright from the flames that I see the red eagle insignia of the Great Japan Youth Association on his breast pocket. A stab of fear. What if he knows Naoki-kun draws *rakugaki*? Boys like him turn in boys like Naoki-kun. But nothing like that matters now.

We run.

Above us the planes seem slow, gliding through black smoke. They could be big lazy birds. Don't they feel the heat? The air is on fire.

A woman rushes at us screaming. I see the flames behind us reflected in her glasses. And I realize: Karo-chan and I don't have our gauze sashes over our eyes. "Which way?" she screams. "Which way?"

"Come with us," I say.

But she runs the other way and nearly gets trampled by horses. They charge down the road, panicked eyes, pounding hooves. They've escaped from a stable. Good for them! We bunch together as they pass.

A reddish-purple flame hits a telegraph pole. Roofs blaze. The police station ahead is lit up by the flames. A policeman runs up to us. "You're doing the right thing," he says. His face is black with soot. His eyes are bloodshot. Ours must be, too.

The fire has disguised us. He races from person to person, giving encouragement. Many sit, or lie in the street, exhausted. Half have children tied to their backs. Who knows how far they've run.

Finally there's the canal, jammed with people. Others line the banks, chanting Buddhist sutras.

I pull Karo-chan closer and ask, "How will we hold on to each other if we're swimming?"

"I can't swim," says Naoki-kun.

I remember—the boy who wanted to join the navy but can't swim.

"Don't do it," says a woman beside us. She's sopping wet. Her face looks haunted. "The water is hot. It's getting hotter."

"Crawl," says our Great Japan Youth. "This way."

We crawl into a *bokugo*. Nothing covers us. Nothing protects us.

No more roar of planes, but fire truck sirens wail as fire crackles, buildings crash, and people scream.

I look at Obasan. "Your knee's bleeding."

Our Great Japan Youth reaches inside his uniform and pulls out a first-aid kit. He hands it to me. "You take care of her now." He leaves, and it feels like he was a dream.

I clean Obasan's knee and tape on a bandage.

The sky slowly turns light with morning. My throat is raw, my eyes burn, and I have no energy. But we are alive. I stand up and look out at the people racing this way and that. All of them are alive. For now, that's everything.

317

CHAPTER

THIRTY-NINE

25 March 1945, Tokyo, Japan

I open my eyes to see Karo-chan asleep beside me. Naoki-kun sleeps beyond her. After the bombing two weeks ago, Obasan insisted that he sleep here from now on. I look across to her spot.

She's gone. And something's wrong. The radio's not on. Obasan has the radio on every waking moment. Nothing else in Tokyo works anymore, but the radio keeps going.

I sit up, and the stench hits me. In the first few days after the firebombing, it was ash; winds blew and ash coated our nostrils. But most ruins have stopped smoldering. Now it's the smell of death. Every available adult is supposed to spend all day digging trenches for burial.

Blindness exempts us. Karo-chan and I stand in the ration line with others who are exempt—half-naked children and wounded adults. The women's fingers worry the frayed handles of their baskets as they mutter to themselves, but we use our fingers to pinch our noses against the stench.

I get up now and go into the front room.

Obasan sits there. "Another evacuation had been declared. All schoolchildren must leave Tokyo."

"I know," I say. The radio announced that after the fire-bombing. "Why isn't the radio on?"

"It stopped working." Obasan stands. As if that movement brings her to life, she hurries around, full of energy. She's already got all her clothes layered on her. But now she reaches into cupboards and fills a small bundle. "I'm going to Sapporo."

My heart stops. "Sapporo?"

"It's in Hokkaido. Where my brother lives. The poet."

I know exactly where it is—far, far north.

Karo-chan comes to stand beside me, and Naoki-kun appears on my other side.

"You're going?" says Karo-chan. "Only you?"

I pull Karo-chan in front of me and close my arms around her.

Obasan's still tucking small things into her bundle. "My dearest children. I'm sorry, so sorry. I tried to find a way. . . . But how can I buy you train tickets? You don't have documents." She pats her chest. "And the trains are horrible now. They stop all the time, and they're crowded. A long trip like that will be hideous and take forever."

"I thought only bomb victims could buy train tickets now," I say. "And the military."

Obasan clutches her bundle. "I got an official letter saying I'm a bomb victim." Her mouth twitches; her face is ashen. "But the official letter says nothing about you. I asked the authorities; I gave you my last name. But they had me listed as the mother of sons, and because I couldn't supply birth certificates, they said no. The only way to get tickets for you is to buy them from a thief."

"Buy them from a thief, then," says Karo-chan.

"I tried! My brother told the professor to give me plenty of money—so I tried. But thieves don't have enough tickets. And ticket lines are full of people trying to bribe their way on. Some wait in line for two days. People cut ahead, and then there are fights." Obasan is breathing hard. "But, oh, my dearest children, it's better this way. Girls traveling with a blind woman wouldn't be safe on a train. Little mobs steal your ticket and sometimes everything you have, and if you dare to fight back, you're left bleeding on the ground. When the trains stop, people have to crawl in and out through windows. Dangerous."

I try to think.

"People have all their belongings with them"—Obasan pats her chest fast—"so they bash everyone else with their luggage. And it's colder up in Sapporo. Travel will be painful." She drops her hand from her chest. "So I made a decision:

you're not coming with me, though my heart squeezes so hard it shatters."

Karo-chan rushes to hug her. Obasan's arms close around her.

I want Obasan's arms around me, too. But I stay put, my mind racing now. Obasan didn't say the most important reasons for not bringing us. If we traveled with her and people saw that we were Westerners, who knows what a mob might do? Even if we made it to Sapporo, her brother could turn us over to the authorities. She said that he blames everyone who isn't Japanese for the war.

Obasan saved us for a whole year. She can't save us anymore.

"You are smart," says Obasan, petting Karo-chan's head. "You can handle things for the moment. And, Naoki . . ."

"Yes, Tanaka-san?" says Naoki-kun.

"Are your hands stained with ink?" She always knows.

"Not anymore."

"My jars are gone," says Obasan. "But there are no buildings left to scribble on anyway."

"I tried," says Naoki-kun. "I failed to convince anyone."

"You can't know that. And you didn't get caught. That's success. You are smart, too. Like Simo-chan and Karo-chan. The three of you, stay together, take care of each other until the professor gets here."

Karo-chan jumps back. "The professor?"

"I sent him a message. I had the neighbor write it for me, though I hoped something would change and I could take you with me after all. He sent a message back. He will take you to Karuizawa with him."

Weeping, we kiss Obasan goodbye. Her hands shake. Her rheumy eyes water. Her voice is faint. My own voice won't come.

She puts an envelope into my hand. "You have your own saved money. But now it's three of you. This will help. The professor knows I leave today, but if anything should happen to him, if he gets detained, find a way to buy train tickets and go north and inland, to Saitama. The Urawa prison camp is there, with American prisoners. So the Americans won't bomb it. Maybe the prison will take you in."

"Thank you." I clutch the envelope. "Thank you. We . . ." I can't speak.

"It's Sunday. The professor should come today. I never told him you are Westerners. I couldn't ask the neighbor to write that. He will be surprised. But you are children; he worries about children; he will not betray you."

The professor won't come. He didn't come last week; we haven't seen him since the great firebombing. But Obasan can believe what she needs to believe.

We embrace Obasan, then watch her walk down the road.

"Obasan is alone," says Karo-chan.

"She'll be all right. We have to go now, too."

"No."

Obasan disappears past neighbors who stand outside their

homes trying to sell their grills and bamboo baskets, ceramics and pots. Anyone who can is leaving, but they take only what they can carry.

"Simo-chan's right. We must go," says Naoki. "Do what she says."

"The professor is coming," says Karo-chan.

"Karo-chan," I say, "Obasan loves us, but she can't find a way to help us now. The professor doesn't love us. Even if he comes today, how can you think he'll be able to help us? Go put on every bit of clothing you have."

"No! This time we stay."

I won't look at her—I won't let my face give away my fear. I layer on all my clothes and search the house as though I know what I'm looking for. Every shelf, every cupboard. There's nothing that might help us, not even matches. I take the money from our box and add it to the envelope. This envelope is the only thing we have. If anyone sees it, the money will soon be gone. Should I divide it among us for safety? But I'm the one who will be most careful with it, so I stuff it inside my clothes as Karo-Chan and Naoki-kun watch.

I gather Karo-chan's clothes on the floor in front of her. "Put them on."

She doesn't move.

I close my eyes and hold my face in my hands. Then I hold my hands in front of her face. "What do you smell?"

Karo-chan blinks. "Maybe a little soy."

I pull her hand to my face and sniff. "You, too. We could be anyone, any girl of Tokyo. But we aren't. I don't know who we are anymore, but everyone who sees us knows who we aren't." I lock eyes with Karo-chan. "We'll go to Saitama. To the prison camp."

"Americans. I hate Americans."

"We have to leave. Tokyo is being destroyed."

"Let's go find Papà."

"The prison guards will kill you," says Naoki-kun. "Besides, you don't know if your father's . . ."

"Enough!" I say. "We'll manage on our own. The three of us. But not in Tokyo."

"We can't manage on our own," says Karo-chan.

"Yes, we can." But Karo-chan sounds right. Staying alive is a game of wits. People often tell me that I'm clever, but right now I feel stupid.

Staying alive is also a game of luck. So much depends on luck. Three women in a cabin in the woods. A blind washerwoman. But luck can run out.

We need help. From nowhere comes an idea. "We're going to other Italians."

Karo-chan's eyes light up. "To Papà's prison."

"No. But to people who will take care of us."

"What about Naoki-kun?"

I look at Naoki-kun. "These people will take you in, too. It's their duty. Say you'll stay with us."

"I'll stay with you. I'll be like a brother."

Naoki-kun has no belongings. I take off my winter kimono and hold it out to him.

He shakes his head. "I'm used to the cold."

I take off my summer kimono and hold it out to him.

"No."

I put both kimonos back on. And I give a small smile. "You could be our real brother, you're so stubborn."

"Stubborn," mumbles Karo-chan. She's putting on her clothes, but so slowly I could scream.

I go into the front room for one last search. The professor stands there. I yelp in surprise. Naoki-kun comes running out and stops. Karo-chan follows.

Karo-chan and I—our eyes are uncovered.

The professor stares. "Western girls. Who are you?" Then, "Ah! Tanaka-san's girls!"

I give Karo-chan the signal, and we pull the sashes over our eyes and go to move past him.

He steps to block our path. "Are you German?"

"No."

"Where do you think you're going?"

What point is there in lying? "The Vatican embassy."

"It's full of Italians! You can't go there." Then he gasps. "Are you Italian?"

"No," I lie. My heart crumples inside my chest.

"Why on earth would you want to go to the Vatican embassy?"

"The Vatican is its own country. A neutral country, not at war with anyone," I say. "It's safe for us."

"Rumor has it that the Vatican harbored spies. Who even

knows if that embassy is still standing? But if it is, it's full of Japanese military police." The professor looks around the empty room. "She's left already." He slaps his palm onto the back of his head and sucks breath in through his teeth, as if to say sorry. Then he sighs, and his hand falls to his side. "How old are you?"

I'm thirteen now. Is that too old for him to see me as a child? "Does it matter?"

"You're as clever as Tanaka-san." He wags his head. "Tell me you're not American, at least."

"We're not! We hate Americans," says Karo-chan.

The professor nods. "My car is packed, ready to take you girls to Karuizawa."

"We stick together," I say. "All three of us."

"We're family," says Karo-chan. "Naoki-kun is our brother."

Naoki-kun blinks, and puts a hand on Karo-chan's shoulder.

The professor looks at Naoki-kun. "There's always room for family."

CHAPTER
FORTY

25 March 1945, Tokyo, Japan

The professor puts Karo-chan and me in the backseat of his car, bundled up with blankets, the gauze sashes over our eyes. Naoki-kun sits in the front by his side.

We go north toward the road to Karuizawa. But the road turns impassable. Knee-high, crusted, ash-covered snow lies everywhere.

"That's all right," says the professor, turning the car. "That's better, in fact. We'll go to Kyoto. They bombed Kobe and Osaka, but they won't bomb Kyoto. Not beautiful Kyoto. They'll want to preserve it so they can visit it as tourists in the future. That's how Americans think. I can find a place for us to stay in Kyoto." He lights a cigarette, and the car fills with smoke. "We'll take the mountain route. Pass fewer people. Fewer nosy people."

The roads toward the mountain are just as bad. The professor has to turn again. "We'll go south along the coast. The traffic of military vehicles undoubtedly made that road passable. We can be in Nagoya by early afternoon, and take the road from there to Kyoto."

"Nagoya?" says Karo-chan. "We'll pass Ofuna?"

"Yes."

"Our father is there, in the prisoner-of-war camp."

"I've never heard of a prison-of-war camp at Ofuna."

"It's secret," says Karo-chan.

"All right. But you said you were going to the Vatican embassy, not Ofuna. If I dropped you at Ofuna, would your father be expecting you?"

Karo-chan won't answer.

"They haven't seen or heard from him in almost two years," says Naoki-kun.

"Not two years!" says Karo-chan. "Eighteen months and two weeks. That's all."

The car slows down, and the professor clears his throat. "There's a blockade ahead. Do exactly as we agreed."

The car stops. Karo-chan and I lie curled up, pretending to be asleep, our arms over our heads to cover the sashes that hide our eyes. The air is dark from Tokyo ash, and military police shine flashlights in, searching for spies.

"Name card."

The professor: "Here, Officer."

"Who are these children?"

"My son and my two daughters."

"Names?"

"Naoki. Sango. Kaori."

Is the flashlight playing over us? I hold my breath.

"You can pass."

The car moves again. After a while the professor says, "You did fine."

We hit another blockade. The same routine.

We hit a third blockade. It doesn't get easier.

We drive a long while. "We're past the outskirts of Tokyo now," says the professor.

"Are you taking us to Ofuna?" asks Karo-chan.

"We passed Ofuna."

"No! Turn back!"

"Think, girl. If I dropped you off at Ofuna, even if there really is a prison there, what would they do to me? What would they do to Naoki? We're harboring Westerners—and you're not German, so whoever you are, you're enemies. And your father isn't . . . waiting for you. I'm sorry to say it, but he could be dead, for all you know. What on earth do you think they'll do to you—two young Western girls?" The professor's voice goes raspy. "Four lives are in my hands now. We are not turning back to Ofuna."

I put my arms tight around Karo-chan, and she strains against me, but she doesn't cry. It's me who's crying.

The professor hits his palm against the steering wheel. "You are not my children. If you three decide together that you must get out of the car, I will stop and leave you by the side of the road. But it's suicide. There have been more than enough suicides in Japan."

We drive on in silence.

"Can we look out the window?" asks Karo-chan at last.

"No."

"Please."

"There could be another blockade at any moment. You might not duck in time."

We drive on in silence. My legs ache in this position. My neck hurts, too.

"It's been an hour since the last blockade," says Naoki-kun.

"How do you know?"

"Your watch is on top of your bag."

"Please," says Karo-chan.

"All right."

We sit up, pull our eye sashes down, and stare out. The world is gray. The winds blew ashes from Tokyo all the way here, wherever here is. It's not as dark as Tokyo, but it feels later than it is, later than midday.

The roads are bumpy from the frozen tracks of truck tires, so we travel slowly. "It's good that we have to go so slow," says the professor. "This way we conserve gasoline."

We pass military vehicles, and Karo-chan and I have to duck down. Every time, the professor says, "It's good there are so many of them. Those big tires help to flatten the way for us on the road ahead."

When we pass cars, the professor says, "It's good to see a car. That means somewhere ahead there must be gasoline stands that serve the public, not just military vehicles."

He says, "It's good there's ash everywhere; without that, the road would be more slippery."

He says, "It's good my car was made in 1940 by Mazda, a prototype that can go a long way on one tank of gasoline."

Everything is good; everything is for the best. He isn't his old complaining self. Still, his shoulders hunch around his neck and his voice grows raspier.

We pass through areas that seem almost normal, except the streets are empty. The professor says, "If this fog weren't here, we'd be able to see Mount Fuji off to the right."

I press my face to the window and wave. Fujiko, Sanae, Kotsuru. Please let them be safe.

Soon we see a big city ahead. "Shizuoka," says the professor. "It hasn't been bombed yet. I bet I can find a gasoline stand. We're almost on empty." The professor puts a hand into his pocket and holds up a bulging wallet so we can see it from the backseat. "Hundred-yen notes." He pulls into a gasoline stand, and Karo-chan and I curl up with the blankets, the sashes over our eyes. Soon we're on the road again. The professor inhales loudly. "We'll be all right, so long as I have money. Right, children? It's a slow journey, but we're already halfway to Nagoya. And the going is less difficult. The car will use less gasoline."

Karo-chan's looking at me, but without expression. Then she sings the song about the crow crying. A pang of longing for

Obasan makes my breath short. Karo-chan is right—Obasan is all alone. Singing is the best way to send energy to her to help her along on her journey. I join Karo-chan, and we sing at the top of our lungs. Soon Naoki-kun joins. We go from one song to the next, through all that Obasan taught us. Even the professor joins in on some songs.

After a long while, the professor asks if we are hungry. I laugh. Who in Japan isn't hungry?

Karo-chan says, "Don't ask unless you have food to offer."

"Look under the jacket by your feet."

We move the jacket aside, and there's a large straw *bento* box. Inside are rice balls. I swallow so hard, my ears pop. The outsides are sprinkled with black sesame seeds. The smell of the pickled plums inside makes me flush.

"Thank you," I say, awestruck.

Naoki climbs into the backseat.

"There's only three sets of chopsticks," I say. "I'll divide this into four parts, and Karo-chan and I can take turns with one set."

"Three parts," says the professor. "None for me."

"Aren't you hungry?" Karo-chan asks.

"I'll eat in Nagoya."

Karo-chan eats first, greedily. Watching her, I almost drool. "Thank you," she mumbles with a full mouth.

She passes the *bento* box to Naoki-kun, but he passes it to me. "I'll go last."

"There's chrysanthemum tea in the jar," says the professor. "It's cold by now, but it's good. Sweetened with sugar."

Real sugar. This is a feast.

Soon we see the outskirts of Nagoya. Naoki-kun climbs back into the front seat, and Karo-chan and I sink down, so that our heads are barely high enough for us to be able to see out the window. The professor doesn't scold us, even though a passing military vehicle might see us before we duck. Maybe he doesn't notice. Oh no. Buildings in ruins. Ash again. I forgot! Nagoya was firebombed the day after Tokyo.

Apparently the professor forgot, too. He stops the car and calls out to a passing woman, "Where's the closest gasoline stand?" The woman gapes at him as if he's crazy. He asks, "The closest rice-soup restaurant?" The woman scurries away.

"Even hundred-yen notes can't buy anything when there's nothing to buy," he mutters.

We drive through town. On and on. Till the engine coughs. We're on the south side of Nagoya when we run out of gasoline. The professor has been muttering to himself for quite a while. It's late afternoon, and the cold outside the car quickly frosts the window. We took off our winter kimonos, but now we put them back on.

"Don't worry," says the professor. "I have containers of gasoline behind the backseat. I've been saving fuel for this drive for nearly a year. I have everything under control." He gets out, opens a rear door, and pours gasoline into the tank.

We drive another half hour and stop to add another container to the tank. "We mustn't add it all at once, you see," says the professor, ". . . in case we come across a gasoline stand where I can fill up the tank and still save the other containers for the future. This is all planned. All under control."

I don't point out to him that if we come across a gasoline stand, he can fill the tank and fill the empty containers, too. I don't point out that there are no big towns between Nagoya and Kyoto, so there won't be any gasoline stands anyway. I don't want to worry him even more.

The road meanders through mountains. "We just crossed into Shiga prefecture," says the professor. "Kyoto isn't far now."

"Shiga prefecture," I say. "Naoki-kun, you said Aiko is in Shiga prefecture. Do you know the town name?"

"It's a tiny place," says Naoki-kun. "Omihachiman."

"I know Omihachiman," says the professor. "Who is Aiko?"

"A friend."

"A good friend?"

"Yes," I say.

The professor is silent a long while. Finally he clears his throat. "Omihachiman has nothing of value. No factories. Hardly any people. It will not be bombed. And you have a friend there. And . . ." He hits his palm against the steering wheel. "You are not my children. I got you out of Tokyo. I did that much," he says. "But you endanger me. I'm sorry. I'm no hero. I can't be expected to do more. And you have a friend in Omihachiman. I will drop you off at the edge of town."

CHAPTER

FORTY-ONE

25 MARCH 1945, OMIHACHIMAN, JAPAN

"The snow isn't so deep here. The wind isn't so bad." The professor peels off money from the pile in his wallet and hands it to Naoki-kun. "Some problems can't be solved with money. But this may help." We try to thank him, but he drives away.

The town lies ahead. The professor didn't dare drop us off in front of a home.

"We can't walk on the road," I say. "A car might come."

We move a good ways off the road.

"If car lights come, drop flat onto the ground, and no one will see us," says Naoki-kun.

The rear lights of the professor's car disappear over the next hill faster than I thought was possible. He was wrong; the snow is deep here. It rasps its way under our school pants and up our legs. There isn't a wind, but the steady cold hurts my face. A curl of smoke comes out of the chimney of the first house.

"You hide outside," says Naoki-kun. "I'll ask where Aiko lives."

Karo-chan and I stand touching sides, trying to fold in on each other. Naoki-kun takes a while. Too long. My feet are so cold, it feels like knives shoot up them.

Then he's with us again. "The old couple said it's all old people on their street. But on the next street, on the corner, a house has children. Wait here."

"I almost froze once before," says Karo-chan. "We're coming with you."

I stamp through the snow, and Karo-chan walks in my footsteps. We go up to the door of the little house. Naoki-kun opens it, just like that, and we all step inside.

A woman stands up quickly. She has a young boy with her. No shadows move behind the translucent partition of the inner room. These two are the only people in this house. The woman's face is lined with worry; the boy goes behind her and peeks out. We're a threat—a half-grown boy and two girls with round eyes—half frozen. A mortal threat.

I bow and clench my teeth to stop the chattering. "Please. We are at your mercy."

"Please," says Karo-chan.

"Go away!" The blood vessels on the woman's neck stand out like ropes, she shouts so loud.

"We are looking for Aiko," manages Naoki-kun. He can hardly talk. He shivers violently.

"There's no Aiko here. Go away!"

"We have nowhere else to go," I say.

"We had to leave Tokyo," says Karo-chan. "Obasan went to Sapporo without us."

The boy says, "There are bears up there. They eat people."

"Obasan won't get eaten by bears. Don't say that." Karo-chan shakes her head. "She'll be all right. She's going to live with her brother. She's blind."

"Get out!" the woman says.

"We can't. We're too cold." I bow. "We have nothing. No one."

"Someone got you here," says the woman.

"The professor did," says Karo-chan.

"Go back to the professor."

"He left us and drove away." I hold out my frozen hands toward the woman, palms upward. "You're our only hope. Please help us. For one night only. Then we'll find Aiko."

The woman's eyes flash in alarm. "How do I know who you are, what danger you bring?"

"She's Simo-chan," says Karo-chan. "She's my sister."

"I'm Asahi," says the boy.

"We are pleased to meet you," I say. "This is my sister, Karo-chan. And my first friend, Naoki-kun, who is now my brother."

Karo-chan smiles with blue lips. "Can we move closer to the fire?"

Asahi looks hard at Naoki-kun. Then he leads Karo-chan to the hearth. Naoki-kun follows.

I meet the woman's eyes. They are dead like stones. Would I let a stranger come into my home and put Karo-chan at risk? Still, I whisper, "Please."

"I'm frightened," says the woman. She looks at Karo-chan and Naoki-kun, and turns to me again.

"We won't hurt you," I say. "Don't be frightened of us."

"Not of you. Of me. Of how hard I've become." Her face is shiny with tears. "Are you hungry? We have miso soup. I can make rice. Hot rice."

We eat quietly. And very little. The huge lunch the professor fed us in the car lingers in our bellies. Asahi watches us, then he goes into the inner room to sleep.

"You can sleep in that corner," says the woman.

We lie down on the tatami mats, three in a row, like fish in a basket. I close my eyes.

"There's no choice." A man's voice.

"But they are children." A woman.

"Remember the swallow chicks and the *mamushi*."

I open my eyes and sit up. A man sits with the woman. He's missing an arm.

"Ah, so you woke," says the woman. "This is my brother."

I get up from the floor and move toward them. I bow my head to him. "What are you going to do to us?"

"You're Christian?"

"My sister and I are Catholic."

"Catholic." He looks at the woman. "This is good. I know where they can go. There's a Catholic mission in Hiroshima where priests go after their own missions are bombed out. They only do this with priests who are friends of Japan. German priests."

Germans hate Italians as much as Japanese do. But surely priests rise above those hatreds. Still . . . "Hiroshima is far away," I say.

"We'll find a way to get you there. From truck to truck, from wagon to wagon. My sister made me promise."

Tears roll down my cheeks. "I have a friend. Aiko. She's in this town somewhere. It can't be hard to find her. This is a small town."

"Exactly. Think about that. In a small town, no one's secrets are safe. People will know you are Western. Do you really want to do that to your friend Aiko?"

I stare at him. Then I drop my head.

He stands up. "Good." The woman walks him to the door. "I'll take care of it," he says to her. "They'll be gone before noon. In the meantime, don't let anyone in or out."

It's not yet dawn, but the woman makes tea. I clean myself and wait for Karo-chan and Naoki-kun to wake. The partition to the inner room slides open, and Asahi comes out rubbing his eyes. We greet each other.

"Do you know what a *mamushi* is?" I ask him.

"The most dangerous snake in the world."

"Do you know anything about swallow chicks and a *mamushi?*"

Asahi's face turns sad. "Last spring a swallow built a nest under our eave. The chicks made the best sounds. But *mamushi* love to eat chicks. And if one came, it would kill us, too. So our mother had to sweep away the nest, and the chicks died."

"Go put your day clothes on, Asahi," says his mother. When he has closed the door, she turns to me. "I see that you understand. The journey will be hard. But you'll pay attention and find a way. You made it this far; you'll make it to Hiroshima."

I open the front door just enough to peek out. The sun rises slowly. The sky is blue and cloudless. Today, out here near the mountains, the war seems far away. But that's a lie. I close the door and wait. When Karo-chan and Naoki-kun wake, we eat breakfast with Asahi and his mother. Karo-chan chatters with Asahi. It reminds me of how she used to chatter with Botan years ago. She thinks we'll stay here. She's already trying to make a friend. Naoki-kun watches me. He suspects.

True to the uncle's word, a truck rolls up the road before noon. The uncle comes in. "Go into the inner room now, Asahi. Go!" Asahi shuts himself away.

"Who are you?" asks Karo-chan.

The uncle doesn't look at her. He hands me a basket. "Wrap your heads good. Look like burn victims."

Karo-chan grabs my arm. "What's going on?"

"We're leaving." I turn my head and rummage in the basket.

"This bandage should cover most of one side of your face, and I'll wind it once across the other eye."

"To Aiko's?" she asks.

"No."

"Where?"

"Someplace better."

"I want to stay here!"

Naoki-kun hugs Karo-chan from behind and looks at me over her head. His eyes ask me what's happening. I look away. "It's all right, Karo-chan," he says. "We'll take care of you."

"You're not coming, Naoki." I look at the woman and pray. She gives the tiniest nod.

"Of course I'm coming."

"You are my brother, and I love you." I'm rummaging around in the basket again. I won't meet his eyes.

"That's why I'm coming."

"That's why I won't let you. We'll manage without—"

"You're crazy!" screams Karo-chan. "Naoki-kun comes with us. You're crazy and mean and I hate you!"

The woman steps toward Naoki-kun. "A Japanese boy can stay here without a problem," she says quietly. "These foreign girls can't. They endanger us. And if you get caught with them, you're old enough to be charged with treason. You'll die."

Naoki-kun shakes his head.

"And I need you," says the woman. "There are jobs around the farm that a boy your size can do. Asahi needs you, too. He needs a brother. Stay here. Please."

Naoki-kun sits on the floor. Karo-chan sits with him and kisses his cheeks. He kisses hers. I step toward him, but he spins to face the far wall.

I walk to him and whisper into his ear, "My heart squeezes so hard, it shatters." I kiss his cheek.

Karo-chan wails as I bandage her head. She wails as I bandage my own head. But I cry silently. We cannot see now. I hope our tears don't make the bandages fall off.

"Your first goal is the hospital of Dr. Fujii in Hiroshima," comes the voice of the uncle. "People in town should know Dr. Fujii. He runs a private hospital and he's the only doctor working there. It's next to the bridge on the Kyo River in the center of town." He puts a package into my hand. "This is extra tape and gauze to make new bandages for your heads—your eyes, especially. I have no idea if Dr. Fujii's hospital is anywhere near the Jesuit priests' mission. But you and your sister must go there next. You know how to walk around the streets of Tokyo, so you'll have no trouble figuring out your way in Hiroshima. It's much smaller."

I want to remind him that we'll be walking the streets blind. But what's the point? I feel something on my head. It must be his hand.

"If anyone questions you, you started out in Tokyo. Tell them you don't know the names of any of the people who have helped you along the way."

"I don't know your names."

"Give Dr. Fujii's name only to the driver who actually takes you into the city of Hiroshima, never to anyone before him. You must not endanger him." He pulls me by the arm.

"Don't pull me," Karo-chan snaps. He must be doing the same to her.

"That's not how you guide blind people," I explain. "Hook our hands over your arms and walk. That way, we'll come along without tripping."

He hesitates. Then he guides us properly out to the truck and says, "War orphans. Firebomb victims. To Hiroshima."

A man's voice answers, "I'm going only as far as Osaka. But I'll pass them on from there."

We lie in the flatbed of a noisy truck, with a blanket below us and a blanket over us. My hands reach out and find boxes.

Karo-chan won't talk to me. But she doesn't roll away when I put my arms around her.

27 May 1945, Hiroshima, Japan

I walk into the kitchen at dawn, and Father Cieslik lifts his chin toward me in greeting. "Good morning, child. Go wake your sister for her big day." He uses Japanese with Karo-chan and me, just like the other priests we've been living with for the past two months, though they use German among themselves. I'm surprised to find Father Cieslik standing by the sink at this hour; he's not generally an early riser. His face is pinched and his eyes look tired; he's cradling his right hand in his left.

Aha! I know why he's up: he had a boil lanced yesterday. I can see that his finger is red and raw. "Would you like me to help wash that finger?"

Father Cieslik looks sheepish, and takes a seat at the kitchen table. "It does hurt a bit. Thank you, child."

I fill a basin with cold water and gently clean his finger. "Am I hurting you?"

"Not at all."

When I finish putting on a bandage, I go upstairs to our small room and touch Karo-chan's shoulder. She jumps awake, and her eyes dart around. Karo-chan has somehow learned to screen out noises when she sleeps, but a touch sends her into a panic. I put my hands on her cheeks till she calms.

Sudden noises jumble my insides, too. But silence worries me more. Silence feels like anything might happen next. Silence at night is the worst.

"Let me help you dress."

"Why?" Karo-chan asks in alarm.

"Nonna helped me dress when I had my First Holy Communion. It's nice."

"You were seven," says Karo-chan. "I'm ten and a half."

"Please."

Karo-chan has been somber since we left Naoki-kun behind, so her silence now is no surprise. But she lets me help her put on the fancy kimono. I wore a glorious white dress to my ceremony. I felt like a bride. But this kimono is just as beautiful in its own way. It belongs to the family of Hoshijima-san, Karo-chan's catechism teacher.

Karo-chan has been preparing for today since we got here. On the first day, we were dropped off at Dr. Fujii's hospital by a truck carrying medical supplies. Father Cieslik was there for a cut on his elbow. When he saw two girls with giant bandages on their heads asking a nurse how to find the mission, he brought us here. And Father Kleinsorge, the parish priest, took us in, just like that. Even after we peeled off the bandages and he saw our faces, he never asked how we'd gotten to the mission or how we'd wound up in Japan in the first place. He accepted us—no matter who we were. I love him for that. He still doesn't know we're Italian. Karo-chan and I never speak Italian, not even in whispers.

What Father Kleinsorge did ask was, "Are you Catholic?" When I told him yes and he realized that Karo-chan was well past seven years old and had not had her First Communion yet, he made her study for it immediately.

I don't know what Karo-chan thinks of the catechism. She worked hard at reading the Japanese and memorized it perfectly. But she didn't ask questions about it. Not the way I did. I never asked Mamma; she was too sick already and I didn't want to bother her. But Nonna was always there, ready with the answers.

Now I say, "I should have helped you learn the catechism."

"I didn't need help," says Karo-chan.

We go downstairs and onto the grounds of this mission compound, Our Lady's Assumption. The chapel is a small wooden building with a little tower on top and five pine trees out front. The tower gives the chapel a sense of dignity. And I love those wispy pines. I walk up to a branch, crush needles in my fist, and put my hand over my nose. I remember the morning Aiko warned me not to smell of fancy food—butter or jam—so I chewed on pine needles. That was the real start of our friendship. Oh, how I miss her. For the rest of the day, I'll have the pine needles' clean scent on my palm and the memory of Aiko's face in my heart.

We go inside the chapel, up to the front, and sit back on our heels on the tatami mats. Beside us on one side sit Hoshijima-san—Karo-chan's teacher—and his family. On our other side sit the six other children in the catechism class. The others in the church are priests, staff, and the families of the children who go to the mission school. It's not crowded; hardly anyone wants to be Catholic anymore.

Father Kleinsorge stands there looking skinny and frail, but he says the Mass with his usual fervor, and all but the youngest children receive Communion. I glance at Karo-chan as we go up to the altar to receive the wafer, but her eyes look ahead. After the Mass, we go into the mission for tea and rice crackers.

Father Kleinsorge asks Karo-chan to step forward—speaking in German. She doesn't move or look at him. I don't, either. Karo-chan made me promise we would not learn German. We will not become new people all over again. So whenever the priests speak German to us, we pretend not to understand even the most basic words that we hear every day all day long. I think Father Kleinsorge knows what we're doing, but he doesn't seem annoyed. He asks again, in Japanese. Then he rings a bell, for everyone's attention. He gives Karo-chan a set of rosary beads. "This marks your new status."

Karo-chan bows. I can't tell if she's pleased.

"I have a gift, too," says Hoshijima-san. He bows. "I managed to save up enough gasoline to take my family on an outing in the countryside today. We are inviting you and your sister. It's a pleasant day. The best of spring. Would you like to do that, Karo-chan?"

Karo-chan hesitates, and for an awful moment I think she may say no. But then she bows her thanks.

We change into school pants and shirts and pile into Hoshijima-san's car with his family. We stop at the edge of woods, and the children explore while Hoshijima-san and his wife rest on a blanket and talk.

His children lead Karo-chan and me on a soft dirt path under leaves dappled with light. We hear the songs of birds, the chittery noise of squirrels that nearly fly from tree to tree. I love breathing this clean spring air.

We arrive at a stream, and rain starts, just the slightest drizzle. We stand and watch the drops fall onto a little pool that has formed in a bulging part of the stream. Something moves.

"Did you see that?" I point.

The head of the creature pops up again. It opens its mouth and gulps air. The water is clear enough to make out its shape. Four legs and a long tail. The front feet have funny little fingers. I can't get a good look at the back feet. The creature is as long as I am tall. And its face is pleasant, sort of smiling.

"That's a giant salamander," says the oldest son.

"Is it dangerous?"

"I don't think so. My father says it's shy. And it never comes out of the water, so as long as we don't swim, we don't have to worry."

The salamander is now out of sight. Karo-chan walks along the shore as close as she can get to where it disappeared. She squats and stares at the water, and I squat beside her. After a while she looks at me, then points with her eyes. Oh! The salamander has lifted his head out again. He's opening and closing his mouth again. His eyes are so tiny. He slips under the surface, and we watch him glide out of sight.

"I expected him to have webbed feet," whispers Karo-chan. "But he has baby fingers. Like some kind of strange gigantic gecko." She stands and hugs herself. "We were lucky to see him. Naoki-kun would have loved to see him, too." I expect her to look sad, but she smiles. Karo-chan is smiling again.

A roll of thunder comes from not too far away. We run back to the car. I'm so glad we came. As we drive away, Karo-chan is still smiling.

CHAPTER

FORTY-THREE

6 AUGUST 1945, HIROSHIMA, JAPAN

Father Kleinsorge is awake, though it can't be much past six. I hear him in his room.

I dress and hurry downstairs and outside, to sweep out the room next to the main chapel. Yesterday I promised Father that I'd clean it. It's important never to disappoint anyone.

I finish just as people start arriving. Karo-chan and I take Communion with everyone. The Communion wafer is slowly dissolving on my tongue when the air-raid siren interrupts Father Kleinsorge's prayers.

Air-raid sirens sound at nine a.m., three p.m., and nine p.m. About an hour after each siren, planes pass overhead. Sometimes twenty, sometimes thirty. People come out into the streets and shake their fists up at them. They can't stand much more. The rectory cook keeps the radio on in the kitchen. Since I help her, I hear the news. More than sixty Japanese cities have been firebombed this year, and it's only early August. Tokyo, four times. Whole sections of that city are gone; no water, no electricity, barely any food. The only big cities that haven't been struck yet are Kyoto, Nagasaki, and Hiroshima. All the little cities near us have been bombed, and the Americans bombed ships in the naval yard at nearby Tokuyama; the skies over Hiroshima were black for a day. It feels like they're teasing us—we're next.

The air-raid siren this morning is early. A mistake? People say that the firebombing will come at night. Half of Hiroshima leaves the city at night, to sleep in the countryside.

Father Kleinsorge stops the service, and everyone goes back to the residence. Father Kleinsorge disappears upstairs, then comes down wearing a military uniform. The first time he did that, I gaped. How can he support war? Father Kleinsorge is a peaceful man. On Saturday nights he holds a record concert at the residence. He plays classical music to a packed room. It's Father Kleinsorge's gift to the neighborhood: for one hour every week, music wins, and people are free of fear.

Music helps all of us. Father Lassalle plays his cello. He dug a special bomb shelter for it in the garden, under the statue of Saint Joseph. He'll never let that cello burn.

And Karo-chan and I sing. The priests love it. We sing to them after every meal.

But despite all this, Father Kleinsorge now wears his uniform. He goes outside to scan the sky. Karo-chan and I join him.

The morning is so clear that the bright sun hurts my eyes. A perfect summer day. A single plane flies over—a weather plane. Father Kleinsorge sighs with relief and takes us back inside. As we eat breakfast—bread made with bean paste, and fake coffee made from roasted corn—the all clear is given, and Father Kleinsorge looks at his watch. "Eight a.m. I'm going to read in solitude from now till the regular alarm at nine." Father Kleinsorge climbs the stairs to his room.

Karo-chan and I weed the vegetable garden. Neighborhood children play on the mission grounds, since school is out till the end of the month. They talk about the emperor in loud voices. One says his mother calls the emperor *baka*—fool. The next says, no, the emperor is *bakayarō*—stupid fool. The next calls him *oobakayarō*—big stupid fool. Insults fly from all sides. I listen in shock. This is their emperor, who is said to be a god.

I work harder, faster. We've finished one row when Karo-chan throws down her hand trowel. "It's too hot to work outside."

"It's our job."

"Come inside, Simo-chan. We didn't sing after breakfast today. Singing is a job, too. It makes everyone happy. If we go inside, we'll find someone we can sing to. Please, Simo-chan."

I stand and wipe sweat off my forehead. "We can finish in the evening."

We go into the residence and pause to feel the cool air. A blinding light invades the room. Then a roar louder than any train, and we're thrown to the ground. I climb on top of Karo-chan to protect her as things crash down on all sides. I cradle my head in my arms and wait. After a few minutes things stop flying through the air. Everything is quiet. And dark as night.

I roll off Karo-chan.

"Are we dead?" she asks.

"No." I rub my throat; it hurts. I scrape grit off my tongue with my teeth.

"Did the house fall on us? Are we buried alive?"

"Reach your hands up. It's still air above us."

"It's dusty."

Slowly the dust settles and the air turns more gray than black. We look around. The big window on the side of the rectory has broken away, and everything outside is gray.

"Are you hurt?" I ask Karo-chan.

"My knee got bumped. Are you?"

Something is wrong with me. I don't know what. And then I see the blood coming from my hand. The little finger of my left hand—something sliced it clear off. As I watch the blood spurt, my hand starts to hurt. "I need a cloth."

Karo-chan looks at my hand. "I'll get one from the kitchen." She stands. "Oh no." We look; a pile of rubble blocks the kitchen.

"We have to go out through that window."

Karo-chan takes off her shirt. "Use this."

I wrap her shirt round and round my hand, and then we climb out through the hole into the garden. We stand there, unbelieving.

Everything is destroyed. The church, all the houses on the block, anything made of wood, collapsed. Those neighborhood children. Where are they? But I can't bear to look too closely; I don't want to see small bodies. I splay my legs to keep from falling.

Tokyo all over again.

But different. In a flash.

"Go inside, Karo-chan," I say slowly. "I'm going to Dr. Fujii's hospital to get my hand bandaged. I'll be back as soon as I can."

"We stay together. Wait here. I have to get Lella. Wait!"

"You can't come with me." But she's gone. My hand throbs something horrible. I walk out to the street. The public bathhouse next door is on fire. The remains of the church catch fire now, too.

Karo-chan appears at my side. With Lella. My crazy sister. "You're right," I say. "We stay together."

I climb a pile of broken stone and wood, and turn in a circle. As far as I can see, nothing but demolished buildings. Wood planks, fragments of glass and shards of pottery, shoes, toys . . . everywhere. Rice paddles and whisks and wire egg baskets and knives and spoons and chopsticks.

I finally let myself see them. They are strewn all around.

Bodies. I can't even tell Karo-chan to look away; anywhere you look, it's the same. The wind is hot.

It looks like the end of the world.

We stand, immobile, for who knows how long. Rain comes, heavy black drops. Karo-chan and I go back to the rectory, climb inside through the window, and hug each other in total darkness. I'm grateful for the beastly pain in my hand; it keeps me from thinking. But gradually my brain works again. We walk through the three floors of the rectory, calling out. No answer.

When we go outside, everything is on fire—a giant sea of fire. People straggle by, bleeding and burned, all headed in the same direction. I remember now: in a bombing, we're supposed to take refuge in Asano Park. We follow them, picking our way through scorching debris. When we get to the park, we stand in one spot and lean into each other. And, thanks be to everything good, there's Father Cieslik and Father Klein-sorge. Scraped up and bruised, but no worse than us. They tell us that Father Lassalle and Father Schiffer are in the hospital, but both will survive.

Father Kleinsorge washes my injured hand in the park pond and rewraps it tighter with Karo-chan's shirt. "You'll be all right. Stay with me and you'll be all right." I choose to believe him. We'll do whatever the priests do, no matter what.

Karo-chan and I hold each other as fires burn outside the park all day. All night.

Somewhere in the middle of the night she whispers to me, "I'm sorry, Simo-chan."

"For what?"

"I didn't mean it when I said you were mean and that I hated you. I wanted Naoki-kun to stay with us. I felt safer with him. I was afraid. But you were right. I'm glad he's not here now. And I'm sorry. I love you."

"I love you, too."

CHAPTER
FORTY-FOUR

"No food," people mutter in the morning. Gradually they dribble away, looking for shelters with food. In the evening we walk with the priests back to the mission. The concrete residence did not burn down, but fire gutted the inside. It's a pity Karo-Chan and I didn't think to take our money—Obasan's money—when we walked through the rectory after the blast. But what am I thinking? Money doesn't matter now.

We go to the air-raid shelter in our garden and take out rice, then pick one of the miracle pumpkins remaining in the garden. The kitchen sink in the residence is still standing, full of dirty dishes from breakfast the day before. When we turn on the water faucet, it actually works. The walls are black, the furniture is all burned up, but the water runs! We cook rice and pumpkin. Emergency workers come by, distributing rice balls wrapped in seaweed. We add this to the meal.

Karo-chan and I walk the ruins near the mission in a large circle and gather everyone we see. We all eat together on the scorched earth in front of the residence, as smoke rises around us. Military trucks pass, picking up the dead. Now and then a building flares up in flame.

On the third day after the attack, Karo-chan and I walk back to the park with the priests and take a boat across the river. I dip my healthy hand into the water, which is still hot. We walk to the nuns' home, the novitiate in Nagatsuka. They have electricity. There's none in Hiroshima, so there's no radio—no news. The nuns tell us that what hit Hiroshima was a special bomb—an atomic bomb. The Americans drop a second atomic bomb while we are at the novitiate, on a city to the southwest of here, Nagasaki. The radio says that one hundred thousand people were killed by the bomb in Hiroshima. They already guess that the number will be the same at Nagasaki. Black rain falls there, too.

Once upon a time, long, long ago, when we lived at the embassy, a German telegram to the Italian ambassador threatened to reduce Italy to mud and ashes. The Americans made good on that threat—but they did it to Japan. Japan is mud and ashes.

I listen hard in case the radio says something about Italy, but I don't hear anything.

There are no trees in Hiroshima now. Are there trees in Rome?

We walk back to Hiroshima as night falls.

The following days blend as we work nearly around the clock to help the wounded. The bomb blasted Dr. Fujii's private hospital off its foundations and into the river, with him in it. He climbed out and even managed to rescue patients. Not many, though. So now he works in the only hospital that still has some structure left, the Red Cross hospital. Karo-chan and I assist Dr. Fujii and Dr. Sasaki. Most doctors and nurses in the city were killed in the blast, so anyone helps however they can. And Dr. Fujii bandaged my injured hand. It feels better.

The radio tells us Japan has surrendered. It's 15 August. We are silent.

That day we set up a generator in the backyard of the hospital so we don't have to work in the dark. News comes from a trickle of volunteers from other cities who bring operating tables and X-ray machines for the hospital. I overhear Dr. Fujii talking to an elderly man as he pulls a thick spear of glass out of his neck and bandages him. Dr. Fujii says, "This bomb was an atrocity, a war crime. When the Americans come, they will apologize. They have to."

The Americans are coming already? That's what surrender means, I guess. I clutch Karo-chan's hand. We'll hide in the rectory. No one lives there anymore.

But what if the Americans arrest the priests? The priests are German, after all.

Well, then we'll hide in the hospital. Whole areas of the hospital have crumbled. But we know where to go.

Over the next weeks, we stay alongside Father Kleinsorge, Father Cieslik, and the new priest, Father Laderman. It's important to be close to one of them at all times, because people trust them; and everyone who sees us with the priests assumes we're German, too. The bandage on my hand helps—we're suffering like everyone else in Hiroshima. So they don't hate us.

One day, we have to run an errand on our own, and we learn that we can walk around freely. No one has the energy to look twice at us. They need all the help they can get from whoever brings it. A strange fever has come, and people develop reddish-black spots all over their bodies. They vomit blood. Dr. Fujii calls it radiation sickness. And Father Kleinsorge suffers from it!

Outside the hospital, small children wander aimlessly, all alone, not even crying. One morning Father Cieslik stands beside us at the entrance to the hospital and watches the children. "We have to do something for them. Come." We walk around for the next hour and gather the orphans into a group. "All right, it's your turn," he says to Karo-chan and me. "Do something. Make up riddles. Something children will like."

Has he gone mad?

"What is the smartest animal in the world?" says Karo-chan to the children, just like that—as though she's been planning this all along.

The children stare at us, listless. Then a girl says, "Snow monkeys. They play snowball, just like children. My teacher told us."

"Good guess. You are smart. Very smart. But this time you are wrong."

After a bit a boy says, "The Akita dog. They're loyal. That's the best you can be."

I remember the mangy Akita dog that day in Tokyo, when the old woman gave Papà and Karo-chan and me three perfect sticks of fish studded with sesame seeds.

"Another good guess," says Karo-chan. "You, too, are very clever. But this guess is wrong."

They guess on and on. Every child guesses now. They cheer for each guess, saying it must be right, saying how smart the child is who made that guess.

When they've all had a turn, Karo-chan says, "It's the *kaba*. Right? *Kaba* is the reverse of *baka*. So it must be. See?"

Everyone laughs. Everyone agrees. A *kaba* is a hippo and a *baka* is a fool. Just flop the syllables. I hug my sister, the riddle wizard.

After that, every day Father Cieslik takes us with him to walk among groups of children. He carries a big tub of water. We scoop wooden cups into the water and offer drinks to everyone we pass, small and big. They bow quietly in thanks. They don't spill a drop. We tell stories and riddles, and the children laugh.

And when Father Cieslik gets radiation sickness, too, we go without him among the children.

We are on our way back to the hospital one day when a woman grabs my wrist as I offer her water. "I couldn't save my sister," she murmurs. Her face is lifeless. She doesn't cry.

I should say what everyone says: *Shikata ga nai.* One simply has to go on. But I can't. My sister is alive; we are among the lucky. I kiss the woman's hand, over and over, till she lets me go.

Weeks turn into months.

On 11 September the radio tells us that Nagasaki is occupied by the Americans.

On 6 October the radio tells us that the American navy landed at Hiro, close by Hiroshima on the coast to the southeast. The next day the American infantry sets up headquarters in Kaidaichi, even closer to Hiroshima. The radio says, "They come to ensure compliance with the terms of Japan's surrender." None of us know what the terms of Japan's surrender are, so we don't know what that means.

The radio says, "The Americans will demilitarize the area, as they have done in Tokyo already." We don't know what that means, either.

The radio says, "The Americans will patrol the streets." We know what that means: nothing. There are no streets left to patrol.

"All we know," says Karo-chan, "is that the Americans are coming."

We keep working at the hospital, boldly moving everywhere the doctors need us to go. Father Kleinsorge and Father Cieslik are healing, but they can't work yet, so we try even harder to make up for their absence.

We label boxes of the cremated remains of the dead so they can be returned to their families. What was done was done. *Shikata ga nai;* it's time to put it behind us.

We scavenge the city for fallen tiles. The hospital collects them so that people can make roofs on the wooden shanties they will build on the ruins of their old homes as soon as the stench and ash are gone. What was done was done. *Shikata ga nai;* it's time to look ahead.

The Americans are here now, but we rarely see them, and only at a distance. Each time, my heart beats fast and loud, but I don't flinch. *Shikata ga nai.*

It's November and winter approaches; the chill surprises me. Every day has been just like the last, like time stopped. But now I realize time is moving relentlessly. So few have shelter, and no one has warm clothes.

Karo-chan and I come across a line of children singing the national anthem. They hold apples cupped in their two hands and nibble on them between words. Their faces are solemn but proud. Their bodies are skin and bones, but they are still standing. When they finish singing, I ask, "Where did the apples come from?"

They run, as though they're in trouble, but a girl shouts over her shoulder, "Yokogawa Station."

That afternoon I tell one of the young aides at the hospital about the apples. He says, "Didn't you know? People gather at night near the Yokogawa train station. They console each other. A black market has sprung up there. It's illegal, but . . ." He shrugs.

Toward dusk, Karo-chan says to me, "Let's go."

"We have nothing to barter with."

"So what?"

We walk to Yokogawa Station and look, trying not to gape at wares and foods that people have somehow managed to find for sale. Karo-chan halts. She jerks her chin toward a couple of men off to one side.

American soldiers. Looking at us.

I put my arm around Karo-chan's waist, and we make an about-face.

A shout comes from behind.

We run, but the soldiers are faster.

They catch us by the arms, then hold on, gently, as they smile and chatter at us. It isn't shouting; it isn't mean. I tell myself that, but I can't control my terror. I know they're asking if we're American, because their word for "American" is almost exactly like the Japanese word and the Italian word. I look around at the other people in the market, hoping someone will help us. They look away.

One soldier points at his chest. "Joseph." Then he points at me and raises his eyebrows.

I can't speak.

He does the same to Karo-chan.

She says, "Karo-chan." She points at me. "Simo-chan."

Joseph blinks. "Simo-chan? Simo . . . na? Simona?" And he says more words in his American gibberish. I make out *mamma.*

"*Si chiama Simona, Sua mamma?*" asks Karo-chan. She wants to know if his mamma's name is Simona.

It's so odd to hear her speak Italian out in the open. I jerk and look around to see if anyone has heard.

"*Sì,*" says Joseph, nodding. And in simple but beautiful Italian, he tells us he is Italian American.

"Please," Karo-chan says to me in Italian. "Please. Please now can I be Carolina again?'"

"Sweet Carolina," I say in Italian, and we hug. The words soothe my heart.

FORTY-FIVE

16 NOVEMBER 1945, HIROSHIMA, JAPAN

In this past week, Joseph and Sam, the two American soldiers, have become our friends. We are friends with Americans! They promised they'd figure out how to help us. On Sunday, Joseph came to Mass, and afterward we sat and talked for a long time. He said the International Red Cross is handling displaced people like us. Slowly, though; the International Red Cross could take months to get to us. But he thinks he can convince the American military to help us right away instead, because Papà was sent to a prisoner-of-war camp. Joseph managed to set up a meeting for us with an American officer.

That's where we are now, walking into a room. Joseph leads the way; Carolina and I follow. The American officer sits behind a desk and talks.

Joseph translates into Italian: "Sit down, please, girls." We sit in chairs side by side. "We have information for you. I'm afraid it's . . . not very satisfying." The officer blinks many times. Maybe he has daughters. "The Allied authorities worked with the Japanese authorities to search for information about what happened to the personnel of the Italian embassy." He scratches above his eyebrow. "We've been thorough."

"Thank you," I say.

Carolina leans forward. "What did you find out?"

"Yes . . . exactly. The ambassador and his wife were transferred from the Tempaku internment camp in Nagoya to house arrest at the Denenchōfu Church in Tokyo in the summer of 1944. They've now been sent home to Italy. They are as well as can be expected."

Carolina and I wait. When the officer doesn't go on, I nod.

The officer continues; Joseph translates: "The prisoner-of-war camp at Ofuna was secret. No one knew about it until the Allied forces raided it after Japan surrendered. It wasn't registered with the government. It kept no records."

I fold my shaking hands to still them.

"When the Allied forces raided it, they found no employees at all." Joseph's voice catches as he translates. "Not in the kitchen." He speaks very slowly. "Nowhere. Just starving prisoners. And corpses." Joseph presses his lips together. "I'm sorry. No one knows what happened to your father."

Carolina reaches for my hand. I hold hers tight.

I won't let this be the end of things. It cannot be. "Can we go there?"

"Of course not. Why would you want to?"

"We could look around the kitchen for traces of Papà," I say. "You wouldn't recognize traces, but we would."

"I'm so sorry. You'd find nothing. The place is filthy, and anything of use was stolen. Besides, we can't allow it."

"We could go to people in the houses near the prison," says Carolina. "We could ask if they knew the cook. We could ask the farmers who sold food to the prison." Her voice rises. "Someone somewhere knows something."

"There is no functioning farm close by. The country was starving when it surrendered."

Does he really think we don't know that?

"I'm very sorry to disappoint you. I'm sorry for your loss. I'm sorry for every child in every war." The officer's eyes are liquid. He's American, but I still believe him. "I understand you will turn fourteen in February, Simona, and you are nearly eleven, Carolina. I understand that your mother is deceased. You are very young to be facing all of this. But you have a grandmother in Italy who will care for you. You have long and wonderful lives ahead. I'll trust Joseph to explain to you what happens next." The officer leaves.

Joseph smiles encouragingly and takes each of us by the hand. "I'm sorry, so sorry about your papà." We are silent. Then he says, "Pack your bags. Because—your *nonna* has already received a telegraph that you're coming home! She knows the ship and the day. She'll be waiting for you at the docks."

"No," says Carolina. She pulls her hand from his. "No!" And she cries.

"We can't just leave," I say. My tears stream now, too. "Not without Papà."

"It's terrible news, I know." Joseph kneels in front of us. He looks right into our eyes. "But, Simona, Carolina, you can't stay. We won't allow you. If your father turns up, the Allied forces will send him home. Just like we're doing with you girls. You can count on that. I promise you, I'll keep asking about him."

Joseph and I look at each other.

They won't allow us to stay. I stand and take Carolina's hand. She looks at me through her tears, gritting her teeth, but she stands, and so does Joseph. There's nothing else we can do. And Nonna is waiting for us. Sweet and gentle Nonna.

Joseph watches us, somber. Finally he says, "I'll go with you to get your things. Your train leaves for Kawasaki this afternoon. You'll board the ship there tomorrow."

"We have no things," says Carolina. "Only Lella."

"Lella?" Joseph draws back in alarm. "There's another of you?"

"She's a doll," I say. "But we can't leave too fast. We have to say goodbye to everyone at the mission."

"There's time."

As we walk out of the room, Joseph puts a hand on my

shoulder and one on Carolina's. "Whenever I was sad as a kid, my mother said something that helped me, so I'll say it to you. *Forza e coraggio*."

Carolina and I look at each other. It's as though we can hear Nonna already.

A month later, our ship reaches Italy. I've been sick the whole time; the seas were rough. Carolina has been my comfort, singing to me sweetly. We've been talking nonstop in Italian, trying to wrap our tongues around the old words again, trying to remember who we are. We stand silent now, as our eyes scan the small group of people on the dock.

And there she is. Yes, yes, it's her, waving like a maniac. She spotted us first. We wave and jump and yell, "Nonna! Nonna!" And that man beside her, he's waving now, too. He wears a mustache—but I know it's our uncle, Zio Piero.

We are alive; we are home; we are loved.

CHAPTER

FORTY-SIX

6 AUGUST 1965, HIROSHIMA, JAPAN

It's barely dawn, and Carolina and I sit on a bench in Hiroshima Peace Memorial Park. The letter in my hands is in Japanese, and the first time I read it, it took me hours to figure it out. But I've read it a dozen times now. I've practically memorized it, like Obasan made us do with her brother's haiku. "Want me to read it to you again, Carolina?"

"Like when you used to read me Nonna's letters, over and over," she says softly. "Sure. Go ahead."

Dear friends,

The season of heat is upon us again in Japan, as it must be in Italy. Seasons carry memories.

I traveled to Kyoto this week, to the opening of an exhibit of manga—subversive manga from the war years.

I saw a series by a certain Fujiko. Unfortunately, her work was exhibited posthumously; she was prosecuted near the end of the war, and sentenced to death. When I saw her name in the newspaper announcement, I thought of the Fujiko in the cabin that you told me about, and I went to the exhibit wondering if it could be her. I am sure it is. And I urge you to return to Japan. You need to see this exhibit and see why I am so sure this is your Fujiko. Please find enclosed the newspaper announcement with the address and dates.

I don't know if you have ever gone back to Hiroshima, but you need to go there as well. You need to sit and look at the Peace Flame in Hiroshima Peace Memorial Park. It was lit last year and will remain lit until all nuclear bombs have been destroyed. It will make you cry in so many ways.

You need to visit Omihachiman, too. I have something I must say to you.

It is my fondest hope that you enjoy the sun, and refresh yourselves in the breeze if there is one.

> With great affection,
> 6 JULY 1965
> Naoki

P.S. Do you wonder how I found you, if, indeed, this letter truly finds you? I will enlighten you in person, if you come.

Please come, Simo-chan and Karo-chan.

Carolina looks around. "We are here. At last."

So many times we talked about coming back to Japan. With every letter we wrote, to every official we could find, asking over and over about Papà, we declared that we'd get back here to search for him ourselves. But even as children, we knew we'd never see him again. If Papà had survived, he'd have climbed mountains, swum oceans, to get back to us. So what does it matter if we have his remains or not? We have memories, and they comfort us.

In 1955, we thought about coming here, to the opening of the Hiroshima Peace Memorial Museum. It was a huge event for Japan, an admission of how wrong the war had been. But I was twenty-three then and a new mother, and Carolina was twenty and still a student, and we simply didn't have the money for such an extended voyage, no matter how much we longed to be surrounded by Japanese people again, to hear the language we treasured, the language that has become our private language in Italy, to use when no one else is around—just like Italian was our private language in Japan.

In 1958 we again thought of coming; the Children's Peace Monument in the Hiroshima Peace Memorial Park was completed that year. No one could understand better than us that children are the ones who must demand that the world seek and maintain peace. But by then I was the mother of two small children, and Carolina was finishing her university studies in jurisprudence. So the timing was wrong again.

Then came Naoki's letter. This was different. Our Naoki. Carolina and I took one look at each other and made plans. Here we are, after twenty years.

Hiroshima Peace Memorial Park is large. A small crowd has gathered since we arrived. They stand in silence as an old man rings a bell. The silence of a group somehow makes the park feel even larger.

Nonna died two years ago, and I miss her terribly. But my family is full. I have a dear husband, Lodovico, who manages a grocery in Lido di Ostia. My daughter, Teresa, is named after my mamma, and she is thirteen years old. My son, Luciano, is named after Papà, and he is nine. They are with their father. Lodovico is perceptive and kind; he never raised the question of whether the whole family should come along. He knows this trip is just for Carolina and me. I feel their absence, even though I'm grateful for it.

Carolina stands beside me. She is a lawyer, one of a handful of women in law in the whole country. She advocates for the rights of children, especially in wartime. She lives in the center of Rome, so we see her often. Teresa and Luciano adore her. And Lodovico loves to debate politics with her.

Now an old man rings a bell. He lights a candle that sits in one of the shallow wells of sand in the park. More and more people are arriving to watch him.

"It's getting mobbed," I say. "Can we go?"

"As long as we go together." Carolina smiles. "And we come back for the lanterns this evening."

We go directly to the mission. None of the people we knew are still there, but the priest who greets us walks us through every room, gracious enough not to ask too many questions. We say prayers for Papà together. Then we go to a memorial Mass at the World Peace Memorial Cathedral. When the mission's church of Our Lady's Assumption was destroyed, Father Lassalle gathered funds to build a new church, so in a sense, this is the replacement of the church where Carolina had her First Holy Communion. We arranged to have Papà's name be printed on cards to give to whoever comes to Mass today. No one in Hiroshima ever knew him, and his death was never confirmed, so, in some impossible world, the cards may be a mistake. But a harmless one. To us, they mean that we love him and always wish him peace.

Afterward, we walk around town and stop to eat sweetfish grilled on a stick. Delicious. The town feels normal. New and clean, as though every trace of the bomb has disappeared. The Atomic Bomb Dome, in the park, is there—but it's part of a past that only memory can see.

When we stop for tea, the waiter says, "Your Japanese is wonderful. Natural, just a bit old-fashioned. Your teacher in Italy must not have come back to Japan for a while."

We don't tell him we've been speaking Japanese longer than he's been alive. "Tell me," I say. "How is it that the town is so fixed up? I expected to see rubble."

"The museum holds the horrors of war. You can go there if you're curious."

He's young and sweet. I don't tell him that we lived those horrors.

That evening we return to the park for the lantern ceremony. People send off spirits of the war victims in lanterns with lit candles. They float on the Motoyasu River, carrying messages of peace. It's beautiful, but I feel my skin prickle.

"It's like when we were in the *bokugo*," says Carolina. "We watched the giant silk balloons float away from Tokyo."

Exactly. I kiss her cheeks.

The next day we take a train to Kyoto. It is a perfect town— old temples, red-lacquered gates, everything preserved. "Carolina, do you remember the professor saying that the Americans would never bomb Kyoto because they'd want to visit it as tourists?"

"I do," says Carolina.

"He was right."

"Yes and no. The Americans talked about bombing Kyoto. But they changed their minds. And the weather chose Hiroshima that hateful morning, anyway. It was perfectly clear for the bombers."

The manga exhibit is in the new National Museum of Modern Art, Kyoto's annex to Tokyo's modern art museum. Fujiko's manga are in a room by themselves. I'd recognize them anywhere. But how did Naoki know this was the Fujiko from the cabin at the foot of Mount Fuji? I scan the paintings on the wall, searching, searching.

"Come here," says Carolina. She stands over one of three glass-encased tables in the center of the room. "Oh, Simo-chan, come here."

A painting of two girls playing *Daruma Otoshi*, that game that Botan taught to Carolina, where the Buddha's head sits on a stack of blocks and you use a hammer to knock out the bottom blocks, one at a time, without making the Buddha head fall. The "hammer" the girls are using is a human bone.

One of the girls has curly hair. The other holds a rag doll under her arm.

Today is a day of many tears.

We rent a car and drive to Omihachiman, where we tried to find Aiko when the professor abandoned us. Where Naoki lives. We park the car at the edge of town, and walk. Agog. The town is built along the sides of a canal. It has a merchant street from the 1600s. It is charming. That one night we spent here so long ago, we didn't see the place at all.

And there it is, the address on Naoki's envelope. It's a craft supply store. We're a day earlier than we told Naoki we'd be, so I wonder if maybe we should come back tomorrow. But Carolina's already crossing toward it. We enter, and she goes up to the counter and presses the bell.

A boy comes hurrying from the back. He bows. "Can I help you?"

"You're too young to be in charge of this shop," I say.

The boy laughs. "I'm just having fun till school starts again. I'll call my father." He disappears.

Naoki comes out, and I gasp. He is tall and thin, a stretched-out version of the boy he was. He wears an artist's apron splotched with paint. "Can I . . ." He steadies himself with a hand on the counter. I understand; my own bones feel like water. He stares, then grins. "Welcome back."

The next hours fly by. We talk and talk, then have dinner with Naoki and his wife, Mayumi, and their son, Kaede.

When I am alone with Naoki, I ask, "Does your son know you named him after a gecko?"

"He does." Naoki laughs. "If we had had two sons, the other would have been Masaki. Does your son know you named him after the best cook in the world?"

I laugh, but it breaks into a sob. "Naoki . . . I've wanted to tell you how sorry—"

"Simo-chan, don't apologize. Let me speak first. That's what I wanted to say to you. I'm sorry for how I behaved when you left me here."

I press my hands to my cheeks. "I didn't want to leave you behind that morning. I was afraid for us without you, but afraid even more for you with us."

"I needed a home. Those people were good to me. They're still my family. You did what was right for me. I know that."

"But you didn't know it then," I say.

"Yes, I did. I just couldn't bear losing you two. I had lost everyone else, and you were sisters to me, as I was a brother to you. I saw how you two made it through anything, everything, because you stayed together. I suffered without a home. But you two were home to each other; I wanted to be part of that. You were right, though. You saved my life. I'm sorry for turning my back on you."

We take each other's hands, and he gently rubs the scar where my finger used to be. We stand, forehead to forehead, till we can manage to talk again.

At last, I ask, "How did you find our address? You amazed me."

"I'm not a magician." He laughs. "The Italian embassy helped."

The next day Carolina and I drive to Mount Fuji and walk past where the little cabin once stood. We stop only briefly—we've had enough of crying—then walk a trail to enjoy the glory of the volcano. We hold hands and look out at the world. At its immensity and unfathomable beauty.

We hike and visit the Shinto temple and rest quietly for a few nights.

Finally we take the train to Tokyo. This must be the busiest city on earth. Thousands of people race by. We get lost in the subway system. But aboveground, we sometimes pass places that remind me of the Tokyo that was ours.

The next day we walk by the embassy, but we don't go in. We walk along the road where Obasan's laundry was. This is as close to her as we can get; years ago I wrote to officials in Hokkaido and asked for her address. They wrote back that a woman by the name of Tanaka, first name Natsu, died in Sapporo in 1956, at the age of sixty-one. She was blind.

There's no laundry on this street. All the shops are new.

But we do find Aiko, at the address Naoki gave us. Her mother still lives in Omihachiman, but Aiko attended university in Tokyo and stayed. We go to her home for dinner.

Aiko's hair is long and shiny; her arms are muscular; she looks the vision of health. "This is my husband, Oto."

I bow and say, "The Oto who was your sweetheart when you were only eleven?"

He laughs.

"We've been lucky," says Aiko.

Her father died. Her brother died. But Oto made it through. I hug Aiko. "I am so happy for you."

She and Carolina and I talk late into the night. Like Naoki, she doesn't ask about my finger. But when we are leaving, she takes my hand and kisses the scar. The intimacy overwhelms me. I hug her tight.

"We must never lose each other again," says Aiko. "Let's send photos every year on the first of January. You two can be in your kitchen and I'll be in mine far across the world—we can make your father's crust with citrus custard and pretend we're sharing it."

Carolina claps. "The perfect way to start the new year."

Before bed, I say to Carolina, "I'm sorry no one knows what happened to Botan."

"So am I. But it's amazing that we found Naoki and Aiko. It's amazing that anyone survived, and we're here together."

On 15 August, Carolina and I are in the Nippon Budokon, a giant arena in Tokyo, to listen to the annual National Memorial Service for the War Dead. In the past, the service was in other cities, but it will be in Tokyo from now on. At noon, everyone goes silent. A single minute of silence all over the country, to commemorate the end of the war.

I want this minute to last. I want to hold everyone who's still alive, everyone who is yet to be born, safe. Now and forever.

Carolina presses against me, and we interlace our fingers.

POSTSCRIPT

While the figures will always remain imprecise, perhaps as many as 100,000 people were killed instantly in the Hiroshima bombing on August 6, 1945, and another 60,000 died of injuries sustained in the bombings over the next weeks and months. Estimates vary, but perhaps around 60,000 people were killed instantly in the bombing at Nagasaki on August 9, 1945, with another 20,000 dying of injuries soon after. The number of people who later died of cancer caused by radiation exposure is also hard to calculate, but it could well be double the total of people killed by the explosions. The March 9, 1945, firebombing of Tokyo, however, was the deadliest air raid of World War II, and of any war in human history. Again, the figures are debated. It killed around 120,000 people, injured perhaps as many as 1,000,000, and left more than 1,000,000 homeless.

NOTES ON RESEARCH

Information on the people living in the Italian embassy in Tokyo from 1940 until they were taken to the internment camps in 1943 is scarce. I therefore felt free to make up Simona and her family. While much of what happens in the embassy comes from documents I read, the personalities of the ambassador and his wife are my own creations and neither is to be identified with the true Ambassador Indelli and his wife.

A few characters in this story are historical, including the Jesuit priests at the mission in Hiroshima. The rectory was the only institutional building of the city that was not reduced to rubble in the bombing, and the water really did still run in those pipes. Somehow the people in the rectory survived their injuries, and only Fathers Kleinsorge and Cieslik suffered from radiation sickness. That's why I chose to place Simona/Simo-chan and Carolina/Karo-chan in that rectory.

The prisoner-of-war camp at Ofuna is also real, and it was indeed a secret, so no records were kept.

Various issues of time arose in writing this. Time in Tokyo is thirteen hours ahead of time in New York, and the international date line falls in the Pacific Ocean. Because of this difference, the date on which an event took place is reported differently in scholarly works, based on which time perspective is used. In this book, the date, day of the week, and time is local to the characters. For example, in the first chapter, the dates and days are given according to time in Italy. After that, they are given according to time in Japan. So according to the Japanese, Pearl Harbor was bombed on December 8. But according to Hawaii, which is east of the international date line, the date was December 7. Further, events were sometimes announced to the public on dates different from when they occurred. For example, Italy surrendered (in the Armistice of Cassibile) on September 3, 1943, but this news was not known to people in Japan until several days later. Always, the dates in this book reflect the realities as the characters would have perceived them.

Materials on World War II are abundant, and I read nonfiction widely (including the outstanding memoir of Dacia Maraini, *Bagheria*), starting my research in 2007, when I first visited Japan and got the idea for this story, continuing through 2012, when I sat down to begin writing it, and on through 2019, when I finally finished it. So many books influenced me, some of which are listed in the bibliography, but the one that was my companion throughout was *A Diary of Darkness: The Wartime Diary of Kiyosawa Kiyoshi*. I also relied heavily on *Leaves from an Autumn of Emergencies*. But really, everything I read informed this story in one way or another.

BIBLIOGRAPHY

Alvarez, David. "Des espions au Vatican." *Historia* 720 (December 2006): 38–41.

Awazuhara, Atsushi. 2007. "Perceptions of Ambiguous Reality–Life, Death and Beauty in *Sakura*." *Japanese Religions* 32 (1 & 2): 39–51.

Bailey, Jackson H., ed. *Listening to Japan: A Japanese Anthology.* New York: Praeger Publishers, 1973.

Cieslik, Hubert. "The day of destruction: An Eye-Witness Account of the A-bomb over Hiroshima." Translated by Francis Mathy. In *All About Francis Xavier,* edited by Francis Britto. Accessed February 14, 2012. pweb.sophia.ac.jp/britto/ xavier/cieslik/cie_d_of_d.pdf.

Cook, Haruko Taya, and Theodore F. Cook. *Japan at War: An Oral History.* New York: New Press, 1992.

Craig, William. *The Fall of Japan.* New York: Dial Press, 1967.

Defense Threat Reduction Agency. "NTPR: Hiroshima and Nagasaki Occupation Forces." www.dtra.mil/Portals/61/Documents/NTPR/1-Fact_Sheets/NTPR %20H-N-2015.pdf?ver=2017-06-14-093753-997.

Duggan, Christopher. *Fascist Voices: An Intimate History of Mussolini's Italy.* Oxford: Oxford University Press, 2013.

Gayn, Mark. *Japan Diary.* New York: William Sloane Associates, 1948.

Havens, Thomas R. H. "Women and War in Japan, 1937–45." *The American Historical Review* 80, no. 4 (October 1975): 913–934.

Hersey, John. *Hiroshima.* New York: Alfred A. Knopf, 1985.

Hillenbrand, Laura. *Unbroken: A World War II Story of Survival, Resilience, and Redemption.* New York: Random House, 2010.

Ikeno, Norio, ed. *Citizenship Education in Japan.* New York: Continuum International Publishing, 2011.

Inaharu, K., ed. *The Japan Year Book 1934.* Tokyo: The Foreign Affairs Association of Japan, 1934.

Jannelli, Pasquale. "Italia e Giappone dopo l'armistizio dell'8 Settembre 1943." *Storia e Politica* 2, no. 2 (1963): 157–182.

Jannelli, Pasquale. "La Guerra nel Pacifico dal diario di un diplomatico." *Storia e Politica* 3, no. 3 (1964): 351–379.

Japan Photographers Association. *A Century of Japanese Photography.* New York: Pantheon Books, 1980.

Kiyoshi, Kiyosawa. *A Diary of Darkness: The Wartime Diary of Kiyosawa Kiyoshi.* Edited by Eugene Soviak. Translated by Eugene Soviak and Kamiyama Tamie. Princeton: Princeton University Press, 1999.

Kono, Juliet S. *Anshū: Dark Sorrow.* Honolulu: Bamboo Ridge Press, 2010.

Lifton, Robert Jay. *Death in Life: Survivors of Hiroshima.* Chapel Hill: University of North Carolina Press, 2012.

Lifton, Robert Jay. "Psychological Effects of the Atomic Bomb in Hiroshima: The Theme of Death." *Daedalus* 92, no. 3 (1963): 462–497.

Manabe, Noriko. "Songs of Japanese Schoolchildren During World War II." In *The Oxford Handbook of Children's Musical Cultures,* ed. Shehan Campbell and Trevor Wiggins. Oxford: Oxford University Press, 2012.

Maraini, Dacia. *Bagheria.* Palermo, Italy: Rizzoli, 1996.

Morgan, Philip. *The Fall of Mussolini: Italy, the Italians, and the Second World War.* Oxford: Oxford University Press, 2007.

Morimoto, Risa, dir. *Wings of Defeat.* Harriman, NY: New Day Films, 2007. DVD, 60 min.

Mullener, Elizabeth. *War Stories: Remembering World War II.* Baton Rouge: Louisiana State University Press, 2002.

Muto, Toshio. "Il contributo dell'Italia alla cultura giapponese nell'epoca moderna." *Il Giappone* 3 (July 1961): 18–24. Accessed January 3, 2012. jstor.org/stable/20750423.

Rinjirō, Sodei. *Dear General MacArthur: Letters from the Japanese During the American Occupation.* Edited by John Junkerman. Translated by Shizue Matsuda Lanham, MD: Rowman & Littlefield Publishers, 2001.

Roehrs, Mark D., and William A. Renzi. *World War II in the Pacific.* Armonk, NY: M. E. Sharpe, 2004.

Shillony, Ben-Ami. "Universities and Students in Wartime Japan." *The Journal of Asian Studies* 45, No. 4 (August 1986): 769–787.

Siemes, P. T. 1946. "The Atomic Bomb on Hiroshima: An Eye-Witness Account." (Continued). *The Irish Monthly* 74, No. 874 (April 1946): 148–154.

Smith, Richard Harris. In *OSS: The Secret History of America's First Central Intelligence Agency.* Berkeley: University of California Press, 1972. See esp. chap. 4, "Italian Sunset."

Tarling, Nicholas. *A Sudden Rampage: The Japanese Occupation of Southeast Asia, 1941–1945.* Honolulu: University of Hawaii Press, 2001.

Tokayer, Marvin, and Mary Swartz. *The Fugu Plan: The Untold Story of the Japanese and the Jews During World War II.* New York: Paddington Press, 1979.

Tsuboi, Sakae. *Twenty-Four Eyes.* Translated by Akira Miura. North Clarendon, VT: Tuttle Publishing, 1952.

Tucci, Giuseppe. "Giacinto Auriti (1883–1969)." *East and West,* 20, no. ½ (March–June 1970): 230–232. Accessed January 3, 2012. jstor.org/stable/29755539.

Walker, Stephen. Shockwave: *Countdown to Hiroshima.* New York: Harper Collins, 2006.

Yamashita, Samuel Hideo. *Daily Life in Wartime Japan, 1940–1945.* Lawrence: University Press of Kansas, 2015.

Yamashita, Samuel Hideo. *Leaves from an Autumn of Emergencies: Selections from the Wartime Diaries of Ordinary Japanese.* Honolulu: University of Hawaii Press, 2005.

ACKNOWLEDGMENTS

Thank you to Barry Furrow (still and always), Faith Apple-
gate, Erin Brangiel, Sam Charney, Libby Crissey, Tashi Dawa,
Chaz Donnelly, Ivy Drexel, Henry Hewitt, Lily Martin, Ma-
sataka Murakami, Michael Noon, Colleen O'Brien, Libby
Parker-Simkin, Bobby Ralph, Abigail Raz, Joanna Riever, Ali-
son Ryland, Edwin Stajkovic, Kayla Strine, Yukiko Sugimoto,
Rachel Sutton-Spence, and Elizabeth Wiseman for comments
on earlier versions. Thank you to Thad Guyer for discussing
matters of the heart and plot with me. Thank you to Brenda
Bowen for discussing so many things about writing in general
and about writing this story in particular, and always being
my confidante and friend. Thank you to Linda and Hajime
Hayakawa and their whole extended family for help with
Japanese language usage as well as comments on the story.
Thank you to Samuel Yamashita, Henry E. Sheffield Professor
of History at Pomona College, for checking historical details,
and for his suggestions on cultural matters and daily wartime
life. Thank you to Jamie Kuramaji, for checking culture and
tradition authenticity in a close-to-final draft. Thank you to
Dana Carey for reading and commenting on every draft and

never showing a hint of being tired of this story. And, most of all, thank you to Wendy Lamb for being my partner all along. Her deep respect for and understanding of the child's sensibility sat on my shoulders through every scene. Any straying beyond is due to my own stubbornness.

ABOUT THE AUTHOR

DONNA JO NAPOLI has published more than eighty books for young readers, including picture books, early readers, and young adult and middle-grade novels. Her work has been translated into nineteen languages and has won many awards at the state and national level. She is a professor of linguistics and social justice at Swarthmore College, and she brings her research skills and her profound interest in language to bear on her novels, particularly the historical ones. She lives in Swarthmore, Pennsylvania, with her husband.

donnajonapoli.com
swarthmore.edu/donna-jo-napoli